# UNDERNEATH THE MOON

## Dan Holt

## MaxHoltMedia

DAN HOLT

Published by Max Holt Media
303 Cascabel Place, Mount Juliet, TN 37122
www.maxholtmedia. com

Disclaimer: This is a work of fiction. Names, characters, businesses, places, events and incidents are either the products of the author's imagination or used in a fictitious manner. Any resemblance to actual persons, living or dead, or actual events is purely coincidental.

The author is totally responsible for the content and the editing of this work and Max Holt Media offers no warranty, expressed or implied, or assumes any legal liability or responsibility for the accuracy of any information contained herein. The author bears responsibility for obtaining permission to use any portion of this work that may be the intellectual property of another person or organization.

Other books by Dan Holt:   SLEEP MODE
        Coming Soon:   UNDERNEATH THE MOON 2

Cover Design:   Max Holt Media
Cover art by:   ID   49926608   © Rfischia | Dreamstime.com (Earth and Moon)

ISBN 13: 978-0-9966104-1-4

# Acknowledgements

I want to thank all of my friends and family who encouraged me to complete the long process of bringing this book to completion. I appreciate those who took time to read and help edit its content.

I want to thank NASA and the many astronauts for inspiring me as I watched the space program unfold over the years and sat transfixed as the first footprints were made on the Moon.

Mostly, I want to thank my wife, Mary, for her patience as I often chose to forego her 'Honey-Do' list and work on this book.

# TABLE OF CONTENTS

## PROLOGUE

*The projectile, hurled viciously outward from the Solar System by the ancient Disaster, gradually slowed as the millenniums passed.  The faint gravity of the distant sun finally pulled the hundred foot wide chunk of iron to a stop, and then brought it back home to be buried deep underneath the Moon's surface. On its return to the Solar System, it circled the Sun, whip-lashed by Venus, and impacted the lunar surface at forty miles per second, opening the proverbial door to Earth's long hidden secret....*

# PART 1

# THE DISCOVERY

DAN HOLT

# Chapter 1

*"Take the Solar System backwards in time fifty thousand years, a few years before the Disaster, and see it when it was all intact. A Solar System in tune; all planetary orbits on plane, concentric, and undisturbed. The asteroid belt still a planet, the ice in the rings Saturn and Neptune still its oceans, the wandering ice-ball comets still its lakes and ponds, Pluto and Mercury still its moons, and the Orrt cloud still its surface...."*

## - NASA'S SECRET -

Douglas Charles Hastings held his finger above the key of the super computer. He glanced at the entrance doors. The night security guard was looking into the room again, as he did every hour. Doug had waved his hand each time. When he did so again, the guard nodded and disappeared. Doug focused on the keyboard again and read the instructions printed on the screen.

## FUNCTION MERGES ALL FILES

Doug had been in front of this keyboard for twelve continuous hours entering the data he'd collected by subjecting hundreds of photographs, taken during the Apollo Missions to the Moon, to state-of-the-art computer enhancement.

He was hooked when his computer work exposed objects hidden in the shadows of the old photographs. The bits and pieces had geometric shape and appeared to be artificial. He'd referred to NASA"s detailed orbital position records, published in the catalogues for each mission, and established coordinates on the lunar surface for the anomalous bits of evidence. After twelve tedious hours all the data was in the memory banks of the super computer.

Doug had to know the results of his search. He pressed the key.

When he saw the indications of the computer processing the information, he got up and went to the window of the Super computer Time Lease Center in Des Moines, Iowa, and looked up at the Moon. He studied the lunar disc in the night sky as he massaged his hands together. Doug stretched to his full six feet of height, put his hands on his back and rotated his lean athletic shoulders and neck, then looked around at the large cool room; a place he had been many times during his computer programming career.

There were twelve cubicles, each with a super computer, a special functions keyboard, and an eighteen by twenty-four inch monitor. His favorite, terminal number seven was busy assembling an enormous base of information. All the others were still and quiet. He glanced at his watch: one-forty a.m. He returned to the computer, sat down in the high back swivel chair, and eyed the monitor. His pulse quickened as he waited for it to assemble the hundreds of enhanced photographs.

A thousand miles away an agent tossed and turned in his sleep. He was hearing the mechanical breathing sounds again. He pushed back the covers and sat up. Standing at the foot of his bed was an astronaut, in an Apollo spacesuit, holding a tank of emergency oxygen under each arm. The agent stared at the darkened faceplate.

"Go away! Go away!" he begged, jolting himself awake. The image was gone. The agent was in a cold sweat, gasping for breath. He grasped the sheet and wiped the perspiration from his face and neck, then looked at the clock: 1:40 am.  He got out of bed and walked out on the apartment balcony and took a breath of fresh air, then leaned on the hand railing. The shadow of the canopy support, cast by the full Moon, cut across his arms.  He straightened up and looked at the lunar disc.

"I had to--I had to do it...."

The brightness of the full Moon made a distinct shadow of the sixty-foot marquee in front of the Time Lease Center fall across a lone car in the parking lot. Inside the building, at terminal number seven, a super computer was gleaning a coherent, geometrically complete image from hundreds of source photographs containing only bits and pieces of anomalous shapes.

The data processing finally stopped.  Two seconds later, there was a burst of light and an image appeared on the monitor.  Doug stared, transfixed, as the image registered in his mind.

Displayed on the screen was the ruins of an ancient crystalline city under a broken and shattered glass dome.

"Oh my God!" Doug breathed then pushed the chair aside and stood to study the image.  He reacted with a start when the guard opened the door and stepped into the room.

"You okay?" the guard asked.

"Ah, yeah," Doug said, blocking the guard's view of the monitor with his body.  "I stood to stretch and almost knocked over the chair."

"You gonna' stay all night?"

"I'm almost finished," Doug said.

"You computer guys are a strange bunch," the guard said in a jovial manner as he leaned to the side for a second look at the monitor.  Doug grinned and nodded, then again positioned himself between the guard and the screen.

"Just doing a little private research," Doug said opening his hands, "just passing the time." The guard smiled without parting his lips and nodded, then turned and exited the door.

Doug quickly returned to studying the image. He looked from side to side at the ruins of the city. They covered almost the whole face of the Moon. "Two thousand miles across," he whispered. Then he studied the bits of reflecting material hanging above the lunar surface. "Two or three hundred miles high!"

Doug became aware that he was breathing with his mouth open: he closed it, then swallowed, and then began to study the details.

Dead center was a large crater. Inside of it was the outline of a distinct equilateral triangle. To the left of it was a pair of roads or highways. He didn't know how far apart they were, but they had exact curves and straight-aways. The roads went from the central crater to a twenty or thirty mile long glass mountain, a complex of some sort. On one end of the huge structure was an opening where a meteor had gone through, no doubt buried deep in the lunar surface. Past the complex, a single road led on to a surface city in ruins, but with distinct streets, blocks, cross streets, and semicircle layouts, much like Earth's neighborhoods.

Doug's eyes went back to the center of the screen and then scanned the other way. There were larger buildings in ruin and decay. Streets, cross streets, and then enormous columns, partially gone, were hanging from something invisible overhead. There was a segment of a building suspended high above the surface of the Moon. On the scale of the curvature of the Moon and the position of the eroded chunk of the structure, the distance from the lunar surface to the bottom of the suspended piece of architecture was over thirty miles.

"Jesus!" Doug said, "What enormous scale!" Breathing heavily, he pulled the chair back in place and sat down. He glanced around the room again and then back to the monitor.

"The city looks melted and eroded," he said quietly. "How can that be? There's no process on the Moon to cause that except the solar wind, the hard particles radiated in sunlight, with no ozone or air to diffuse them. But even in a hard vacuum it would be a very slow process. That means it would have to be...." he paused and took a breath.

*"Thousands of years old!"*

Doug leaned back in the chair, eyes fixed on the screen, as the implications of the discovery began to sink in. Abruptly he glanced around the room again, downloaded the image to his external disc and instructed the computer to print five copies while he grabbed the phone and dialed his home in Davenport.

Karen, Doug's wife, sleepily answered the phone.

"Karen! You're not going to believe this!"

"Doug?"

"Yes, it's me. You're not going to believe what's on the Moon!"

Karen cleared her throat, "What?"

"An enormous glass city!" Doug said. "It was under a dome." There was silence on the phone for a few moments. Doug took a deep breath and cleared his throat.

"Karen...Karen?"

"Ah, I'm here... ah, are you sure?"

"Yes. I'm looking at it right now. I'm still at the center. This computer combined all the enhanced imaging together and it's there, Karen, it's really there! There're ruins of a huge city on the Moon."

"I want to see it."

"I printed five copies and got it on disc. I'll be there in a couple of hours."

"Okay. Oh, Doug...watch your driving; you been up since yesterday morning."

"Believe me I'm wide awake, but I will be careful." He hung up the phone and erased his work before turning off the computer. He collected the disc and printed copies and left the Time Lease Center.

On his way to his car, Doug looked up at the Moon. Focusing on it as he hurried along, a smile formed on his lips and then slowly faded as a strange feeling swept through him. A feeling abruptly interrupted when he stepped off a curb and staggered off the edge of the parking lot, then fell to his hands and knees. The document tube, containing the five prints, landed in front of him on the grass. He stared at it for a moment, took a deep breath, picked it up, and went on to his car.

Arnold Gavin, the security guard standing just inside the glass doors of the Time Lease Center, watched the car's lights come on, and then make a wide U-turn in the empty parking lot, and drive away in the early morning hours. He glanced up at the Moon and then back down to watch the car disappear around the corner. He then hurried to his office and picked up the phone.

Agent Allen Brewster was just drifting back to sleep when the phone rang. He fumbled blindly for it. As the clock fell off the nightstand; its cord drug the ashtray off onto the floor.

"Ohhh" the agent said, placing a hand on his

irritated stomach. "Ulcers, acting up again." He rose up on his left elbow, reached across his chest, grasped the lamp and followed the stem up to the switch, and turned on the light. The phone rang again. He picked it up. "Brewster." he said sharply.

"This is Gavin," came from the receiver.

"Gavin, who?"

"Arnold Gavin at the Time Lease Center, Mr. Brewster."

"At four in the morning!" Brewster said angrily.

"Yes, sir, you said to call you immediately if I saw anything unusual." Brewster moved the mouthpiece to the side, burped, then blew out the stale air and swallowed. He placed the phone back into position as he pictured the idiot on the other end.

"What is it" he said.

"Well, Sir, there was this guy. He came in here yesterday morning and worked on computer terminal number seven all day and up until three-thirty this morning."

"So; some of those computer geeks can stay awake for days!"

"But," he said weakly, "It's what I saw on the monitor when he finished."

The Agent shouted into the phone: "Well, what did you see!"

"A huge glass domed city on the Moon that looked like it had been bombed." Brewster sat straight up in bed, ignoring the sharp stomach pain.

"Who was the guy?" There was a pause then he heard Gavin again. His voice sounded stronger.

"Douglas Hastings. He lives in Davenport. His address is 1224 Cherrywood Lane."

"Okay," the agent said. "Let me know if he comes in again."

"Yes, Sir." He said, and the line went dead.

The agent put the phone back on its cradle and lit a cigarette. He went to the bathroom, opened the medicine cabinet, took out a large bottle of Maalox and took a swallow, then returned to the side of the bed and sat down.

So far, this thing of enhancing the Apollo photographs, done by several sites on the Internet, had been groups in scientific circles bringing out anomalous objects and treating them as something controversial that should be researched. That in itself is, more or less, containment. They marketed tapes and books on the enhancements and created some public interest, but, so far, it had been a relative few and no real threat. Up until now, no one, especially anyone like that brain-dead Gavin, had called the results a 'city that looked like it had been bombed.' He'd have to find out who this Douglas Hastings is, how much he knows, and could he become a problem.

Allen Brewster had received explicit instructions. The public could never know what is hidden underneath the Moon. Not for a long, long time. If it became public knowledge, according to the opinion of the agency's top people, it would be the end of civilization, as we know it. *'the end of civilization as we know it.'*

God, his stomach hurt.

He'd have to check out this guy and see what he was going to do with the information. He'd go to the Time Lease Center and see how much this Douglas Hastings knew. He'd report. He'd watch. This guy would probably get excited for a while then die on the vine. After all, the evidence was a quarter a million miles away in space. He could never check it out. Probably no reason to even bother watching him. However, Agent Allen Brewster was still getting paid. He was still the guardian of Earth's ancient secret.

Still the author of his own actions--back then.   Still, the nightmares....

Karen was standing in the doorway when Doug drove up into the driveway.   He got out of the car, held up the document tube, and then hurried to the door and into the house.   Karen followed him to the kitchen table and seated herself when Doug pulled out a chair. He removed a copy from the tube and laid it in front of her.   Karen's eyes went to the print, and then darted from feature to feature for several moments.   She looked up and caught Doug's eye.

"This is real!"

Doug nodded.   "Someone built a city on the Moon, two thousand miles across and several hundred miles tall, thousands of years ago, out of glass."

Karen blinked several times, then her eyes went back to the print.   "So enormous.   Built to hold a lot of people."

"Yeah," Doug said, "so big that any one photograph would show only bits and pieces, since it's so eroded and old.   From a distance, since it's transparent material, pure glass, it would blend into the surroundings.   However," Doug continued, tapping the print, "These structures, the castle looking thing, the columns, the geometry of the remains of the city blocks, could be seen from orbit.   Therefore the astronauts saw it.   They knew.   They may not have put it together right away, since it was completely unexpected; they may have seen it repeatedly during the initial orbits of the Moon before they realized they were looking at intelligently made structures down on the surface and some suspended quite high.   But, they knew."

Karen looked at Doug's face for a moment, then back to the print.

Doug concluded: "This has been deliberately hidden from us--the public."

Karen's eyes were wide. "Do you realize what you're saying?"

Doug has been on the trail of discovery for just over three years. He and Karen had done well in their eighteen years of marriage and decided on early retirement to pursue personal interests. Doug had sold his small company, Computer Control Services, Inc., to David Henson, his best friend. Three months later, Karen retired from the Chicago Linguistics Institute. They shared a passion for uniqueness. Karen did a lot of Flea Market and Garage Sale shopping for unusual items and had built up quite a collection. She was still doing some linguistics work, but was hooked on collecting items that 'speak' as she had put it.

During the last couple of years prior to his retirement Doug had gotten caught up in the wave of new public interest in the Apollo moon missions. He was browsing the Internet when he ran across enhanced imaging of the Apollo photographs. He became intrigued and studied all that was available on the Net. He'd ordered all the tapes, books, and pamphlets available, and digested them. Still not satisfied, immediately upon retirement, he took on the challenge of doing the enhancing himself. He decided that he would begin a search for photographs taken of the Moon. He had to know if it was actually real.

Ironically, the search was a short one. Doug called his long time friend, Dave Henson, and told him about the new project. Dave responded with, "If it's Apollo Moon photographs you're looking for, search no further. I know where there's a trunk full of them. In fact, Pop has every one that was taken."

Doug would never forget his exhilaration the afternoon he'd looked into a trunk in the spare bedroom of a modest suburban home in Houston. There, underneath a hand embroidered tablecloth, were stacks of Apollo catalogues and pictures.

Doug met Dave Henson when Dave joined Computer Control Services, the company Doug had started. While working on several programming tasks, they hit it off. Dave was also an expert with computers and that common bond was the vehicle that caused them to interact away from the workplace. Their wives became acquainted and friends almost instantly. Both being professional women, Karen with her linguistics training and Dave's wife with a background in geology, they spent a lot of time together.

The trunk full of Apollo photographic records belonged to Dave's father, who worked at NASA as an internal courier and had been a space enthusiast during America's rush to get to the Moon. He collected every photograph he could get his hands on from the Apollo missions. He carefully protected every picture and catalogue and displayed them proudly on the bookshelf in his den. When the Moon program suddenly came to a halt, he'd put them in the trunk and tucked them away, more or less forgotten.

Isaac Jacob Henson, Dave's Father, was delighted to see new interest in the collection he so eagerly assembled years earlier. He agreed to turn the trunk over to Doug for his project upon securing a promise that he would get to know everything that developed. Doug concurred and began the tedious task of enhancing every photograph.

"Yeah, I know what I'm saying," Doug said as he glanced to the print and then to Karen's face. "When that computer finished the processing and the image appeared on the monitor, it hit me. There's no way they could have missed it. They saw at least some of it." Doug touched his stomach.

"I'm starving," he said.

"Me, too," Karen said. "Let's have breakfast then you'd better lie down for a while. We have the barbecue tonight, remember? Dave and Jean will be here at six."

"You're right, I'm a little heavy on my feet," Doug said as he stretched again. "I don't know if I can clear my mind enough to go to sleep." he picked up the enhanced photograph. "This is going to blow Dave away."

# Chapter 2

*"At the Research Center, on the larger of the four blue and white worlds of the ancient Solar System, the chief scientist watched the intensity of the magnetic field increase. When the specifications outlined in the study were reached, a hyper-dimensional window opened. The mathematical prediction had been correct. A brilliant stream of energy flowed from the window into a containment tunnel around which the complex had been constructed. Suddenly, the entire research center rose several feet, then paused, before starting to rise again. Something was wrong. Something terrible…."*

## - THE COVER-UP -

Arnold Gavin feigned the secret agent look seen on countless spy and conspiracy movies. Allen Brewster glanced at him and then toward the ceiling. He focused again on Super computer Terminal number seven as the bearded, pot bellied man with the long ponytail worked toward bringing up the work of Douglas Hastings. The man at the terminal easily resurrected the deleted file and hit a key sharply. He then rolled the swivel chair back and looked up at the agent.

The image of the ruins appeared on the monitor.

"That's it," Gavin said, then caught himself and resumed his 'look'. "That's the picture I saw when the guy finished. When I came into the room, he tried to block my view of the screen. I'd already see it, though, through the door." Brewster studied the screen a few moments.

"This guy's really good," he muttered. His eyes went to the twenty-mile long glass complex. He broke away then locked eyes with the guru.

"Make me a couple of prints, then copy it to disc and delete it from the computer, completely this time." The guru nodded and rolled his chair back into position. Brewster turned to Gavin.

"You're to forget all about this. It's Top Secret, it didn't happen."

"Yes, Sir," Gavin said dramatically.

The guru glanced at Brewster, maintaining a straight face, then turned back to the computer to carry out the agent's instructions.

## Chapter 3

*"The ancient intelligent Being blinked in disbelief
when the image of his home planet suddenly
expanded outward to twice its size and then, like
the burst of a balloon, accelerated in all
directions, in pieces. He recoiled from the
monitor, caught his breath, and then looked up
through the transparent ceiling of the lab complex
as if to see a piece of it go by. There, in the
beauty of space, was Earth, the plush,
comfortable Primary, the Moon's partner in
space, soon to be co-victim...."*

## - DAVE HENSON -

Dave Henson hung up the phone. The barbecue
would be a good break from his routine. It'd been a
busy week. Left handed, he shuffled through the
notes again. He got up, stepped over to the office
window and did a couple of squats. He'd been sitting
at the desk for hours. He could run the hundred yard
dash in ten seconds flat when he was in college. Still
lean and athletic at five-foot-ten and a hundred and
seventy pounds, he wondered how much he'd slowed
down at forty-five. He returned to his desk.

He leaned back in his office chair, rethinking his
nine a.m. appointment in Des Moines Saturday
morning. He'd agreed to do a preliminary review of
computerizing the production and distribution of a
small company that had grown slowly over the years
but remained behind the times. Sheer numbers had
now forced modernization of its accounting system.

Dave had done such before. Less than a year
after acquiring Computer Control Services, he began
specializing in customizing small distribution needs.
He was very successful at marketing custom systems

of his own creation.   He loved his work and took great pleasure in seeing his systems working well.   He'd met Doug years earlier and recognized his computer skills.   Doug was gifted with computer programming and they continually enjoyed interacting on the professional level, as well as being close friends. He'd liked Doug from the start, and had noticed his unusual independence.   It seemed to fit and he wore it well.   Doug had a way of keeping the edge off his disagreements with colleagues.   Maybe down deep his friend had some hidden talents; the talents of a diplomat.

Dave grew up in suburban Houston.   During his early teens he'd watched his father's enthusiasm during the Apollo Moon Program and witnessed the collection of the paraphernalia displayed in the den. He'd seen many of the geometric anomalies as Doug had progressed with his research.   Now, Doug had methodically   enhanced   every   photograph   and combined them.   He had the results all together and Dave would see it today.   His pulse quickened as he thought about it.

He picked up his briefcase and evaluation portfolio and headed for the supermarket to pick up steaks, at Jean's request.

The two couples sat at the backyard table while the last flame of charcoal was burning out.   Dave and Jean studied he photograph for several minutes. Doug remained quiet to allow them to digest what they were seeing.   Jean glanced up at Karen, who motioned for her to go with her into the house.   Jean glanced at the photograph again, then stood and followed her.

"It's huge," Dave said.   "I knew something was there, but this is overwhelming."

"I know," Doug said. "I stared at it for a long time and had this feeling I can't describe. I was awed--overwhelmed. It means there were others--a civilization, *advanced* civilization, here, a long, long, time ago. I have to follow up on this; I can't just let it go."

"Are you thinking of the press?"

"I don't know," Doug said. "Somehow, I don't think that's the thing to do. The implications here are not trivial but the press has seen it before, at least in bits and pieces."

Dave nodded. "Have you called Pop?"

"I put a copy in the mail to him today; he'll have it Monday."

Dave's eyes went from Doug to the back door of the house. Karen and Jean came out carrying a platter of meat, barbecue sauce, and grill tools still bearing droplets of water. Jean picked up the print again. Doug watched her face momentarily. At five-foot-eight, she looked half a head taller than Karen's five-six. She had a slender build and square shoulders. She was a good geologist. She would see a lot in an enhanced photograph like this; especially like this.

Jean focused on the photograph. Karen watched her study the scene for a moment then took a breath.

"Just think, a huge city made of pure glass."

"The building material of choice on the Moon," Doug interjected. "Lots of sand available."

"God, it must've been beautiful," Jean said and then pointed at the suspended structure. "This looks like a castle."

Doug glanced at Jean, then at Dave. "The best I can tell by the coordinates, it's suspended some thirty miles above the surface of the Moon."

"Just imagine," Jean said, "walking down the street and all the buildings transparent and glistening." She focused on another anomaly. Dave leaned close as she pointed it out.

Doug looked at the area. There were bright spots scattered between the central crater and the piece of building hanging above the surface. He studied them momentarily.

"I wonder what the women were like." Jean said. "If they had women--if they were male and female, I mean."

"They were real, just like us," Doug said.

Dave nodded. "In that picture you can see that they laid out streets just like us, they had roads just like us, they need air to breath, just like us."

"I've got to know more about them," Doug said. "What did they look like? What language did they speak? And most of all, what happened to them? I've got to know more about their culture."

"Just suppose," Dave said. "that there's a central library or records room of some sort; archives, that's survived all this time."

"You're making my mouth water. Doug said.

Karen stood up. "Guys, speaking of mouth watering, let's start the steaks. The grill's ready and I'm getting hungry."

"So am I," Jean said as she pushed the platter of steaks toward Doug. He placed the steaks on the grill, seasoned them, and then returned to the table. He leaned forward and placed his palms on the table on each side of the print.

"A gigantic Arcology," he said.

"Arcology?" Jean said.

"Architectural Ecology," Doug said as he glanced at Jean. "It's a closed environment built to live in that's completely contained and separate from the environment around it. Do you remember the special on TV about the one in Arizona? It was called the Biosphere. The people stayed in it for several months. They were testing to see if people could survive in a closed environment in the future on Mars or on the Moon."

"We're lucky," Dave said, "that some of the ruins are still there for us to analyze."

Doug, tending the grill, looked around. "You're right. Too bad the discovery was kept quiet. A whole generation has passed since the astronauts walked on the Moon, a whole generation that didn't get to know about it."

"I wonder why." Dave said. "Why didn't they shout it to the world?"

"I don't know. Maybe they were afraid of worldwide panic. Remember, this was back in the sixties. Put yourself in their place. They expected to land on a dead Moon and when they looked out the window, they were landing in the middle of a huge city, in ruins. Maybe they were just plain scared. Just suppose one of the astronauts had shouted into the radio. *"Houston, there are buildings here! We just went by one several miles tall!"* What do you think would have been NASA's reaction?"

Dave was silent or a moment. He looked at the suspended structure in the photograph. Doug glanced at the picture again.

"Houston would have asked them to describe it. Just imagine their reaction to this kind of news. If you remember, the first astronauts that returned from the Moon were kept in isolation for a long time to see if there was any biological contamination."

Dave nodded. "I remember that."

Karen and Jean were looking back and forth from Doug to Dave. Karen spoke: "I don't see how they kept it from leaking out; thousands of people have been involved with NASA."

"There are lots of websites about it," Doug said, "I've studied them all. It's just that there's been nothing *official.*

Richard 'Dick' Bantan, private eye, pulled his car over to the curb a half block away from 1224 Cherrywood Lane, shut off the engine, and prepared to wait. He opened his thermos, poured a cup of coffee, lit a cigarette, and then looked toward the house. It was almost sundown.

Earlier, a man had walked into his office in Des Moines, laid ten one hundred dollar bills on his desk. He had given him a phone number to report to and the name and address of Douglas Hastings. The man wanted to know who Doug's friends were without him knowing about it. Dick asked his client's name. He didn't get an answer and didn't ask again when he saw the look in the man's eyes. He needed the money. *"Probably some big company politics; none of my business,"* he thought.

Doug placed the platter of grilled steaks in the center of the table. Moments later the two couples were enjoying the food with the sun low on the horizon. They were quiet for a few moments.

Dave broke the silence. "I don't get it. NASA's always looking for funding." He gestured his fork toward the photograph. "What better way to get it? It just doesn't make sense."

Doug nodded toward the print. "Maybe the answer is there."

Dave glanced at it. "What could it possibly be?"

Doug paused for a long moment. "I want to find

out."

They ate in silence for a few moments.

Doug changed the subject. "Dave, how early do you have to get up in the morning?"

"He's already set his alarm for four-thirty," Jean responded.

"Yeah," Dave added, "I have to be there at nine a.m., I want to be on the road at five. This company I'm calling on is a perfect candidate for one of our computer systems. They've grown and started taking a lot of small direct orders resulting in a ton of additional paperwork. We can do them a lot of good and I want to be a little early to prepare myself."

The two men discussed the different programs that Dave could offer, analyzing the call as they'd done for years, prior to Doug's retiring. Doug loved the rapport with Dave, a chance to stay in the game and stay sharp on the fast changing computer programming and sales world.

When the Sun disappeared below the horizon they gathered up everything in the glow of the yard light and retreated into the house. Karen fixed them all a drink. As they sipped them, the conversation turned back to the Moon.

"There's a full Moon tonight and it's a clear evening," Doug said. "Come outside, I want to show you something." He led the way out into the back yard, then located the Moon and pointed.

"Look at the dark areas; just gray dust now. But, back then those areas were forest--reduced to gray dust by suddenly being exposed to a hard vacuum and then subjected to the raw radiation of the sun for thousands of years. They were under cultivation then--green things to make oxygen. Imagine the effort and the technology to transport everything there to get it started." Doug was talking rapidly with excitement in his voice as the others focused on him and listened. He paused and took a couple of breaths, then continued:

"First they dredged out the areas for the sand to make tons and tons of glass for the construction of the city and the dome over it, and then prepared and planted the areas to sustain the population in the finished domed city. It staggers my mind to think about such an enormous engineering project. Just think of the technical development to be able to erect a dome that size. And, they did it in a hard vacuum...."

"You're really caught up in this thing, aren't you?" Dave said.

"I can't help it. I'm not off the deep end, okay? But, this is very, very significant. This is not your every day revelation."

"True," Dave replied, "very true."

When they returned to the house, Dave and Jean announced a early retreat and went out to their car. Doug and Karen followed. The two couples exchanged pleasantries and Dave and Jean drove away into the clear, moonlit night. Doug glanced up at the Moon again. He heard a car engine start half a block down the street. His eyes found it when its lights came on and it pulled away from the curb. It went the same direction as Dave and Jean had driven away. It was a light green plain automobile. He was unable to see inside the car as he watched it disappear around the corner two blocks away. He was looking at the ground, harboring a touch of uneasiness when Karen slipped her arm around his waist. He glanced at her. As she looked up at the Moon, his eyes followed. He put his arm around her shoulders and they gazed at the Moon for a long moment, then their eyes met. He saw something in them. Fear? No. She had learned of something awesome; something out of context, and she wanted everything to still be okay. She had her head on his chest.

"I'm okay," he whispered in her ear. He put his hand on her hair and held her for a moment. She raised her head up again, cleared her throat, and then kissed him. They walked back to the house together. Doug paused at the door and looked again toward where he'd seen the car turn off the street. It had made a turn at the same corner where Dave had turned. Karen looked up at him with question in her eyes. Doug looked down at the sidewalk, then at Karen.

"Did you see that car pull out from the curb and drive away just as Dave and Jean left?"

Karen glanced down the street then up at Doug again. "No, ah, I didn't notice."

"Probably nothing," Doug said as they turned and went into the house. Karen did the last tidying up in the kitchen. Doug checked the back yard again. Back inside, he looked at Karen for a moment, then picked up the phone and dialed Dave's number. Dave answered the phone with his usual briskness.

"Dave, Doug. Did you notice anybody following you on your way home?"

"What?"

"When you and Jean drove away a car pulled out from the curb half way down the block and followed you."

"I didn't see anybody," Dave said. "I wasn't looking, though."

Doug heard Dave ask Jean the question. She said the same.

"Maybe I was just a coincidence." Doug said.

"Probably," Dave said. "How would they know? You haven't told anybody yet"

"You're right. Good night."

Karen woke up with a start. She reached over toward Doug; he wasn't there. She rubbed her face and looked at the clock; it was two o'clock in the morning. She turned on the nightstand light and sat up on the side of the bed. She rubbed her face and the back of her neck, then slipped on her robe and went to the kitchen. Light from the office door illuminated the hall and dimly lighted the dining room. She drank a glass of water, then stepped into the office doorway, leaned up against the jam, and crossed her arms.

Doug, in his robe, his hair in disarray, looked up from the print spread out before him. "A building," he said softly, *"thirty...miles... tall."*

Just outside Wichita, Kansas, an astronaut sat alone in his living room, in his robe, holding a photograph of his wife and two children; Jenny, Marvin, Jr., and little Patty; Patricia Lynn. In the 4 x 5 picture, they were beaming with smiles. He'd been looking at them for an hour.

It had been just over two years since it had happened. They were gone, just gone in an instant. Just three days earlier he'd returned from a shuttle mission where he had floated around and around the Earth seventy-two times, three of them outside the spacecraft in a pressure suit, and he was still here. They had gotten in the family car to go to the supermarket, and in a horrible instant, they were gone--forever. God, it had hurt for a long time. He glanced at the clock; two a.m., then back at Jenny's face.

"Jenny," he whispered, "Renee will be here for breakfast in the morning. I told her about you. She's wonderful, Jenny. You would like her. I know you would.  I don't think you would mind if I fall in love with her...."

Karen, still standing in the doorway, studied Doug's face, glanced at the suspended structure on the print, and then back to his eyes.
"You want to go there, don't you?"
"There's gotta be a way."

DAN HOLT

# Chapter 4

*"The immeasurable detonation of the planet hurled much of the debris toward the Sun. Upon arriving at the nearest planet in its path, fate would have two of the giant projectiles on the correct trajectory to settle in low and medium orbits around it. The larger of the two carried the remains of the Research Center, whose horrendous mistake had destroyed its home planet. Thousands of years later, when awareness and the ability to think arose again, the newcomers would find these two in the night sky and, ironically, name them Fear and Terror. The newcomers would place them in their records as Phobos and Deimos and call them moons of the planet Mars. As the newcomers grew in knowledge, their tiny robotic probe, which in their fondness for names they called Viking, would circle Mars and learn of its lifeless condition, then turn and look at the grooves in Phobos with an accusing eye...."*

## - ISAAC & AL -

Isaac Henson sat in his living room looking at a picture of an ancient crystalline city on Earth's Moon. He didn't know how to feel. When he was young and so hungry for discovery like this, he'd been denied. He had eagerly hoped daily during those years. Then the hope began to go away and was finally gone.

Isaac, an energetic person, still very agile at fifty-nine, bounced his light, five-foot-eight inch body from the recliner and went to his office. He picked up the phone and dialed his son's home in Davenport, Iowa. Jean answered on the first ring.

"Jean, is Dave home?"

"He sure is, Pop. He and Doug are in his office

working on the new system for a client in Des Moines. Hold on, I'll get him."

Moments later Dave came on the line. "Pop, you okay?"

"Dave, I knew we would find something when we landed on the Moon! You remember me telling you that?"

"I remember, Pop. It looks like you were right, because it's there and it's so tremendous and magnificent that I think it overwhelmed those who discovered it."

"They had no right to keep it a secret from the rest of us," Isaac said pointedly.

"No, they didn't," Dave said quietly, "but they did conceal it from the public and, as it stands now, that was a long time ago."

Isaac paused. "Yes, it was a long time ago. If it wasn't for Douglas' computer enhancement of my collection, I still wouldn't know about it." He continued with excitement in is voice, "You know, I had quite a treasure in that old trunk, didn't I?"

"No doubt about it."

Isaac abruptly asked to speak to Doug for a minute. Doug took the phone. "Hello, Pop Henson, how're you doing?"

"Okay." He paused. "Douglas, I received the last picture you sent me. It's great! It's really something that you were able to put it all together like that. What's the next step, what are you boys going to do about it?"

Doug took a deep breath and exhaled slowly.

"Pop," he said, "Dave and I have been talking about that for several days now. We intend to follow up on it. We'd like to hear your thoughts."

"Well, what you ought to do is set up a private venture and go back to the Moon," Isaac said seriously.

Albert Billington carefully tied the string to the top of the mast with the long tool supplied with the kit. Building a ship in a bottle was a real challenge to him and he just had to do it. At sixty years old, a full head of graying hair, and carrying twenty extra pounds on his six-foot frame, he still had steady hands and keen blue eyes.

Staffing had been his challenge for thirty years at The National Aeronautics and Space Administration. From nineteen sixty until nineteen ninety, Al had driven a desk on what he felt was the most glorious journey a man could be lucky enough to take. Upon retirement, he and his wife, June, had done some traveling, seeing some of the things on their years old bucket list, and then finally settled down to seek out one small challenge after another.

"There," he said, stepping back to admire his work.

"Phone for you!" his wife called out. Al had not heard it ring.

"I'm coming," he said, looking at his handiwork again.

"Hello," he said, sitting down in his recliner, "Al Billington here."

As he listened to the voice on the other end of the line, memories began to replay in his mind. It was Isaac Henson with a rush of words about something that he had to show him.

"I.J," Al said, "It's been a long time. How are you doing and what are you talking about?"

"Al, I'm doing fine and I've got to show you something," Isaac said. "Do you remember me talking about all the pictures of the Moon I was collecting and the catalogs and all?"

"Yes, I do," Al said cheerfully. "Everyone would

remember that. It's all you talked about back then."

"Well, I want to show you one of those pictures."

"I.J., I've seen all the pictures, but I'd like to see you again. Come over and bring Thelma. June will be glad to see her."

There was silence on the other end of the line for a moment. "Al, you have not seen this picture. We're on our way."

Al called out to his wife as he hung up the phone. "That was I.J. He said he had a picture he wanted to show me."

"A picture of what?" June said from the kitchen.

"He said he had a picture of the Moon that I haven't seen." Al got up and went into the kitchen. June glanced over her shoulder. "Oh...how's Thelma?"

"I invited them over."

"Good. I haven't seen her in a long time. I wonder if she's still dressing up teddy bears like she used to." Al shrugged his shoulders.

Isaac and Thelma arrived just over an hour later. Al opened the door when they pulled into the driveway, then stepped out and down the walk as they were getting out of the car. "I.J., you look the same, how do you do it?"

Isaac smiled, extending his hand. "You look good yourself, Al. It's good to see you again."

"Oh, I've put on some weight," Al responded, shaking hands "but I feel good."

June and Thelma hugged each other and began talking.

"Come on in. We'll get something to eat and talk," Al said.

They went into the house and Al took Isaac straight to his new project. Isaac bent down and looked at the detailed sailing ship inside the glass bottle.  He thought how patient one would have to be to assemble such detail through that small bottleneck.  He studied the intricate detail momentarily then blinked.  He realized he was viewing the ship through…glass.  He turned to Al.

"Come over here and sit down at the table," he said.  "I want you to look at something."

Al sat down, looked at his friend, and smiled.  Isaac pulled the photograph out of the document tube and laid it in front of him, then leaned back in the chair and remained silent.  Al glanced down at the picture and then back at Isaac, then picked up the photograph.  For moment he was quiet.

"Where did you get this?" he finally said without looking up.

Isaac began to explain about Douglas Hastings.

"No, no," Al interrupted, "I mean, where did you get this shot of the Moon?   I haven't seen it."

"Oh, every time I ordered one of the catalogs, I'd follow up by ordering each of the photographs separately.   That photo number is one that was overexposed in the catalog.   Then Dave's friend, Douglas Hastings, computer enhanced it and was able to assemble the bits of evidence from all the photographs into a three-dimensional picture."

"But I asked about those overexposed pictures in the catalogs," Al said, "and the told me that they didn't come out."

"I don't know, when I ordered that number, that's the picture I got."

"I had that feeling back then."  Al slowly shook his head.  "I couldn't imagine being able to send a spacecraft to the Moon and not being able to get the light settings right on the camera."  Al laid the picture down on the table and placed his hands on each side of it, palms down, and stared at the images.

"My god, I.J., look at this, there're ruins of a huge city on the Moon!"

Isaac smiled. "I know." Al's face hardened.

"All the years at NASA and not a thing about this. I'm going to make a serious phone call."

Al was half way up from his chair when Isaac put his hand on his arm. "No, Al."

Al sank back down in his chair, studying Isaac's face. "I.J., we can't let them get away with this."

Isaac stared at Al for a moment. "They already have."

Al searched Isaac's face. Isaac continued:

"Think about it. Many people knew about this. All the astronauts that made the trip to the Moon saw it for themselves. Not one of them has made a public announcement. Of all those people, some had to have argued for disclosure to the public, yet it hasn't happened. Why?"

Al leaned back in his chair, took a deep breath, and exhaled slowly as he looked at the picture again, and then stared out into the room. "I feel queasy."

Isaac nodded. "It takes some getting used to."

After a few moments, Al resumed studying the photograph, bending close to examine detail in several places. Isaac watched as he studied it. Al cleared his throat and looked up.

"Who is this guy you started to tell me about? I believe you said he was a friend of your son. Does he work at NASA:"

"Oh, no," Isaac responded quickly, "he's a computer man like Dave. Dave brought him down to see me. At the time, Dave told me that Douglas wanted to computer enhance the photographs and see what was on them. He and Dave have been friends for a long time so I let him take them. He said he'd send me copies of everything he found. That photograph," Isaac pointed to the picture on the table, "is one of them."

Al sat straight up in his chair. "You mean there's more!"

"Oh, yes," Isaac replied. "Dozens of them. That one there shows the most stuff together."

"I'd like to see them all."

Isaac got up from his chair. "I expected you to say that. Let me get them out of my car."

Al followed as Isaac went to the car and retrieved the six file pockets filled with photographs. Al was looking up at the Moon. Isaac looked up also. Then Al looked down and their eyes met. Al smiled. Isaac smiled and nodded.

Back inside the house, Al laid the file pockets on the table, "Can I keep these pictures for a day or two and look them over?"

Sure," Isaac said, "just give me a call when you're finished and I'll pick them up."

DAN HOLT

# Chapter 5

*"The cumbersome creature made a break for the trees, running on two legs with an occasional dip down for a couple of strides on all fours and then back to the newly learned art of upright locomotion. He, and a dozen others quickly concealed themselves. Then the dominate one peered through the leaves and watched the shiny ball ascend into the sky. When it was out of sight, he turned and sniffed the leaves next to him...repeatedly. For the first time, they had scent...."*


## - MELVIN SIMPSON -

Doug sat as his desk looking over the photographs again. His mind kept going back to the phone conversation with Pop Henson. *"Organize a private venture and return to the Moon,"* he'd said. Doug thought about actually being on the Moon and exploring the ancient city. He thought about the wonders and treasures that an advanced civilization might leave behind. He felt exhilaration as he imagined sophisticated artifacts and trying to figure out what they were and how they worked.

The more he thought about it, the more he knew he couldn't leave it alone. There was a cover-up of the discovery on the Moon, a thirty-year-old cover-up. Thirty long years. There has to be more to it than just the fact that the city's there for the cover-up to still be ongoing. *But, what?*

Doug opened his Contacts file and located the information for Melvin Simpson, a friend and associate he'd known for years.

Melvin sat in his office. His desk was stacked

neatly with financial reports. He loved it; he enjoyed painting the financial portrait of a company. When Martha, his wife, passed away six years earlier, Melvin buried himself in his work and became even more efficient in his ability to handle complicated accounting jobs. He was very comfortable with numbers, they worked with him, and they listened to him. Melvin wasn't that good with people. People were unpredictable, difficult for him to manage. But, a pile of reports had names and places and they all stayed where they belonged and reacted as they should.

He removed his glasses, cleaned them, readjusted them on his nose, then got up and went into the receptionist area to refill his coffee cup. His receptionist glanced up from her computer and smiled, then went back to the chore of putting Melvin's work in client-ready form. Her hands moved rapidly over the keyboard, pausing just as quickly when the phone rang. Melvin noticed her quick movements, admiring her. He loved a quick mind.

She cupped her hand over the phone and turned to him. "It's a Mr. Douglas Hastings," she said. "Do you want to take his call?"

Melvin smiled. "I haven't heard from him in a long time. Yeah, I'll talk to him."

Melvin returned to his office and picked up the phone. "Doug, how's the retirement going? Have you been rocking chair shopping yet?" Melvin laughed into the phone and took a sip of coffee.

"Melvin, I need to talk to you," Doug said seriously.

"Sure, Doug. What's up?"

"How about me telling you all about it at dinner. Do you have plans this evening?

"No."

"Seven p.m. at the Tiger's Paw?"

"Seven's fine," Melvin responded. "Doug, anything wrong?"

"No," Doug said slowly, "It's just a little awkward to try to explain on the phone. And also, Melvin, do you mind if Dave comes along?"

"Dave Henson?"

"Yes."

"Sure. I haven't seen him in while either."

"Okay," Doug said. "We'll see you there at seven."

Melvin hung up the phone and stared at it for a moment. He didn't like unknowns, always a hangnail in his business, but he found himself enjoying the mystery.

Doug hung up the phone feeling just a little uneasy. He was about to take his personal vigil outside the protected world of his and his best friend's close relationship. What would be the reaction? He knew Melvin, but mostly on the professional level. The phone on the desk rang. Doug picked it up, his mind still addressing the problem.

"Hello."

"Douglas Hastings?" a voice on the other end of the line said. Doug's mind came rushing back to the moment.

"Yes."

"Mr. Hastings, this is Albert Billington, National Aeronautics and Space Administration, Personnel Staffing, retired."

Doug set straight up and took a breath as the voice continued: "I.J. gave me your phone number and I thought I'd give you a call."

"Who?...Who's I.J.?" Doug said.

"Isaac Jacob Henson," was the response. "He showed me the computer enhanced pictures of the

Moon that you worked up. I asked to call and talk to you. He gave me your number."

"Oh, you're talking about Pop Henson in Houston," Doug said, leaning back in his chair.

"Yes, we called him I.J. when he was working at NASA," Al replied. "He said you and Dave were looking into following this up and I just wanted to volunteer to help and be part of it if I can."

"Okay," Doug said. "Ah, we're still getting focused...organized on this thing. You worked at NASA in personnel staffing?"

"Yes, I did," Al said, "for thirty years. I never knew a thing about this. Things didn't seem right sometimes but I'd just dismiss it because I couldn't imagine such a thing. After seeing these pictures where you brought out what was really photographed, it floored me for a little bit. But, looking at them now, it clears up a lot of things that were a little confusing back then. You did a great job. This discovery of yours has put some spice back into my life. I would like to be a part of this. If you want to organize a private venture to do a research mission to the Moon, I offer my services any way I can help." He paused. "Let me give you my address and phone number."

Doug reached for his note pad and a pen. He wrote down the address and phone number, thanked Al for the call, and hung up. He sat back, looking at the spread of pictures again, digesting the new development, then he picked up the phone. He called Dave and told him about the unexpected call from Al Billington and about Al's NASA connection. Dave remembered the name and person from his teenage years. Doug then related the conversation with Melvin Simpson and asked Dave to accompany him for the evening.

Doug hung up the phone, glanced at his watch,

sighed, and went to the kitchen to get another cup of coffee. He took a sip as he leaned on the cabinet. The thing growing inside him just got another spark. The projection in Albert Billington's voice was inspiring. After all, he was a professional man with thirty years at NASA.

Doug and Dave were escorted by a young attractive woman to a booth on a raised floor, one step up, and around a latticework divider to a half-moon table where Melvin Simpson was sitting, sipping a screwdriver. Melvin smiled and extended his large hand. Doug noticed his fifties hairstyle. The tall gangly man with the dominant Adam's apple still looked the same.

"Melvin," Doug said, shaking his hand, "How have you been?"

"Fine, just fine," he said, and then shook Dave's hand. "Dave, long time no see. Sit down and I'll order your drinks. What will you fellas have?"

Melvin signaled the waitress. She appeared and took the order.

"I've had the longest afternoon of my life," Melvin resumed, "What..." Doug laid the document tube on the table. Melvin stared at it. "What have we got here?"

When Melvin looked up, Doug continued. "You were, what, twenty-three, twenty-four, in nineteen sixty-nine?"

Melvin nodded. "Twenty-four, why?"

"Were you watching TV the day Neil Armstrong stepped out on the Moon?"

Melvin glanced at Dave then back at Doug. "Of course I was--everybody was."

The waitress arrived with the drinks, took Melvin's empty glass, placed a fresh napkin in front of him, and then served him another Screwdriver. She then set drinks in front of Doug and Dave and went away. Doug opened the tube and removed the enhanced picture, then spread it out on the table.

Melvin stirred his drink with a tiny plastic oar as he studied the photograph. His facial muscles slowly caused wrinkles in the middle of his forehead as he scanned it from side to side. He looked up at Doug, and then at Dave. He opened his mouth, took a half breath, and then closed it again. Doug watched him as he leaned closer and studied the detail. Melvin tried to brush something off the picture. When it remained, he studied it for a few moments. He picked up the photograph and held it at arm's length. As he studied it, a smile formed on his lips, and then went away as he blinked his eyes several times.

"These are ruins; ruins of a city." Melvin said.

Doug nodded, watching his reaction.

"Ruins of a huge city made of glass!" Melvin exclaimed.

"By the scale of the size of the Moon," Doug said, "the city and the dome over it were about two thousand miles across and several hundred miles tall."

"All of the astronauts who went to the Moon saw it," Dave added.

Melvin just stared at the photograph. "I haven't heard anything about it."

"I know," Doug replied, "No one's heard about it. It was kept from the public."

There was silence for a moment as Melvin's surveyed the photograph.

"My God," he said quietly and fell silent.

When the waitress appeared Doug quickly covered the photo with a napkin. They ordered another round of drinks, and then placed their orders for dinner. Through the rest of the evening Doug filled

Melvin in on how he came by the pictures and the processing he'd put them through. Melvin listened intently and began to relax and digest the scope of the discovery. The three men discussed the discovery's possible repercussions at length, and then eventually got around to routine matters and updates on what had transpired in the three years since they had visited together.

Doug paid the check and then turned to Melvin.

"I just wanted you to know about this. You're a serious-minded man and I want the privilege of calling you from time to time. I intend to follow up on this. I'm not sure yet as to what move to make, but I'm not going to just let it go."

"Doug, I'm glad you called me. I must say, I'm overwhelmed. But, you know, I saw that 'Castle on the Moon' on the front page of the National Inquisitor on the supermarket shelf. I just laughed it off as another one of their outlandish stories."

"Well," Doug said, "it's as real as it can be, and I'd sure like to know more about it. I'd like to know about the people who built it."

"I would, too," Melvin said as they went to their cars. "Doug, you and Dave keep me posted. If there's anything I can do to help, call me. Say hello to the wives for me."

"Sure," Doug and Dave echoed as Doug unlocked his car. Melvin steered his car to the street and entered traffic. As Doug's eyes followed, they came to rest on a light green car. He stared for a moment, then glanced at Dave and pointed toward the automobile.

"That's the car I saw follow you the night we had the barbecue!" Dave looked at the car Doug was pointing to.

"You sure?"

"Yes, that's it."

The car's lights came on, and then it pulled into traffic and went in the same direction as Melvin had driven away. Doug quickly started the car and followed.

"What are you doing?" Dave said.

Let's see if he's following Melvin."

"You think we should?"

"Yes, yes we should," Doug said and followed several car lengths behind the green car.

It was apparent that what Doug suspected, was indeed happening. The green car followed Melvin until he turned into his driveway. It slowed momentarily and then drove away. Doug continued to follow. Two turns later, the occupant of the green car realized that he was being followed. He suddenly accelerated, made a fast turn, ran a red light, and was gone.

"Son-of-a-gun!" Dave said.

"Looks like they are still sensitive about the discoveries on the Moon," Doug said.

"How did they know? Have you told anybody?"

"Just you, and then Melvin, tonight."

"Maybe Pop or Al Billington mentioned it to somebody," Dave said. "I'll call Pop when I get home."

A few minutes late, Doug accelerated the car from the entrance ramp onto the Interstate. Joining the traffic at highway speed, he noticed the rhythm of tires on the joints of the road. He thought about the magnificent roads in the lunar city. He wondered if they had joints, if they were made of concrete, or something else; glass, maybe. He ran a hand through his brown hair and glanced at the rear view mirror.

Dave spoke: "I remember Pop talking a lot

about Albert Billington."

"Oh, yeah?" Doug said, watching his mirrors as he changed lanes. "He sure sounded like the professional type when he called me this afternoon."

"That's exactly how I remember him. When I was around him, he was NASA in my young mind. What he was doing was very important and serious."

"He said he was with NASA for thirty years and knew nothing about the discovery," Doug said.

Dave nodded. "He'd know all the astronauts and everybody else that trained with NASA."

Doug agreed. "Yeah, he would."

They drove the rest of the way to Dave's house in silence. When Doug pulled into the driveway, he shut off the engine and turned to Dave. "Let's organize a research trip to the Moon."

Dave was silent for a moment. "I knew you were going to say that sooner or later. Do you realize what kind of task you're talking about? Look at the millions of dollars that NASA spent, and look at the vast pool of expertise they utilized to get there. That's not to mention that somebody's upset that we know about it."

Doug was nodding before Dave finished. "I know what a vast enterprise it was. I know that an enormous cost was involved in going to the Moon, however, I've been doing some thinking on this for a while now and I believe there just might be a way to do it."

Dave's eyes blinked the question.

Doug took a breath. "To do it, first you have to have the money. To get the money, you have to talk to those who have it and give them a good reason to *invest* it."

Dave straightened up and then nodded.

"Second," Doug continued, "you have to have

the expertise. There are many who already have the training to do it, compliments of NASA and the taxpayers. Only a few got to actually participate in NASA's activities, but many were trained. I thought about this again when I saw Melvin's reaction. If this was presented to enough people with the where-with-all, there's a chance of putting something together."

"For the enormous project it would be, they would have to be something very alluring or nobody's going to risk serious money." Dave said.

"Right. What gets serious money is a chance of serious profit."

"Do you think," Dave said, "that after all this time, there will still be things that can be recovered--things of value?"

"Underground," Doug said, nodding, "Plus the scientific value."

Dave's eyes widened as Doug continued. "Basements under the buildings. Support equipment for the enormous structures and facilities, that's underground. Under the surface, it would be protected from meteors and the solar wind. And in a hard vacuum with no moisture, equipment wouldn't deteriorate."

Dave paused for a moment and smiled. "I hadn't thought about that."

"I believe we can count on it," Doug said. He glanced at the house, and then at his watch. "Well, it's getting late and I know Jean and Karen are waiting. Let's talk more this weekend."

"Okay," Dave said, "call me Friday afternoon."

Allen Brewster hung up the phone. His local investigator had gotten himself noticed. He'd have to let things cool for a while. So far, Hastings had talked to his best friend, another geek, and an accountant. No problems there. However, it was a little surprising that he would chase the local investigator he'd assigned to the initial surveillance. This computer expert had spark. He'd check up on him again in a few days.

The agent poured himself a stiff drink. Most of the time, it'd get him through the night without having the nightmare. In the nightmares, he'd never seen the face. He didn't have to....

Doug awoke early, the Sun splashing its first rays across the city. Karen was sleeping soundly. He kissed her on the cheek and she stirred, but the long deep breathing of sleep continued. He slipped out of the bedroom closing the door behind him, went to the kitchen, and put on a pot of coffee. As the coffee maker started with the familiar sounds, He opened the front door, went down the walk, and picked up the morning paper. Across the street a dog barked a couple of times as if looking for something to break the monotony. It then lazily walked back upon the porch and lay down. Doug opened the paper.

The headline, *"Ancient Alien Ruins Discovered on the Moon"*, was not there. Doug smiled at himself. He went back inside and sat at the table with a cup of coffee. The paper was spread out; he was reading it but not seeing it. His mind was racing along on the subject of how a return to the Moon could be made to really happen. He knew that just telling friends, who would tell friends, and so on, wasn't going to result in an organized effort to follow up this discovery and go back to the Moon to research the ruins that were there. There was, however, an avenue that he felt had definite possibilities; the lure of advanced technologies and advanced materials. Both, he felt, were on the

Moon, waiting to be recovered.

Doug heard the bedroom door open. He got up and poured a cup of coffee and set it in front of Karen as she sat down at the table across from him.

"How long you been up," she asked.

"Not long," Doug smiled, "about half an hour."

"Hungry?"

He nodded and turned another page on the newspaper.

"I woke up hungry," Karen said, getting up and carrying her coffee to the stove. "I want some pancakes this morning. How about you?"

"Huh?"

"Pancakes? I want pancakes. You?"

"Oh, yeah, I'm hungry," Doug took a deep breath and sighed. "Sorry."

"Don't worry about it," Karen said. Doug got up and set the table and helped with breakfast.

After finishing the pancakes and bacon, Karen pushed her plate back and refilled her cup with coffee, then took a sip. "Jean and I are going to Clinton to the flea market and then to Cedar Rapids to an antique show tomorrow, if you don't need me to be here."

"Oh, no," Doug said, "that's fine. I'm supposed to call Dave this afternoon. We wanted to get together this weekend and plan this thing."

"Going to pursue it, huh?"

"I have to try."

"Well," Karen said, "Give it your best, but don't get so serious that you ham it up." Doug opened his mouth, took a half breath, and then paused.

"You're right. Melodramatics isn't going to get it done. The people I ask for help are going to have to feel about it like I do."

Karen nodded, smiling.

# Chapter 6

*"The debris from the planet's explosion rushed toward the Earth and its moon like a blast from a cosmic shotgun. The inhabitants of these worlds, except for a few whose personal routines exposed them to that moment of detonation, were unaware that their end as an intelligent species was near. The oncoming projectiles were so large and so violent that these cultures would be eradicated almost instantly. The Earth would have witnesses for a few days; the ruptured Moon Arcology would decompress to a hard vacuum in an hour...."*

## - THE PROFESSOR -

Karen and Jean left early for Clinton and their day of 'treasure hunting.'

Doug and Dave sat in Doug's office discussing ways to go about getting investors interested enough to supply the enormous amount of money needed for the expensive project.

"We're talking about a research venture," Doug said. "Let's look at it from that standpoint. What we need is someone who knows how to organize a research project."

They both looked at each other momentarily, then said in unison:

"Professor Charles Liggins."

Professor Charles Liggins picked up the phone and said hello, still reading the newspaper. He didn't recognize the voice at first.

"Who is this?" he asked, his mind releasing the article before him.

Dave Henson identified himself. "Professor,

it's been a long time since I've seen you. How have you been?"

"I'm doing fine," Charles said. "Sorry I didn't recognize your voice. How have you been and to what do I owe the honor of this call?"

"Charles, I'm at Doug Hastings' home. We've been doing some research and would like to discuss it with you. Are you busy today? We'd like to drive over and see you."

"No, Dave, come on over," the professor said. "What kind of research?"

"We'll explain everything when we get there. See you in a couple of hours."

They exited the interstate and drove into a well kept middle class neighborhood and into the long circular driveway of Charles Liggins, Professor of Anthropology, University of Iowa, Des Moines.

The Professor opened his front door as they were closing the doors on the car. "Well, gentlemen, come in," he said warmly.

Charles escorted them into his study. Doug looked around the tastefully decorated room. In the middle were two small couches arranged facing each other. In between them was an oval shaped polished oak coffee table. The Professor's desk sat on one wall facing the room. Behind it, bookshelves, floor to ceiling, covered the entire wall. On the adjacent wall was an open antique roll-top desk, its cubbyholes stuffed with opened letters. Above the antique desk was a picture of the Earth, taken from the Moon. Doug nodded approvingly and looked at Charles, noticing his brown hair was graying around the temples. He'd put on weight around the middle of his six-foot frame but still had the thin wiry legs he'd developed when spending so much time in the field.

He knew about organizing research efforts.

Charles invited them to seat themselves, then he left the room and returned with three cups of coffee.

"Now, gentlemen, what about your research?" he asked curiously.

Doug cleared his throat. "Were you teaching during the Apollo Moon Program?"

Charles glanced at Dave, and then back to Doug.

"Yes, I was," Charles said, and then took a sip of coffee. "I remember it was in my second year of teaching when the race to the Moon started. Those were very thrilling days for me when LBJ galvanized everybody to beat the Russians to the Moon." Charles paused for a moment. "Why do you ask?"

Doug pulled the photograph of the finished image out of the document tube and handed it to the professor. "We've been doing some computer enhancing research on the photographs taken during Apollo and have discovered this."

Charles studied the picture for a long time without taking his eyes off it. He glanced up at the framed picture above his roll-top desk, at Doug and Dave, then back at the photograph. He took another sip of coffee, wiped his mouth with his fingertips, and then adjusted the picture to study the detail at the bottom.

"Professor," Dave said, "Doug's been working on this for three years. What you're looking at is the final result. There're lots of other pictures showing all parts of the Arcology on the Moon. It appears that the folks that took the pictures chose to keep it quiet for whatever reason. It's been a long time now and the advances in computer technology are what finally let the cat out of the bag, so to speak."

Charles took a deep breath. "I'm shocked! I

thought there was nothing there. The prospect of what this means is staggering. What I mean is, somebody built this on the Moon, and it wasn't us." As Doug nodded silently he continued. "Have you called anybody, the authorities, the newspapers, anyone?"

"No," Doug said. "We've talked to Melvin Simpson and you."

"What are you going to do about it?"

Doug set his coffee down. "Professor, there's a reason I've kept this to myself." Doug stood and stepped over to Charles' desk then turned and put his hands in his pockets. "I've been working on this a long time. As the evidence in the pictures of the Moon started to come out, I had a lot of time to think, and it became clear that NASA's known from the start, at least those at the top. Maybe they were afraid of panic, cultural shock, or maybe just didn't know what to do about it back then. As you can see, it's overwhelming. Obviously, it was built by an advanced race. But, as time passed, and our technology grew, and the public has become more science and space oriented, why hasn't it been released?"

Charles watched as Doug went back to the couch and sat down. Doug pointed at the photograph spread out on the oak coffee table. "All of the men who went on the missions to the Moon, saw this for themselves."

Charles scanned the picture again.

Doug paused. "Think about it, all those people knew, thirty years ago, and none of them have made an announcement to the public. No one can tell me that those men didn't want you to know, at least some of them. Yet, they remain quiet. I think there's more to it than just the fact that it's there."

"What do you mean?"

"Well," Doug said, "why continue to keep it quiet

for over a quarter of a century?"

Charles leaned back in his chair and let out a long, slow breath.  Doug, noticing his discomfort, paused momentarily.  The professor stared at the floor, breathing noticeably, as if fighting off the truth.

"Charles, somebody knows that we've discovered this."  Doug related the incident at his home the night of the barbecue and then the incident when he and Dave dined with Melvin.  Charles stared at Doug for a moment, and then looked out into the room and blinked a few times.

"That...ah...I don't know...ah...could be serious.  Did you call the police?"

"No," Doug said.  "They ran when they discovered we saw them.  I think they were just trying to find out who we are.  I don't know how they found out we'd made the discovery."

"Where did you get this?" the professor asked, indicating the enhanced photo.

"I did the final three-dimensional work at the Time Lease Center here in..."  Doug stopped short. "The guard!" he said and turned to Dave.

"What?" Dave responded.

"The guard came into the room just as I'd finished assembling the data and had the results on the monitor.  He had never entered the room before when I worked with the super computers on some of the sophisticated programs for Customers.  On our way home, I'm going by there and check that out."

"Just be careful," Charles said.

"They're not going to play cloak and dagger with me," Doug said.  "I'll blow this thing wide open." Doug paused for a moment.  "Professor, Dave and I want to organize a private research venture to the Moon."

Charles searched Doug's eyes.  "What?"

"We want to organize another mission to the Moon and research this." Doug repeated, pointing at the photograph.

Charles stared at Doug for a few moments, and then glanced at Dave. He picked up the photograph again and studied more detail. "This is huge."

Doug and Dave glanced at each other.

"It covered almost the whole face of the Moon, as seen from Earth." Doug added.

"I could spend the rest of my life digging in these ruins." Charles said.

"The only thing," Dave said, "you'd have to be in a space suit."

Charles looked up. "I wouldn't care. Here," Charles tapped the area of the surface neighborhood, "I wouldn't be digging for stone tools or pottery; I'd be digging for…there's no telling what you might find."

"Wonders and treasures beyond imagining; I just know it." Doug said. "Professor, you've organized several research projects here on Earth. How would we go about organizing such a venture?"

"You're talking about a venture here that's on a much larger scale. You have the problem of getting there."

"It's already been done," Doug responded. Charles paused and was quiet for a few moments, then got up, picked up the empty coffee cups and disappeared into the kitchen. He returned with them filled again. He sat down, looked at the picture, took a sip of coffee, and mumbled: "There just might be a way."

Doug glanced at Dave, then at Charles again. "Professor?"

Charles leaned back. "It just might work."

"What?" Doug said, leaning forward.

"I have a friend in Chicago. We were in college

together. He's an organizer, a promoter, the best in the business. His name is Michael Sheridan. I had dinner with him about two months ago and he told me about some new technology being developed at a magnetics corporation just outside Chicago. Michael's very excited about it. He said it was a self-sustaining drive involving magnetics. They're keeping it under wraps until they've finished the testing. I don't know how far along they are, but if you're seriously going to try to get a private venture together and go back to the Moon, maybe you should present this to Michael. They have the resources. If anybody can do it, they can."

"Do you think he would see us?" Doug said.

"I can give Michael a call Monday and let you know."

"Okay," Doug said, "I'll put a presentation together."

"Now," Charles said, picking up the photograph again, "tell me again how you found out about this."

Doug drove away from the home of Professor Liggins, excited about the chance; the possibility of an answer to something growing inside him. Getting a quarter of a million miles to the Moon to see, for real, the city of glass he'd seen on a computer monitor a few days earlier. And, to find out, perhaps why such a wondrous and glorious discovery was kept from the public. He drove to the Time Lease Center and parked.

"Come on," he said to Dave as he got out of the car. Dave followed as they entered the Time Lease Center and went straight to the guard's office. Arnold Gavin looked up when Doug and Dave stepped through the door. There was momentary recognition in Gavin's eyes.

"Remember me?" Doug said pointedly.

"No, Sir, I'm sorry, I don't. What can I do for you?"

"I was here a few days ago for some computer work. You walked into the room where I was working."

"Oh, no, Sir. You must be mistaken. I don't enter the rooms while clients are working."

"It was two o'clock in the morning," Doug said loudly. "I was the only one here; I was on terminal number seven, and you walked into the room!" Gavin leaned away, fear in his eyes.

"I'm sorry. You're wrong." Gavin said defensively.

Doug took a deep breath and stepped closer to Gavin's desk.

Dave put his hand on Doug's shoulder. "Let it go," he said. Doug glanced at Dave. Dave smiled at the guard. "Sorry we bothered you. Have a good evening."

Gavin nodded, his eyes wide. Dave pulled Doug toward the door. Doug paused, glanced at the guard, and then followed Dave into the hall. Dave steered him down the hall and on out of the building.

Doug stopped and pointed back toward the door of the Time Lease Center. "That wimp came into that room!"

"I know, I know," Dave said. "He's obviously following instructions from someone. Did you see the fear in his eyes?"

They went on to the car and began the trip back to Davenport. Doug was quiet until they entered the Interstate; he was focused on the road. He took a deep breath, and then exhaled slowly.

Dave glanced at him. "You were about to come unglued back there. We don't need that."

"I know…thanks."

Dave nodded and grinned. Doug nodded then gripped the steering wheel and growled.

Doug drove in silence for a while before speaking. "New technology," he said. "Technology has come a long way in the last thirty years. My desk-top computer has more power than all of NASA had in the sixties."

Dave nodded. "I wonder about the engine drive Charles was talking about. If they're keeping it quiet, it must be something advanced."

"I sure hope so," Doug said. "I'm going to try to sell them on going back to the Moon. They are developing new technology. If I can convince them that there's some advanced technology to be had on the Moon, maybe they'll consider it."

"That depends on how they feel about it after they see the evidence."

Doug glanced over. "Yeah, it does. If they commit to the venture, it will be the evidence that does it."

It was late afternoon when they pulled into Dave's driveway. Jean and Karen were standing behind Karen's car, opening the trunk. As the guys got out of the car, Jean looked one to the other with feigned consternation.

"Are you guys following us?"

"Oh, no," Dave said. "That would be too much hard work."

Jean cradled her hands on her hips as Dave laughed.

Doug looked into the trunk of the car at the array of unusual items. "Hey, you girls made quite a haul."

"It was nice," Karen said and kissed Doug, "but I'm tired. How was your day?" She adjusted Doug's shirt collar and pushed his hair back.

"Very interesting," he said.   "I'll tell you about it later."

Allen Brewster had taken drastic action only once concerning the lunar secret.   The act had gotten him the center seat responsibility.   The agency felt he was the man for the job when they were informed about the way he'd handled the first threat of the secret getting out.   It got him the job and it got him the nightmares.   The haunting nightmares; the only thing he couldn't control.

The phone interrupted his thoughts:   "Mr. Brewster?"

"Gavin.   What is it?"

"Hastings came back to the Center."

"More computer work?"

"No.   He came to my office.   He had somebody with him."

"Who?"

"I don't know.   He acted like the guy was his friend."

"That'll be Henson," Brewster said.   "What happened?"

"Douglas Hastings asked me if I remembered him," Gavin said.   "I told him, no.   He started to get mad and the other guy told him to let it go.   Then they left."

"Did he say how he found out you reported it?"

"No, he acted like he was trying to prove to the other guy that he had been at the Time Lease Center. I denied everything."

"Okay, keep me posted."

"Good-bye, Sir."

Doug was up early Monday morning, eager to hear from Professor Liggins.   He knew Charles would call as promised, although it would probably be in the afternoon. Doug was sipping his morning coffee as he was putting together his presentation. He wanted to be very thorough. If the fundraiser was to consider taking on the project, he'd need to feel the project was well researched, solid, and had a reasonable chance of a return to its investors. Doug firmly believed that the Arcology on the Moon qualified in all those areas. He must present enough information so that the promoter would feel the same. He wondered how old he was. He must ask Charles when he called with the details. What was his disposition during the Apollo Moon Missions? Doug picked up a note pad and started a list of questions to ask the Professor when he called. He was deep in thought when Karen slipped her arms around him from behind. He reacted momentarily from the surprise but relaxed just as quickly to the familiar arms.

"Ready for some breakfast?" she asked. Doug nodded.

The phone rang; he picked it up after the first ring.

"Doug? Charles Liggins".

"Good morning, Professor," Doug said. "Good news I hope."

"Oh, yes. I just got off the phone with Michael a few minutes ago. He will see you tomorrow at ten."

"Great," Doug said, trying to keep his excitement under control. "I'll be there. I appreciate you doing this for me. Also, I need to ask you a few questions I didn't think about when we were there." Doug went down his list with Charles, making notes as he went. When finished, he thanked him and hung up, already concentrating on the new objective. The phone rang again as soon as it touched its cradle.

"Doug," Dave said, "when Charles calls, give me

a call here at the office and let me know…"

"He already called," Doug interrupted. "I just hung up. He said Michael Sheridan would see us tomorrow morning at ten."

"There's an early flight to Chicago in the morning," Dave said.

"I'll make the reservations right now," Doug said. "I'll call you back.

The twin turboprop entered its final approach to O'Hare. Doug opened his briefcase and retrieved a leather bound note pad, then went over his notes as the plane taxied to the terminal.

They got a cab at the airport and headed for Michael's office. The driver pulled under the awning of the forty-story Wheaton Building. The deep red awning clashed with the greenish glass architectural covering of the building front. They exited the cab and entered the building.

"There's the building directory," Dave said pointing at a pyramid shaped marble monolith in the center of the lobby.

"Executive Profiles, Inc.--Michael Sheridan, President--Suite 1401," Doug read aloud.

"This place looks like something out of Star Trek," Dave commented.

"Maybe that's an omen."

"You don't need an omen or anything else; you're armed with real facts about a real discovery."

"Until now, I've known the people that I've revealed this to. Because of that, I already had their trust."

"He's going to give you the same credibility as he does the Professor," Dave said as they walked toward the elevator. Doug took a deep breath as the doors opened.

When they were escorted into the office, Doug noticed the promoter's stocky build and athletic movements as he walked over to greet them. He was just shorter than Doug's six feet height. His thick blond hair was parted on the left and combed back neatly. He had an innocent face and electric eyes. There was also another man in his office, tall, six foot three inches with a medium build, hard features, and deep set brown eyes. The man nodded. Doug looked back at Michael.

Michael shook hands with them and spoke with a resonant, well trained voice. "Good to meet you, Mr. Hastings, Mr. Henson." Michael turned and extended his hand, palm up. "This is Frank Gordon, owner of Gordon & Gordon Magnetics, an inventor."

Doug stepped forward and shook the hand of the tall man with thinning hair. He had a steady gaze and the look of question in his eyes.

They seated themselves. Michael spoke.

"I asked Frank to be here this morning. Charles explained his relationship with you and said you wanted to talk about an application for the new drive Frank's developing. I must say, Frank's a little concerned."

Doug glanced at Frank, then back to Michael. He opened the document tube, removed the enhanced photograph, and spread it out in front of the two men. They both leaned forward and studied the photograph for a few moments, glanced at each other and then back to the picture to study detail.

Doug paused a few moments, then spoke: "That photograph was taken during the Apollo missions to the Moon. I acquired hundreds of photographs that were taken during those missions, enhanced them separately, and used a super computer to assemble all of them according to their coordinates."

"I'll be damned!" Michael exclaimed.

"It's a city, a city on the Moon," Frank stated.

"Yeah!" Michael said. "Does anybody else know about this?"

Doug explained about Melvin, Isaac and Al Billington, and went on to explain the source of the photograph now lying on Michael's desk and the three years of computer work that led up to it.

Michael seemed to adjust very quickly to possessing exclusive knowledge of a staggering fact. Frank sat quietly and listened intently. Michael asked pointed questions about the possibilities that Doug outlined. Doug was delighted that the organizer dug into the prospects surrounding the discovery on his own volition, not waiting for Doug's planned presentation.

A little over an hour into the discussion, Michael got up from his chair. "Could I ask you gentlemen to excuse us for a few minutes?"

"Of course," Doug said.

"If you would, wait for us in the reception area. We won't be long."

Doug and Dave took their seats in the waiting area. Michael's secretary brought them coffee.

"Evidently," Dave said, "they're interested."

"I sure hope so."

Doug looked up expectantly when the door of Michael's office opened and the promoter came out, smiling.

"Gentlemen, we want you to come with us. We want to show you something. Can you do that?"

"Sure," Doug said.

"We're going to drive out to Frank's test facility," Michael said.

The four men drove past the airport entrance and continued on, Michael at the wheel of his three year old Town Car. They talked until they reached the company and Michael drove into the entrance of the sprawling complex. He then drove down to the end of a huge building, to an obvious addition, and parked the car.

DAN HOLT

# PART 2

# THE INVENTION

DAN HOLT

## Chapter 7

*The intelligent Beings embraced in their customary fashion, muttering phrases of affection for each other in a language unspoken for thousands of years. "Remember," the larger of the two was saying as the projectile was breaking open the dome two hundred miles away, "what we have left of ourselves in this place. What we are and who we are will be discovered someday...by someone who will care."*

## - MAGNETIC INERTIAL PROPULSION -

Frank Gordon, owner of Gordon & Gordon Magnetics, opened the side door of the two story research facility. He escorted the three men inside and closed the door behind them.

At the end of the room Doug saw an overhead crane, hanging motionless, its hook empty. The rails it ran on went the length of the room. At the edge of the room were several ramp ladders on wheels, and several small glassed-in cubicles; offices, he surmised. The room was cool, slightly cooler than the air conditioned office they'd just left. Doug noticed the faint smell of carbon in the air, and something else, an electrical smell. He heard a muffled hum and as he looked around, he saw it.

There was an object suspended in mid-air that looked like two large bells with the open ends butted up to each other and fastened together. The twin bells appeared to be about eight feet from top to bottom and four feet from side to side. Mounted on each side of the object, along the centerline, were two football shaped pods about two feet tall and a foot and a half in diameter. They looked like ears sticking out of the odd shaped device.

Doug studied the object. He could see no cables holding it up and no platform underneath. It was floating in mid-air, completely motionless. He turned to Michael, his mouth open, and blinked the question.

Michael smiled. "That's Magnetic Inertial Propulsion--a power plant--engine, developed by Gordon & Gordon Magnetics. It's been hovering there for twelve days, as of today."

Frank glanced at a console on the right side of the room. "288 hours." he added.

Doug turned to the object and studied it for a moment, and then nodded at Frank. He turned back to the device and walked toward it and around it. Dave followed. They circled the device completely and then stopped and stared. The object was dead still, in mid-air, as if it were a picture that was painted on the wall behind it.

Michael's voice interrupted the steady hum.

"If you fella's are going to the Moon, you'll need a way to get there."

Sitting back in Frank's Gordon's office, Doug looked at the inventor's hard features and deep-set eyes. "Tell me about Magnetic Inertial Propulsion. How did you discover it?"

"I had been experimenting with gyroscopes and magnets for years," Frank said. "I was in college when I first conceived the idea of trying to combine the two forces. After years of research and many trials, I found a way to integrate them. I installed a ring of eight magnets inside a special made gyroscope. I balanced it and placed a steel ring inside, in working proximity of the magnets. I designed the steel doughnut so that a section of it was moveable. I discovered that when I adjusted the moveable section in the ring away from the magnets, with the gyroscope spinning, it resulted in thrust. I put the gyroscope out of balance in one direction. That's when I knew it could be harnessed as a drive system. So I built a full size prototype; the one you saw in the test room."

Michael cleared his throat. "Frank showed the invention to me. I'd been promoting Gordon & Gordon's products for several years. When I saw it was a completely new power system, I encouraged Frank to market it. We mutually agreed to thoroughly test it first."

Frank nodded. "As soon as the test was set up," he said, "I realized it performed even better that I anticipated. The gyroscopic design gives it complete stability. It stays exactly where it's set to run. Another thing, the energy needed to run the rotor system is small. The thrust is centrifugal; it's free energy. It's the same force that keeps a top standing up while it's spinning. The only power consumption is to keep the rotor turning against the resistance of the gears and bearings. I've devised a way for the rotor assembly to generate its own power supply."

Dave straightened up in his chair as Frank became quiet and turned to him. "It's impossible for a generator to supply enough electricity to run its own self," he said. "Ah, at least, that's what I understand," Dave added.

"That's true," Frank said. "However, I've found a way to overcome enough of the resistance encountered in the generation of electricity to allow the rotor to supply its own. That's what the two extensions are that you saw on the sides of the housing."

"What do they do?" Doug said.

They are armature assemblies with permanent magnets so configured to attract the armature in a circular motion; in effect, a motor that does not need power. They are not very strong, but, they supply enough energy to take the rotor past the threshold of resistance. The mechanism inside the magnet ring supplies thrust, as I explained. There's a field coil around the outside of the magnets that generates the electric power. The gyro motors give it the boost it needs to supply enough electricity to run itself.

"In other words," Michael said. "This invention is not just another engine to sell; it's the replacement of the jet engine and rocket engine; it's the next step."

"Here's another feature to this type of power plant," Frank resumed. "There's no fuel problem. The engine recycles its own propellant; its propellant being centrifugal force, therefore, it doesn't run out. That means we can make the trip under constant acceleration and have artificial gravity all the way except for a brief midpoint reversal of power. Also, that will greatly reduce the transit time to the Moon."

Doug sat back and blinked and swallowed as Michael paused, and then spoke with conviction:

"What better debut could we give Magnetic Inertial Propulsion than to develop a vehicle for lunar exploration?"

Doug leaned forward and put his hands flat on the desk.

"Then you'll take on the project and get financing for a private venture to the Moon?"

Michael looked at Frank, Frank nodded. Michael looked back, smiling.

"Okay!" Doug said. He then stood and they all shook hands.

Later, sitting at a table at the Holiday Inn, the four men placed their orders.

"I'll begin organizing the corporation and

arranging the money," Michael said. "I'll need a prepared list of possible finds on the Moon from you, Doug." ✓

Frank added, "We'll need a company to build the ship. I have a design drawn up for the actual testing of the drive, but in this case, it will have to be space worthy. I'll need some consultants for the hull strength. The craft will hold six people."

"Okay," Michael said. "I'll need the drawings and specifications so I can determine who has the facilities and engineers for the job."

Frank nodded. "I'll have that to you in a few days."

"The ship will hold six people?" Doug asked. Frank nodded again.

"Well," Michael said. "If you, Doug, and Dave went, that'd leave three places for trained people to go along. Also, Doug, introduce me to Melvin Simpson. We're going to need an independent accountant on this venture."

We're going to do it!" Doug said as he and Dave walked through the terminal on the way to the late evening flight home. "We're really going to do it."

"Yeah," Dave said. "I wonder what Frank Gordon is worth?"

"The professor said that Michael told him that Frank was rich when his father left him the company," Doug said. "But, what I'm excited about is the fact that the man's a genius. That drive he's developed is a giant leap forward."

They stopped and both called home with their arrival time and arranged for their wives to pick them up at the airport. Doug particularly noticed the roar of the jet engines of the planes departing and arriving. "Magnetic Inertial Propulsion." he muttered softly.

"What?" Dave said as he hung up the phone.

"When Frank's drive is fully developed and part of our culture, all these planes will be obsolete."

"It will take a long time," Dave said then glanced out the windows at the activity of the busy airport.

"Yeah, well beyond our lifetimes."

Doug and Dave and their wives left the airport in Davenport and went for a late dinner. The guys spent some time relating the events of the day.

"The ship will have the feel of normal gravity, caused by the constant acceleration at one g, all the way to the Moon." Doug explained the self-maintaining drive. "We won't be floating weightless the whole way like they did on the Apollo missions."

"Sounds like they know what they're doing," Karen said.

Doug nodded. "Oh, yes. Frank Gordon's a genius. He's wealthy and can afford to do things right. They're arranging for a company to build the ship and then they'll test it thoroughly. We're bringing in some NASA experts. Things will be done properly. In fact, we're probably looking at a year or two before we actually go."

"At least," Dave agreed.

"You see," Doug said enthusiastically, "this type of craft gives us hovering capability. We don't have to rocket down and be limited to a small area. We can hover over the surface of the Moon and move around and look around, like a helicopter does here on Earth."

The two couples became quiet for some time, sipping their after dinner drinks, as the events of the day began to sink in. The quest had now become a reality, an impending event that was really going to happen. They would glance at each other, and then look back at their drinks. Doug shifted his position and asked Dave.

"You scared?"

Dave paused a moment, glancing at Jean and Karen. "A little."

"Me, too, but I've got to do it."

"I'm going, too." Dave said.

"NASA people will test and approve the ship?" Jean asked.

"Of course," Doug answered. "And, we'll have trained people with us who know about going into space."

"You're both in good shape." Karen added.

"God, it's going to be something," Dave said. "Something I cannot...not do."

After Doug and Karen left, Dave and Jean retired for the night, discussing the day's events. Dave related again the scene in the test room, dramatizing the invention and its implications. When he finished, they were quiet for a few moments, then Jean turned out the light on her nightstand and moved closer to Dave and said, "When I was a little girl, I wanted to be an astronaut. I told everybody that I was going to be an astronaut and go into space."

"You never told me that," Dave said. "Did you ever pursue it?"

"No. My father was never interested in anything like that--he had his friends and he drank quite a bit. Mom took care of the family and just made ends meet. As I got older and helped her, I just kind of gave up the idea and went on with my life. Later, I went back to school and completed my degree in geology."

"I like your Mother. I never got to know your Father. I never saw him much." Dave slipped his arm around her.

Jean laid her hand on Dave's jaw and rubbed the side of his nose with her thumb. "I'm glad that you're going to the Moon. You're going to be an astronaut." She laid her head on Dave's chest. "You'll have to tell me all about it," she said quietly.

Michael Sheridan sat in his plush suburban home, sipping an after dinner drink. The house seemed unusually empty that night.

His daughters, Michelle and Nikia, were living with their mother in California. They'd decided to live there after the divorce two years earlier. His son had stayed with him but was now in college at San Jose State and saw more of his mother than he did his father.

Michael had mastered the art of PR and fundraising so well that the opportunities had started to run together. This new drive had fueled his enthusiasm; at last, a real challenge. This wasn't going to be easy and he was glad. He had to get this done. He had to show himself that he was still the best.

He frowned as the images in the picture Doug had shown him formed in his mind. What could possibly be the motive to conceal such a discovery? He shook his head as if tossing off the thought.

He got up and went over to the window and looked out at the well lighted Chicago skyline in the distance. He spoke in a smooth, resonant voice, although there was no one to hear. "I'll have to school Doug and Dave on giving an effective presentation on this research project to some of the big investors." He felt a thrill as he thought about setting up the meetings, watching the prospects be informed of the awesome facts, and then taking the floor to do his job.

To get it started, he would call some of his

regulars who had a standing request to invest in anything that Michael had going.

DAN HOLT

## Chapter 8

*"At the moment of detonation, a beautiful, peaceful, rural lake was heaved into the void of space as if rejected by the Solar System. Deep frozen instantly, it would return briefly every seventy-six years as if asking for re-admittance. Eons would go by before it was reinstated as a resident by a newcomer named...Halley."*

### - COMMITMENT -

Dave and Jean drove up the Hastings' driveway. Dave got out of the car and picked up the morning paper from the edge of the yard. Doug opened the door.

"Good timing, breakfast is ready."

"Mmmm, I'm starving," Jean said.

The four gathered around the table and began breakfast, talking about the private venture to the Moon and the impact on society of Frank Gordon's new drive when it was fully developed and practical for everyday use. They finished breakfast and the guys went into the office to get Michael's list together. When they were done, Doug faxed a copy to his office. Twenty minutes later the phone rang.

"Okay, Doug," Michael said, "we're going to need some type of paperwork to get this project going."

"What kind of paperwork?"

"This Research Project needs to be some kind of body or entity in which people or companies can invest. It needs to be a corporation; a legal entity that can borrow money, etcetera."

"Okay," Doug said. "Can you do that?"

"I can arrange it. Frank and I discussed it at length. What I have in mind is that you, Dave, Me, and Frank hold, say, sixty percent of the shares and the rest can be sold to investors."

"Just let me know what to do," Doug said, with a new excitement in his voice.

"Okay. I'll give Frank a call and get things rolling. Also, as soon as you can, I need to know our first priority."

"We'll get right on it," Doug said, "and we'll be calling you very soon." He hung up the phone and related the conversation to Dave.

Dave sat up in his chair. "Okay, now things are starting to happen!"

Doug pulled a writing pad from a cubbyhole. "Let's get Albert Billington on the phone and ask about some expertise to help put the thing together." He dialed the number and Al's wife answered. She said he was at Dave's father's house so Dave dialed his dad's number. Moments later they were on speakerphones updating Al and Isaac. Al received the news very enthusiastically.

"Mr. Billington." Doug said, "I want to…"

"Call me Al," came from the receiver.

"Al," Doug said, "I want to take you up on your offer of help. We need to know everything involved in going to the Moon. We have the means as we told you, but we need the math worked out and we need somebody that has the training to counsel us."

"That's no problem." Al said. "Lots of people trained, few were used. I'll make some phone calls and get back to you. How much do you want me to tell them?"

Doug thought for a moment. "Can you contact some people that you feel would do a private venture and have them get in contact with me without telling them about what we've discovered?"

"I sure can," Al replied, "I had a good rapport

with many of them--they'll call."

"Okay," Doug said. "Let's see if we can do it that way."

Frank nodded toward the phone upon Michael's request. Michael pushed the speaker button and dialed the number for Douglas Hastings.

"Doug, Michael Sheridan. I'm in Frank Gordon's home. I talked to Frank here and we're all set. I'll get my attorney to work on it right away. Frank can hear you and wants to talk to you."

"Okay," Doug said.

"Doug, I'd like to invite you, Dave, and your wives here for the weekend as my guests. It'll give us time to talk and get better acquainted."

"Hold on a second," Doug said, "everybody's here." He checked with the other three, and they agreed. "We'll be there and we're looking forward to it."

Frank, sitting in his home office, nodded when Michael excused himself to return to the city. He walked him to his car and watched him drive away, then looked up at the faint lunar disc in the late morning sky. He felt exhilaration at the latest events concerning his invention. He'd labored for years, seen many failures, but just kept trying. Now he had it. He had it perfected and due to some wonderful events, it was *really* going to be something. As he gazed skyward, a feeling swelled up inside him.

"Dad," he muttered, "you would be proud of me. All you ever saw was the failures and you never tried to discourage me. You had faith in me. Well, Dad, I did it. I got Magnetic Inertial Propulsion to work. I wish you were here to see it." Frank focused again on the Moon. "And, Dad...guess where it's going to take me...."

He went back into the house. Sandra was sitting in the living room reading a novel. She glanced up at him and smiled. He liked it. She smiled every time he looked at her. In fact, that's why he had approached her and introduced himself at an annual machinery show years ago. He'd caught her eye and she flashed that smile. They'd spent the whole day together checking out machinery. She, the mechanical type, and he, the biological type. It was well into their first year of marriage when he discovered that her smile was a character trait. Everyone got a warm smile from Sandra. But that's okay; he got Sandra.

Doug drove the rental car into the wide driveway of the Gordon home. Frank came out of the side building as they were getting out of the car. "I was just setting up the original magnet rotor to show you," he said to Doug and Dave. "Here, let me help you with your luggage."

Inside the house Doug admired the vaulted ceilings, large living area, bay window, and across the room a fireplace and mantle. Above the mantle was a three by four foot painting of a stately looking gentleman with a mustache, receding hairline, and hard features. At the bottom of the artwork was a gold bar etched with black scroll lettering: 'William Eugene Gordon.'

Sandra Gordon looked at Karen and Jean, put her hands together and smiled warmly. "Oh, you're both so thin and pretty."

They laughed at the unexpected greeting from her, an obviously friendly woman, a little on the stout side.

Sandra put her arms around both Karen and

Jean. "I'm so glad you could come, I want to know everything about you." She then showed them their rooms. As the women started a tour of the house, Frank, Doug, and Dave went directly to the outbuilding to see Frank's original model of his invention.

When Doug entered the shop, he noticed the wall covered with pegboard. There were dozens of different types of tools hanging neatly on their individual pegs. On one side of the twenty by twenty foot building, a workbench went the full length of the wall. It was stacked with dozens of different shaped magnets. Fluorescent lights hung by chains directly over the workbench and there were two long ones centered in the room. He noticed two calipers, a small and a large, lying beside the object they'd gathered around. Doug examined the device mounted on an eighteen by eighteen inch table. The table was mounted on four coil springs that had been attached to the workbench. He saw Dave look under the suspended table.

"It's small," Doug said, mentally doing a comparison with what he'd seen in the test room at the company.

Frank nodded. "Yes, this was my first setup to see if the principal really worked."

Doug took a close look at a rotor mounted on a shaft. It looked something like a small ceiling fan motor, only the inside was hollow. On the outside ring were eight magnets evenly spaced. Inside the rotor was a solid steel donut with the magnets almost touching it. In the donut hole was an adjustment screw with a knob mounted on it. An electric motor was mounted with a gear positioned to spin the rotor. The entire mechanism was centered on the spring suspended table.

Frank gestured toward the mechanism. "You

see that the whole thing is mounted on a table sitting on springs. See this arm I fastened to the table? It runs across a fulcrum and to a set of scales. The scales measure ounces of force. I spun the rotor at eight hundred and seventy-five RPM and turned that adjustment screw which pulled a two inch section of the steel donut away from the magnets. I discovered that as I turned the adjustment screw, the scales registered ounces of force in the direction of the gap in the donut. Watch."

Frank flipped a toggle switch on the side of the motor. The rotor was up to speed in a few seconds. He reached into the hole in the center and turned the adjustment screw. The scales increased simultaneously. Doug's eyes went from the scales back to the mechanism.

"How much force?" he said breathlessly.

"The numbers on the scales are ounces." Frank re-stated. "The needle is on fifteen and a half ounces now."

Frank rotated the screw a quarter turn; the scales went instantly to twenty-six ounces.

Doug recoiled and took a breath. "The one in the test room," he asked, "how much power?"

Frank cleared his throat. "On that one, everything is much bigger and has much stronger, heavier magnets. The whole assembly weighs over three thousand pounds. The rotor's in a vacuum chamber to remove air resistance and is spinning at fifty-three hundred RPM. It's levitating its own weight running at less than two percent of its capacity."

Doug's looked back to the model. He leaned down for a side view of the spinning rotor; then his eyes went back to the scales. The needle remained dead still on the number twenty-six.

Frank pointed at the still spinning rotor. "This is

the future of propulsion." he said as he turned it off. At the click of the switch, Doug watched the table sink down on its springs as the rotor slowed.

"A tremendous breakthrough!" he said.

"An opportunity." Frank said. "Let's go into my office and discuss some of the details." ⬋

In the office, Frank continued. "The rotors and their booster units supply electricity to an electric motor which maintains the RPM of the rotors, and keeps a bank of four batteries, wired in parallel, charged. If the booster units failed, the batteries would take over automatically and power the rotors."

"Rotors?" Doug asked, "You mean there will be more than one on the actual ship?"

"Two. You have to have two to have control in all directions. There has to be one vertical and one horizontal."

"The gap has to be pointing in the direction you want to go."

"Exactly, or a combination of two or more of the gaps for directions in between the points of the compass."

Frank took a blank sheet of paper and sketched out two circles, one inside the other. The sketch looked like a doodle of an atom. He then put small circles on the four points of each of the circles.

"Okay," he said, "if you wanted to go northeast and climb at a forty-five degree angle at the same time, these three would be engaged." Frank checked three of the small circles, the two computer experts watching intently. Frank then sketched a large oval around the two circles. "The craft will have to be round because..."

"A flying saucer!" Doug said.

"A flat disc shape or round like a ball because it would need to have the same drag in all directions in the atmosphere."

Doug smiled. "We're going to the Moon in a flying saucer. If anybody knew this they'd think we're crazy."

Frank blinked a couple of times as a smile formed on his lips. "Anyway, that's the best shape for this type of propulsion. All directions are the same to the craft. Now, here's where you fella's come in. The craft will have to be computer controlled."

Doug and Dave nodded.

Frank continued. "Once you start those rotors and bring them up to speed, they're set, just like setting a gyroscope. That means the ship will rotate around the rotor core and its vacuum chamber to be oriented in any direction."

Frank was talking in a lecturer's tone, his voice rich with adventure. "The computer will have to constantly update the controls so that forward activates the right controls to go in the direction that the *pilot* considers forward; the direction the ship is facing."

"I think I understand," Doug said. "When the pilot raises the ship up, say, one hundred feet, and then goes forward, the computer must activate the control on the front side of the vertical rotor. But, when the pilot makes a left turn, the rotors stay oriented as they are and the ship banks to the left, and then rotates around the rotor. The computer then must make the forward control activate the control on the left side of the horizontal rotor so that the propulsion is forward relative to the pilot."

"Exactly! The computer must do that while it's activating the controls opposite the force of gravity to maintain altitude."

"Now this is a programming challenge," Doug said as he glanced at Dave then back at the drawing. "We must begin right away. This is going to take some time."

"Let me show you the prints themselves," Frank said. He got up and went to the far wall of the office and opened a cabinet.

Doug glanced around at the office. He noticed that there were two computers. A small one with a simple black and white printer, and a later model, large-scale computer equipped with a full page scanner and color printer. There was a round table in the middle of the room with rows of storage discs in one set of shelves. Another set of floor to ceiling shelves was stacked full of drawings of machinery. There were mechanisms, magnets, control linkages, and dozens of different shapes of spaceships, automobiles and boats, all of them with a bulge in the middle where a rotor would be mounted.

Doug was impressed with Frank; this man could dream.

Frank returned with a group of prints that were rolled up with a rubber band around each end. He removed the two rubber bands and spread the stack of prints out on the large round table and seated himself. Doug and Dave joined him. The top, thirty-six by forty-eight inch, print was a three dimensional view of a disc shaped craft, complete with all the details of the interior.

"I had a plywood mock-up built and delivered to the test room," Frank said. "It helps me clarify the available space in my mind. I'll show it to you."

Doug leaned forward and scanned the print, following his eyes with his fingertip. There were numbers with tiny arrows pointing to segments of the print that the inventor had drawn to scale inside the ship. Dave's eyes followed his progress. Then the two men studied the list on the right side of the image.

1.    Hull substructure.
2.    Drive substructure
3.    Drive and integrated back-up boosters.
4.    Control Panel mountings.
5.    Atmospheric plumbing diagram.
6.    Venting system
7.    Oxygen   and   Compressed   air   control
      assemblies.
8.    Air lock and Excursion system.
9.    Water tanks.
10.   Food supply
11.   Radio equipment.
12.   Radar system.
13.   Video system
14.   Storage tank mountings.
15.   Seats and safety harness.

"I see the air lock," Doug said. "We need the capability to retrieve things."

Frank nodded. "You need to contact your NASA man and have him locate someone who can produce pressure suits. With those, we can simply go outside and bring things back into the ship."

Doug nodded as he and Dave continued studying the drawing and its details.

"We need a good NASA pilot," Frank said.

"I sure wish we could get someone who has been there before to go with us." Dave said seriously. "At least someone who has been in space before."

The phone rang.

"Hello," Frank said. Doug saw him nod and listen for a few moments.

"Okay, come on out." Frank hung up the phone. "Michael is coming out and bringing his attorney. He said he wanted to talk to us." Doug nodded and moved the top print off the stack and started looking at the detail drawings of each system as Frank explained their functions. Forty-five minutes later, Michael arrived with his attorney.

Michael shook hands with the three men and introduced the lawyer. "This is Jimmy Sawyer. Jimmy's done a lot of legal work for me and is here this weekend to get all the information to go ahead and take care of this for us."

Doug noticed the forcefulness of the young attorney as they shook hands. His grip was strong, his smile rich, and his eyes sparkled. He appeared to be a man that believed he could do anything. He had black, wavy hair, cut short and neatly combed. He had a lean five-ten build and an agile look about him. He looked smart. Doug liked him.

Michael quickly outlined the proposal he and the attorney had drawn up. "Jimmy's suggested we name the Corporation 'Technical Research Association.' I want to ask Doug to brief Jimmy on the discovery from the NASA photographs and Frank to explain Magnetic Inertial Propulsion."

When the attorney heard the word NASA, he glanced at Michael. Michael held up his hand.

Doug nodded, went to the guest room and returned with the tube to find the three men seated at the round table.

Doug laid the picture in front of them. Several moments passed. As the attorney studied the photograph, his face went from a puzzled expression to one of question. Doug explained the eighteen by twenty-four inch image.

Jimmy was surprised. "This is the first I've heard of it."

"No one knows about it," Doug said. He briefly explained the origin of the photograph and many others like it.

"Michael kept me in suspense about this," Jimmy said. "Now I understand why. It blows my mind that it was kept quiet." He studied the images on the photograph again.

Frank began simply. "My father started a magnetics company when I was a little child. He made me a partner when I got out of college. I've been researching magnetic and gyroscopic forces for years. Out in the shop beside the house is a model of my invention. At the company, which I own outright now since Dad passed away, there's a full size prototype. I've invented Magnetic Inertial Propulsion."

"Never heard of it."

"I'll show you." Frank led them to the research lab.

He continued. "It delivers force by deliberately causing a magnet loaded rotor to be out of balance in a controlled direction," He said to Jimmy as the group stood around the table suspended on springs.

"Say that again."

Frank reached over and flipped the toggle switch on the small electric motor. As the rotor started turning, Frank explained the principal to Jimmy, then turned the adjustment screw and pointed to the scales. Jimmy watched the table rise on its springs, and then his eyes went to the scales. He eyed the needle sitting dead still and then watched the rotor. He then knelt down on one knee and strained to see the magnets passing across the gap above the adjustment screw. He was silent for a few moments.

"It gets power when the magnets pass over this gap?" he asked.

"Yes," Frank said. "The magnets suddenly lose their attraction to the steel core inside when they arrive at the gap. They're momentarily out of balance while passing across it. I call the event, *Moment of Inertia.*"

Jimmy glanced at Frank then back at the rotor before asking, "Does anyone else know about this!?"

"Only the people in this room."

Jimmy stood. He then reached down and touched the table with his fingertips. "This is big...really big." After a moment of silence, he pointed at the spinning rotor. "You have a full size model at the company! You're going to the Moon, aren't you?"

Jimmy glanced from face to face. The four men said nothing.

"Michael, are all of you crazy!"

"We hope not," Michael answered. "We are getting help from some NASA people."

Jimmy exhaled and took a breath. "Oh...I see."


"Technical Research Association." Allen Brewster read the name from the report a Chicago contact had dropped off moments earlier. Looks like Hastings is starting another group to propagate alien artifacts in the Solar System. Good. The more there are the less influence they have. Of course, Brewster would subscribe to all their newsletters, check their materials, and check on their activities from time to time. But, it appeared there was no real threat here.

*"God,"* He thought. *"The public loves this type of stuff.. It's amazing they never react seriously when they hear about it. Of course, it's never been released officially, and probably never will, not for a long, long time. Only a handful of people know what's really there."* He thought again about the meeting, long ago, when he'd spelled out the facts. He was so awed himself by what he'd seen. It had given him a mind-set, a mind-set that had made him do what he had done. The image in the recurring nightmare

formed in his mind. He shook his head, and then lit a cigarette.

When the Apollo program suddenly came to a halt, Allen Brewster's job had begun; a job he became obsessed with--almost to the point of psychosis. It became all-important. *Keep it hushed up.*

Chapter 9

*"....and their appearance and their work
was as it were a wheel in the middle of a
wheel."* Ezekiel 1:16

## - THE ASTRONAUT -

Colonel Marvin D. Andrews. The letters carved
in varnished wood looked back at the retired Air Force
officer as he reached to open the mailbox located by
the highway two hundred yards from his modest
country home. Renee Blanchart placed her finger in
the letter C and traced its outline, then smiled at
Marvin.

Marvin collected the stack of mail, closed it and
started back toward the house. Renee looked at
Marvin and grinned, then started sprinting down the six
hundred foot concrete ribbon that ran from the main
road to the front yard. Marvin joined in the race.
Renee had gotten a ten yard head start and was swift
on her feet. They were fifty yards from the house
when Marvin overtook her, then outdistanced her by
ten yards. He stopped, turned, and opened his arms.
Renee jumped from ten feet away and landed in his
arms in a cradling position. Marvin swung her around
twice, kissed her and grinned back at her.

"It took you longer this time," Renee taunted,
breathing heavily. "You're slowing down."

"No, I'm not," Marvin retorted, breathing easily.
"You're speeding up."

"I gotta' go," Renee said, kissing him again.
"I've got to get back to the shop." Marvin set her back
on her feet.

"Bye," Marvin said. He watched Renee get into

her candy apple red nineteen sixty-nine Mustang convertible, toss her pony tail off her shoulder, and drive out the long driveway.

Marvin went into the house leafing through the stack of circulars and advertisements. He saw an envelope with blocked letters stamped in red: "Please notify sender of current address." His eyes went to the return address:

*Albert Billington*
*NASA, Staffing - Retired*
*1514 Huxley Court*
*Houston, Texas*

His mind flashed back to NASA, the world of vigorous training, the two missions on the space shuttle, a space walk to test working with tools in weightless conditions, and the endless politics of many wanting and few getting. He was glad the pressure was gone. Even so, Colonel Marvin Dean Andrews would not have left willingly.

The astronaut was an even six feet tall, curly blonde hair, no part, cut short, and wide set blue eyes. He was trim but muscular, two hundred ten pounds and had stayed in shape. He'd been notified during a debriefing that he had an emergency phone call. He learned from that call that his wife and children had been in a car accident. Later, he'd learned that they all had perished instantly.

He was so affected by the horrible loss that NASA and the Air Force had decided to retire him after twenty-one years; prudently, of course. He'd fought it for a while, but soon realized that on such a job, he had to have complete backing. He knew he wouldn't have that and it would be just a matter of time. He'd accepted retirement and bought his quiet little place, still not sure what he wanted to do. He had more or less fallen into the woodcarving hobby when a friend saw his mailbox plaque and suggested he carve items for the shops nearby.

He'd met Renee Blanchart when he began delivering wood carved gifts to the shops. Renee managed a gift shop at the edge of Wichita. She was forty-one, blonde, slender, and physical. She lived with her Uncle Jason, the owner of the shop. Renee had lost her husband in a car crash two years earlier. Her Uncle Jason had been with him at the time but had survived the accident. He was seventy now and came to the shop only occasionally. Renee was the mainstay of the business. Renee lost her father, a test pilot, in a plane crash when she was fifteen and had lived with her Uncle until she married Fred Blanchart. Because of her husband's death, and the age of her Uncle, she had moved back in with him and cared for his business. Renee and her Uncle Jason enjoyed the peace and quiet of county living four miles down the road. Marvin and Renee became friends, and soon began seeing each other. He liked her; no, he loved her.

Colonel Andrews closed the front door, went to the kitchen, and got a drink of water. He sat down at the table and tore open the letter.

*Colonel Andrews, Please call me if you receive this letter, my phone number for you is not current. Urgent.*

The letter was signed by Albert Billington and gave a phone number. Marvin glanced at the return address again. He picked up the phone and dialed.

The colonel recognized the voice as he heard,

'Al Billington here.' Al always answered the phone like that.

"Al, this is colonel Marvin Andrews, I got your letter. What's up?"

"Colonel!" the voice on the line blurted out. "I was afraid I wasn't going to be able to reach you! How are you?"

"I'm doing okay. I see from your letter that you're retired. How are you doing, Al?"

"I'm just fine. I'm so glad to hear from you. When I couldn't reach you I thought I'd lost contact for good."

"Your letter said it was urgent that I contact you. What's up?"

"I wanted to ask a favor of you, Marvin. I put down urgent in the letter because I feel that it is, and I think you'll agree."

"What is it?" Marvin said pointedly.

Al spoke seriously, "Marvin, a group of friends of mine need a man with your training and experience. I want to ask you to meet with them and let them explain the project. It would mean a lot to me and to them if you'd take the time to talk to them."

"What's the project?"

"I had rather that they explain it to you, Marvin. You've known me for a long time; I'm asking you to do this as a favor to me."

"Al..." Marvin hesitated. During his personal tragedy while at NASA, Al had listened. Al had cared. "Okay, I'll do it. When and where?"

"Great!" Al shouted.

Marvin pulled the phone away from his ear, smiling.

"Thanks, Marvin, let me get back to you in an hour with the details. Are you working or can you go anytime?"

"Sure," Marvin responded, beginning to feel good about the call. "I've got a little business going, but really it's more of a hobby than a business. You remember when they retired me, don't you?"

"Yes, I do," Al said quietly. "Everybody was a little upset about that for a while. Marvin, trust me, I think you're going to like this meeting. What's your phone number?"

The colonel gave him his phone number and hung up. He got up from the table, stepped out on the front porch of his neatly trimmed home and looked across the sprawling wheat field beyond the highway, wondering what Al was talking about. Al was an older man, retired from NASA. It was probably some type of benefit and they wanted the advertising value of an astronaut being involved.

"Oh well," he said out loud, "it's for Al and Al's a good man."

Doug was busy at his computer. He was programming segments of the programs needed to control Frank's newly developed drive when the phone rang.

"Douglas, Al Billington, I've got some good news for you."

Doug wrenched his neck and cleared his throat, breaking away from his programmer's trance.

"Hello, Al, what is it?"

"I got lucky, Doug, I got in contact with an astronaut who's retired from NASA and the Air Force and he'll meet with you."

Doug sat straight up in his chair. "A real astronaut!"

"Colonel Marvin Dean Andrews. He's been in space twice and he's done one space walk."

"Fantastic! What's he doing now?"

"He's living in a small town just outside of Wichita, Kansas. While he was at NASA, he lost his family in a car crash. It affected him for a while and NASA and the Air Force retired him. He had twenty-one years in the Air Force. He's in his forties. He's a good man, Doug. He's meeting with you as a favor to me. All he knows is that some friends of mine need his expertise on a project. He agreed to talk to you."

"When?"

"Well, I told him I would call him back with the details. When do you want to meet with him?"

Doug paused for a few moments. "It would be the best if we could have him meet everybody at the same time and, hopefully, he'll help us out."

"I think he will. I think he'll jump on it. He's a good man and he took his activities seriously at NASA; fought the retirement for a while."

Doug asked hopefully, "Can you set it up so we can meet this coming Saturday in Chicago? We could all meet him at the airport."

"Sure," Al said confidently.

"Can you be there too, Al?"

"I wouldn't miss it for the world."

"Call Pop and ask him to come also."

"I'd be delighted!" Al said gleefully. "I'll let you know what flight Colonel Andrews will be on."

Doug hung up the phone then picked it back up and called Dave at his office.

"We've got a real astronaut," Doug said proudly, then answered several rapid-fire questions. He did the same with Frank and Michael.

While on the phone with Michael, Doug learned that a company had been located to build the ship and Michael needed to set up a meeting with the company's designers and engineers to go over the details.   He also was informed by Michael that a corporate fund was in place to cover all travel expenses involved during the research project.

"The Colonel will be on the nine-ten a.m. flight landing at O'Hare," Al said when Doug answered the phone.

"We'd better go to Chicago Friday night," Doug said.   "I'll call Frank and have him get some rooms for you and Pop."

"Okay, let me know."

"I'll call you."

Doug called Melvin Simpson and Professor Liggins.   Melvin, now involved with the accounting of Technical Research Association, would be there.   The professor was out of town but his wife would give him the message when he called.

Saturday morning, Al, Doug, Isaac, and Dave watched the line of passengers file off flight 907 at Chicago O'Hare.   Michael, Frank, and Melvin waited in Michael's office while Karen and Jean waited with Sandra at the Gordon home.   The whole group of enthusiasts anticipated the Colonel's introduction to the research effort.

Colonel Andrews walked down the ramp, enjoying the break from his normal routine. It was okay to do a benefit once in a while.   He'd done several over the years, mostly small, but they were fun.   He wondered what type of benefit it was and if there'd be media coverage.   When he entered the terminal, he saw Al right away and as he got closer, he recognized another friend.

"Hello, I.J.!" he said.   "How in the world are you?"   He turned to Al.   "How have you been?"

They shook hands, smiling broadly

"Colonel," Al said warmly, "I'm so glad that you came. This is Douglas Hastings and Dave Henson; they're computer experts. I'll explain all that later."

Marvin turned to Doug and Dave and extended his hand. Doug took it first, then Dave. The colonel nodded as he shook each of the men's hands, and then turned back to Al.

"Well, I'm enjoying the break," Marvin said warmly. "You asked I.J. to come too, I see."

"Well...yes," Al smiled. Marvin raised an eyebrow. Al continued. "Let's go to Michael Sheridan's office and we'll explain everything to you."

"Lead the way," Marvin said, putting his arm around Isaac's shoulders as they walked through the terminal. "I.J., good to see you, do you still have your collection?"

Isaac pointed toward Doug. "Doug has it right now."

Marvin glanced at Doug, then back to Isaac. "By now it's probably becoming valuable."

Al interrupted. "Colonel, if I remember right, you've been on two shuttle missions."

"Yes, I went up once to deploy a satellite and various other tests in zero g and another time to test our ability to use hand tools outside the spacecraft."

Marvin discussed his experiences in space with the group of men until they reached the Wheaton building. Sitting around the conference room table in Michael's office, the introductions having been made, Al began.

"Colonel Andrews, "I'm glad that our friendship was enough to get you to come here and meet with us. I also hope that what you're about to see will be enough to get you to join us."

Marvin searched Al's face. Al gestured toward

Doug and leaned back in his chair. The colonel turned to Doug expectantly. Doug began speaking, nervously at first, but quickly became solid as he approached a subject in which he was well versed. Doug briefly explained how he'd gotten interested in the photographic records of the Apollo program and the computer work he'd done with them. Then he removed the enhanced photograph and spread it out on the table.

"This is what we found," he said.

Colonel Andrews studied the photograph for a couple of minutes. He picked it up and leaned back. I heard talk about this. Several of the astronauts got calls about it. The story had come out in one of the tabloids or something. We asked the powers that be at the time about it and they simply denied It. We thought there was nothing to it."

"We'll, Colonel," Doug said, "it's there and it's real." Marvin's eyes went back to the print.

"Now I understand why NASA's so full of politics. They've gotten something started that they can't stop without being in a lot of trouble."

"Colonel...Marvin," Al said, "forget about NASA. We have something far more important and far more exciting we want to show you. We feel there are huge amounts of treasures of technology, records, equipment, and advanced materials, underneath the surface of the Moon."

Doug stood and leaned forward and placed the palms of his hands on the table and looked at the picture. Marvin's eyes followed.

"Things underground," Doug said, "that are shielded from the meteoric bombardment and the radiation of the Sun." He looked up and met the colonel's eyes. "We're going after it."

Marvin glanced at Al, then back to Doug.

"How're you going to get there?"

"That's the next thing we want to show you." Doug gestured toward Frank. "Frank Gordon's an inventor. Let's go to his company and we'll show you."

The group slid their chairs back to stand. Marvin turned to Frank. "Do you have an Apollo spacecraft?"

"Something better, Colonel."

Colonel Marvin D. Andrews stood in the, now partitioned off, end of the test room at Gordon & Gordon Magnetics. He heard a steady hum coming from somewhere in facility but couldn't determine its source. Centered in the area was what appeared to be a huge skeleton of a soccer ball waiting for the white panels to be installed. Inside the frame was a wheel, six feet in diameter, standing vertical. Around the outside of it was a wide steel band, then mounted on the bearings was another wide band with eight rectangular magnets evenly spaced around it. Outside that wheel was a second wheel, mounted horizontally, with another pair of wide bands with the same type magnets ringed around it, mounted to the outside rigging.

It was a wheel inside of a wheel. I looked like a giant atom. Marvin was intrigued.

"Frank, what is it?" he said as he studied it.

"I...we decided to keep it quiet until we were sure that it's a solid, dependable principal of propulsion." Frank put his hand on the Colonel's shoulder and started walking toward the partition. "Step into this next area and I'll show you the test going on with the rotor."

When Marvin stepped through the door, the ever-present hum grew louder. He looked up at the 'twin bells,' noting the absence of support framing or cables. His eyes went from one booster unit to the other, then to Frank.

"That vertical rotor you just saw in the other room is inside there, in a vacuum, running at under two percent of its capacity. The test chamber it's supporting weighs over three thousand pounds. It's been hovering there for eight months."

Marvin walked over to the suspended object, then all the way around it. He glanced at the group of men watching him, then reached up and placed his hand on the bottom of it. It was cool to the touch. He pushed on it. It didn't move at all.

It was firmly anchored to…nothing.

Marvin studied the bottom of the odd shaped device, then reached up with both hands and grasped the heads of two bolts, gripped them, and lifted himself off the floor. The object remained motionless. He lowered himself to the floor, dusted his hands together, and looked at Frank.

"What's keeping it stationary?"

"It's a gyroscope, with thrust capabilities," Frank said. "I can show you the mathematics on it."

Marvin studied Frank's face for a moment, and then looked again at the suspended object.

"I want to see the ship!"

"Michael's contracted a company to build it. We're meeting with their people a week from Monday to discuss the details and give them the specs for it. All I have here now is a plywood mock-up. It will show you the general shape of the spacecraft."

"Colonel," Al spoke up, "we'd like you to join us. Help us layout the design of the ship for the mission and test it properly. When it's ready, we'd like you to pilot the ship to the Moon for the research effort."

"Colonel Andrews's head reeled momentarily.

The thrill and satisfaction of going into space had been taken from him by a personal tragedy.  Everything he had trained for, for years, was gone as a result.  But now, a dream of a lifetime was being offered him, and he knew it.  He looked around at the group of men, then up at the odd-shaped device in mid-air for a long moment.

"Count me in."

# Chapter 10

*"On the lunar surface, an impact of a high speed particle occurred, as they have been occurring for eons, but this time the particle struck the last molecule of strength that suspended the two mile by two mile pane of lunar glass to the overhead rigging. The pane slowly cambered downward, popped out of the latticework and majestically fell to the lunar surface 200 miles below, silently smashing into the ruins of the ancient crystalline city...."*

## - THE SHIP -

The truck with McNeal Ceramics stenciled in huge letters on the side backed up to the dock at the test room at Gordon & Gordon Magnetics as the group of men talked idly among themselves. Two engineers from McNeal Ceramics were assigned for certification of the completed ship. They were present to verify that everything had arrived as ordered. Frank had also brought in a radar expert and an electrical engineer. The group got quiet when the driver opened the truck's rear doors and handed his bill of lading to Frank. The March winds ruffled Frank's hair as he signed the bill and took his copy.

Dozens of vehicles had backed up to this dock in the past few months. Michael Sheridan has been busy. Delivery vans, bobtail trucks, and over the road eighteen wheelers had been bringing the results of his efforts to Gordon & Gordon Magnetics, Doc C.

Eight months had gone by since the specifications for the ship had been delivered to Samuel J. McNeal. The ship was to be built as his company and delivered to Frank Gordon, a deal arranged by Michael Sheridan; in exchange for samples of all materials discovered on the Moon to be delivered to Sam McNeal for examination in his labs and the rights of the use thereof.

The fifteen crates were taken off the truck and stacked near the walls of the test facility, along with many others already there--oxygen tanks, lubricants, seats, panels full of gauges, and doughnut shaped field coils, seven foot in diameter, in gleaming copper. To the uninformed, it would have appeared to be an aircraft hanger; a place for repairs or nothing that unusual, until the crates were opened and assembly began.

The truck gone, the door closed, Frank opened a crate and took out one of the outer panels and turned it over and over in his hands. "They look heavier than they really are." he said.

"The same as on the space shuttle," Marvin said, "except for the lead lining you see sandwiched in the middle for radiation protection. Just like the Space Shuttle, this entire ship is covered with ceramic tiles with thick foam insulation inside to protect it from the direct sunlight in space."

McNeal Ceramics' engineers examined the received parts and pre-assembled systems and then left. They would return later and certify the assembled outer hull. The electrical engineers and radar expert checked all the electrical systems and were satisfied. They left the facility.

The six men began assembling the framework of the ship. As the days rolled by, the bottom half of the ship began to take shape. When all struts were placed according to the labeling by the manufacturer, Marvin and Doug began to torque bolts as Frank checked the specifications. Torque was applied until the preset wrench clicked the specified foot-pounds. When all the struts were assembled, they went back to all bolts and checked them again. Satisfied, they backed away and surveyed the rigging. It looked like a giant bowl.

"It's ready for the rotor assembly." Frank said, then stepped into a glassed in cubicle and picked up the phone.

Doug looked at the rotor assembly sitting twenty feet away in an aluminum cradle. The assembly, now enclosed, looked like a deep-sea diving bell without portholes. Where one would expect to see portholes, there were spindles sticking out. The polished steel axles, four of them, six inches in diameter, were sticking out on the four points of the compass.

The eight-foot diameter black ball; the rotor pod, had two gear tracks around it; one vertical and one horizontal. Just above the spindles there were steel eyeholes fabricated into the outer casing. On each one there was a thick nylon lifting strap attached.

The door of the test room opened and an older Spanish man came in. He gracefully went up the ladder to the cabin of the overhead crane, as if he'd been up there many times. Doug heard the electric motor start and then creep slowly down the rails toward the rotor pod.

When the crane was in position, the hook was lowered two feet above the center of the pod. Doug, Dave, Marvin, and Isaac each got a ramp ladder, rolled them into position and hooked the nylon straps to the crane. Frank signaled and the crane started winching upward. When the slack was taken up in the straps, the operator stopped and looked at Frank. Frank walked around the rotor pod checking it and the position of the crane, then nodded. The operator triggered the controls. Doug heard the heavy motor whine as it lifted the black sphere clear off the supporting cradle. He saw the rotor pod swinging gently. Doug and Marvin grasped the tight straps and brought it to rest. Frank nodded again and the operator raised the load above the height of the waiting structure.

Doug glanced at the substructure in the middle of the bowl. There were four heavy aluminum triangle mountings with half-moon bearing cradles waiting for the spindles of the rotor pod. The crane operator moved the load over the center of the bowl and began lowering the mechanism into the bottom half of the ship. The four men climbed inside the bowl and stood on the metal floor, hands up, waiting to guide the spindles into their respective cradles. A couple of inches above the cradles, the operator stopped the load and watched Frank. The waiting crew tugged on the spindles until they were aligned with the waiting U-shaped mounts. Frank motioned and the crane operator lowered the rotor pod into the cradles. When it made contact, a solid sound echoed through the test room. There was something comforting about it. Doug glanced at Al standing just outside the struts of the bowl. He had the upper half of a bearing in one hand and the torque wrench in the other. His eyes were sparkling.

After they unhooked the rotor pod, the operator moved the crane to the end of the room, and then came down the ladder. Frank waved at him; he nodded and went out the door.

The assembling of the framework and setting the rotor pod and its power supply was tedious work. Saturday afternoon of the sixth week found them connecting the last of the wiring on the panels in the crew's control center.

"Let's take a break before we start putting the outside hull together and start the testing," Frank said.

The five other men, the strain of the intense work showing on their faces, nodded in agreement.

"Let's all get a good night's rest and meet at my home tomorrow morning at ten for a late breakfast."

Thomas Thornton was over the ten foot wire fence in seconds. A physical young man, he quickly crossed the grass to the side of the test facility of Gordon & Gordon Magnetics. Leaning against the side of the corrugated metal building, in the dark, he massaged his reddened hands. He had to see what had brought this unusual group of people to this building every day for the past six weeks. They had arrived just after dawn and left well after dark each day.

Thomas, twenty-four, got out of the Marine Corp a year earlier and joined the CIA. He had an edge on him, and a ego problem. He just had to be somebody, he didn't care how. Now his chance had come to make a name for himself. He'd been assigned to a real heavy, a forty-year agent, to assist without question. That 'without question' touched something deep inside him; a chance to be a 'real' agent. His partner, Allen Brewster was awesome; that look he had--CIA.

Tom crept to the back of the building and around the corner. There was an open field behind the company. He quickly surveyed the area and found that all was quiet. He made his way along the backside until he reached a personnel door. Just past that, he made out, in the darkness, two twenty-foot hanger-type doors, making a forty-foot opening, if they'd been open. His attention returned to the personnel door. He pulled a leather tool holder from his inside suit coat pocket and opened it. His fingers quickly located the tiny steel shaft.

He slipped the hardened tool from its slot and inserted it into the lock of the metal door. In thirty seconds the door was open and Tom was inside the test room. He slipped a pencil-sized flashlight from the holder and swept the room. When the light swept across the framework of the partially assembled ship, he stopped and aimed it back at the project. He outlined the ship with the light then paused.

"What is this?" he said in a whisper. A thrill swept through him. He carefully studied the rigging and interior. Having formed a mental picture, he crept back out the door, locked it, and was quickly back over the fence and to his car.

Early May brought an unseasonably warm Sunday to suburban Chicago. Marvin Andrews hummed: "Up we go, into the wild…" He smiled, realizing the parallel to what he and several other adventurous dreamers were about to do. He felt strangely comfortable about the undertaking; all of his training and his built-in Common sense seemed to tell him that they were doing things reasonably, and in a sound and prudent manner. Plenty of testing would be done. Marvin was now an integral part of Technical Research Association and its success was important.

He hummed the tune again as he turned onto the street leading to Frank's home. He pressed the gas pedal on the rental car.

He would test the equipment to guarantee it would deliver as expected. If the engine on this car stopped, he would be inconvenienced for a while, no harm done. If the booster units in the ship failed, they were all dead and that was final. He was glad that there were two back-up clusters installed as part of the ship's design. Frank Gordon was a very bright man. It's not surprising that he could figure things out.

Doug, Frank, Dave, Isaac, and Al sat around a table under a large shade tree in Frank Gordon's front yard. The array of chairs was as different as the personalities and backgrounds of the men occupying them. There were two kitchen chairs, two folding chairs, four lawn chairs, and Frank asked Doug to help him carry his favorite recliner out into the yard. Doug obliged and Frank was enjoying occupying it in the fresh air of the Illinois morning.

Marvin drove up the long driveway and stopped the car. All the men held up their coffee cups. Marvin got out of the car and looked at the array of chairs and the group sitting in them. He looked at Frank, put his hands on his hips, and smiled. Frank kept a straight face and took a sip of coffee.

"Good morning, Colonel," Isaac said enthusiastically. "Which way is it to the Moon?"

Marvin pointed straight up, laughing. "That way, Mr. Henson, that way." He glanced around at the group, wondering if they had any idea that their names would be household words around the world if this project went as planned. He could think of no group of people more worthy of the honor. They were real, honest, and caring; the highest traits of the human experience. They were a breath of fresh air for Colonel Andrews-astronaut.

Marvin took a seat and greeted the others. As the group talked idly about the past week's project, Karen stuck her head out the door and motioned. Marvin glanced up and Doug and Dave got up and hurried to the house. Doug, Dave, Karen, Jean, and Sandra came out of the house carrying the food and hardware for an open-air breakfast.

The group ate in idle conversation.

The meal finished, the table cleared, discussions began again on the ship, the project, and the intriguing possibilities waiting on the Moon. Marvin was silent for a few moments. A picture formed in his mind. A picture of the skeleton of the ship, with its systems, rotor pod, wiring, storage tanks, and equipment exposed, waiting for the outer hull to give it grace and style. He turned toward Doug and caught his eye. Doug turned to face him.

"I've been going over again, in my mind, the crew of the ship for the mission," Marvin said. "We have a pilot--myself, propulsion system--Frank, computer control--you, computer safety systems--Dave, and we'll need somebody for telemetry. We have one seat left."

"Doug nodded. "Who else do you think we need?"

"We need a ship's safety officer," Marvin said. "It needs to be someone to mind the details; operate the air lock during excursions, check the space suits before exit, and check them after an excursion. He would have to pay attention to every little detail so that something simple isn't overlooked. He would never leave the ship. The ship and its atmosphere are his only concerns. It needs to be someone to see that every procedure is followed; a systematic checker of everything, to avoid making a mistake and losing all our oxygen or cabin pressure."

"Who do you think it ought to be?" Doug asked.

"Me," Isaac spoke up.

The group turned to Isaac. He continued. "I helped put the ship together; the air lock, all the valves, the gauges and reserve tanks, the plumbing for the pumps, and the spools for the suits. I know how it all works."

"Do you want to go?" Marvin asked.

"Yes I do, Colonel. I would have gone on Apollo if they'd let me."

Marvin reached and shook hands with Isaac. "I can't think of anybody I'd rather have."

Isaac stuck both arms up with hands in a fist and shook them, smiling. Marvin noticed Dave and Jean looking at Isaac and smiling broadly.

The group talked at length about Isaac's election to the crew and what his duties would be. Marvin noticed it seemed to breathe even more enthusiasm into the group. Marvin motioned to Frank.

"Frank, what's the name of the ship?" All eyes in the group went to Frank's face.

"I haven't addressed that yet," Frank responded, looking around at the others. "Let's name it."

"Yeah," Jean said enthusiastically. "We'll have to get some champagne and christen it, too."

"Yes," Karen said. "I dub thee…what?"

"Well," Doug said, "there's lots of obvious names; Voyager, Explorer, Lunar One, Discovery, and on and on, but they're names that have been used many times."

"What's this spacecraft all about?" Dave offered. "It's a research vessel. It's a completely new shape; compared to the shape of all the spaceships that have flown before. It's an experiment in Magnetic Inertial Propulsion, and a research venture by a private group."

"Research One," Isaac said. "It ought to be called, Research One."

They all sat back, nodding to each other. Marvin watched Isaac momentarily. He was in good physical condition. His enthusiasm had kept him very active over the years and his body had delivered the motions faithfully, keeping itself in tune and healthy. He was a small man and moved like a man twenty years his junior.

"Research One it is," Frank announced, following the nodding unanimously around the table.

"A flying saucer!" Allen Brewster said almost jokingly. He looked at the young man with a burr haircut. He had a muscular build, very smooth face and distant eyes; eyes with the glaze of an obedient zombie. Thomas Thornton had been with the CIA less than a year. Several of his fellow agents called him TeeTee until he put couple of them in the hospital. Brewster didn't particularly like him, but Tom would have no problem taking care of ugly business if he needed it done.

Brewster had followed the organization of Technical Research Association and all who were recruited and now involved. Some pretty heavy names. Sheridan had friends in high places, including Washington. Frank Gordon had personal friends in the state legislature. Professor Liggins was well known in the hallowed halls of Iowa. And there's the astronaut. And Douglas Hastings and Dave Henson were both very successful men. They were well known in the computer world. They had programmed a safety sub-routine for the space shuttle computers. Then there were the two retired office types from NASA. It was a little puzzling that no literature had begun to flow from the Association. All the rest of the similar groups had publications, websites, and outlets for tapes and books. There was something different here. But, what?

"A flying saucer," the young agent from Chicago repeated as he straightened his tie. He had instructions to assist Allen Brewster without question. All reports were to be personally delivered and then considered not to have happened. Thomas Thornton was eating it up.

"You're sure?"

"Yes, Sir, a flying saucer. I entered the Magnetics company and looked for myself. No one has any idea that I was there. They don't know that we know."

"Is it real, Tom?" Brewster said, and then awkwardly: "Does it look like it would really fly? Maybe it's an attraction for an amusement park or something--spins on magnets."

"No, it's real," Tom said dramatically in spite of himself. "The outer hull is not on it yet. You can see all the stuff inside and..."

"What kind of engine?" Brewster interrupted.

"I don't know. There's a black ball in the center of it about eight feet high. It's all sealed. I couldn't see anything. But the inside of the ship looks like Star Trek. It has view screens, panels, gauges, levers, all kinds of stuff. Also it has lots of tanks all around it.

"That's exactly what an amusement park ride would look like," Brewster said. "It could be a display for the Association."

"It looks serious," Tom said.

Allen Brewster was quiet for a moment. The young agent waited for instructions with a straight face. "Keep an eye on them, but make no waves," Brewster said. "They cannot know that you're monitoring them."

The next month saw the ship completed, certified by the consulting engineers, and ready for tests. For two days, Doug and Dave loaded the programming into the three on-board computers. They ran simulations until they were satisfied that the programs were flawless. They had forty-one and a half years of combined experience in front of the programmer's keyboard, but still, this *had* to be right.

"One more thing," Doug said, as he hurried to his car, then back up the ramp and into the ship. Dave watched him pull a copy of the enhanced photograph, done at the Time Lease Center, out of its document tube and unroll the print.

"We're going to visit a city, we don't want to forget the map," Doug said and moved down to the wall of the ship by the navigator's seat. A few minutes later they exited the ship and approached the group.

"The main control program is installed and operational," Doug said. "Also, all the sub programs for safety are on line."

"Sub programs?" Frank said.

"Yes. Programs that are linked with the radar system that won't let the ship collide with anything. Also, the programs that limit the acceleration and deceleration are done."

Frank's face showed question again.

Dave spoke up. "We had the programs set limits to how much you can accelerate. With the power of the rotor pod, it's possible to accelerate, or decelerate, too quickly and cause blackout." Dave Glanced at Marvin. He nodded.

"It's ready for local operation, meaning, you have to stay on Earth. Without a telemetry program, gravity's the reference for the controls. To go to the Moon we'll need a telemetry program to be the point of reference for the controls. The computers will fly the ship into space and to the Moon. Then, we'll take over again for local operation there." Doug turned and faced the finished silvery ship. Dave, Marvin, and Frank followed his lead.

"We need an egghead; an expert in orbital science."

"I know just the man," Marvin said confidently. "He worked with JPL during the Voyager missions, working out the telemetry for the multi-planet trajectories and mapping programs. He's good, really good. He left during some of the budget cuts of the time."

"What's he doing now?" Frank said.

"He's creating orbital science learning programs for universities around the country. However, as soon as I give him a call, he's going to be mapping the highway to the Moon for Research One."

Doug's eyes scanned the name on the side of the disc, then looked into the colonel's wide set blue eyes. "What's his name?"

"Daniel Stubblefield. I'd be very comfortable with his numbers. He knows his business."

"Well," Doug turned to Frank, "there's crew member number six."

Frank nodded.

Frank walked around the finished ship. He experienced an emotional moment at seeing it complete. Research One was saucer shaped, twenty-four feet in diameter, twelve feet high in the center sloping down to six feet high at the edge. It looked the same from the top and from the bottom. It was painted a heat reflecting silver. The surface of the ship reflected his image. Underneath was the tripod landing gear. On the bottom of each leg was a ceramic tile for the foot. When the gear was retracted, the tiles went into place in the underside of the hull, making the ship completely smooth and aerodynamic.

In front, there was a windshield of thick-layered lead-filled acrylic, formed into the hull. It was eighteen feet from side to side, a quarter of the way around the ship. It extended from four feet onto the bottom of the ship, up the six foot front side, and then four feet up the topside of the ship. It was a curved windshield, fourteen by eighteen feet. The massive piece of handiwork was traded to Gordon & Gordon Magnetics for a comparable amount of lunar glass. *"A promise to keep."* Frank thought.

The three, four-foot diameter portholes were included.

Frank stood in front of the ramp on the Northwest side of the ship. The entranceway was eight feet wide with a nine foot clearance, full open. On the Northeast side was a secondary ramp three by six feet.

He looked again at the three aluminum tube legs with their feet on them and then into the ship. The solemn, mysterious looking black ball; the rotor pod, dead center inside the ship, made you feel that the outside shape of the vessel was as it should be. Smooth, shiny, graceful. It looked like it had just paused for a moment in this room to be seen, its three legs just barely touching the floor, and then would fly away. For a brief moment, in fantasy, he was afraid it would. In its heart was Magnetic Inertial Propulsion. If it did fly away, nothing could ever catch it.

Thomas Thornton was through the rear door of the test facility in twenty seconds this time. He returned the tiny hardened tool to its slot and reached for the light. When he turned it on, the silvery ship seemed to glow. He stared for a long moment, and then quickly moved around to look into it through the ramp opening. He slowly ascended the ramp and peered inside. An indescribable feeling gripped him as his eyes probed the saucer shaped craft. Breathing with his mouth open, he carefully crept into the interior of Research One. He turned to the right and began making his way around the perimeter of the vessel. He placed his hand on the glassed in chamber on the right, then moved past it. The four-foot diameter window reflected the beam from his flashlight. Following that was a double row of tanks, all plumbed together.

He continued around the ship until he came to the control panels at the massive windshield. He swept the light along the COMM panel. The tiny beam came to rest on duel monitor screens in front of the right-most seat. He studied the panels for a few moments, then cautiously reached up and flipped a switch. The monitor lit up and a wire frame representation of the ship appeared on the screen. It looked like a hologram.

There were several green dots scattered around on the image. One of the dots blinked and computer began running a diagnostic. He flipped the switch back to the off position; the monitor went dark. He moved toward the two center seats. There was a monitor in front of each. Just above and centered over the two was another monitor. His eyes went down to the panel at the base of the screens. He flipped another switch. A few seconds later, a low hum found his ears, growing in pitch rapidly. He quickly lunged forward and switched it off. His stomach hit the twelve-inch wide table pivoting his chest into the back of the seat. He grunted from the blow of the solid mountings. He recovered momentarily then aimed his light out the windshield to see if the saucer had moved. "This is not an amusement ride. This is a real flying saucer."

"Isn't she beautiful," Doug said as the group prepared to itemize everything again one final time before the maiden flight. The builders of the ship admired it for a few moments in silence. Frank broke the stillness when he picked up a small toolbox and started for the ship to remove the inspection panels from the rotor pod. Doug went into the ship and seated himself in front of the pilots monitor and switched on the system. Dave switched on the safety monitor and rotated the chair to seat himself. His eyes fell on a four inch square black module at the base of the secondary monitor. A red pin-dot size light was flashing.

"Doug!" Dave shouted.

"What?" Dave pointed at the module. Doug's eyes went to the flashing light. Dave was in his seat. His fingers flew over the computer keys.

"Someone turned on this terminal at eleven-fifty-one last night!" he said. "It was on for thirteen seconds." Frank and Marvin were already standing behind Doug. Isaac and Al were coming up the ramp.

"What is it?" Isaac said.

"Somebody was in the ship last night," Dave said.

"My, God," Frank said. "Let's check the doors." They quickly exited the ship and went to all the doors. There was no evidence of entering. They were all locked. Marvin and Doug went out and searched the grounds then returned to the group. The group was silent for a few moments as the impact and implications sunk in.

"Someone has been watching us," Doug said. "They came in here last night and entered the ship. We'll have to check everything again to make sure they didn't do anything to sabotage it."

"That word scares me," Marvin said.

"We've got to move the ship and everything associated with it," Frank said. "I'll have a crew here in an hour with a float trailer."

"Where to?" Doug said.

"I have a building just outside Aurora. It's remote. I still use it for assembling magnet production lines to be moved here. It's eighty by a hundred feet with a fifty-foot ceiling. We'll move everything today."

"Suppose they're watching right now and will know where we go with it?" Al said.

"I don't think so," Doug said. "Whoever was here is on their way right now to report to his superiors."

"Probably true," Marvin said. "However, I'm going to comb the area while we are waiting for the equipment to move the ship."

"I'll go with you," Doug said.

"Me, too," Dave said.


The three returned to the company an hour later. A lowboy float trailer was backing into the test room through the hanger door opening.

"Nobody around," Doug said. "However, they now know it's here."

"It won't be in a couple of hours," Frank said. "We'll move the mock-up into its place."

Doug looked at Frank for a moment, and then glanced at Dave. Dave lips formed a smile. "Is there any of that silver paint left?"

Frank stopped and looked at Doug, then at Dave. His facial expression didn't change. "Behind the half wall divider, in the corner.

DAN HOLT

# Chapter 11

*"The ancient Being looked around at the expansive chamber, waved his hand across a grid to bring up the lighting, then, with eyes of pure science, scanned the row of bottles containing the life giving fluid...."*

## - EARTH BASE ONE -

Frank called Michael while the crews were in route to move Research One. He filled Michael in on the intrusion into his test facility. It'd been a while since Frank had heard such deep concern in his friend and colleague's voice. Michael was ready to go to Washington if necessary.

"Michael, we don't need this thing to get out of hand," Frank said.

"Well, Frank, from Doug and Dave's account of the only episode that they know of, I thought it was some activity from a troubled CIA They're just touching all the bases as they are supposed to. You know, they have fallen in favor a great deal since the dismantling of the Soviet Union."

"I don't care about that," Frank said. "To me, this is a breach of my privacy. As an inventor, my inventions and discoveries are my property."

"I know, Frank. I have some people I can get to look into it. They're good. They'll find out what's going on."

"Okay," Frank said, then outlined the plan the group at the company had agreed on. He heard Michael chuckle.

"I like it," Michael said.

Four hours after the mover's trucks pulled out of

the test room with its cargo, covered with tarps and blocking to look rectangular, Doug watched the driver position the large vehicle in back of a faded tin covered building several miles outside Aurora, Illinois. A second truck, carrying all the support equipment for the ship, waited at the edge of the abandoned parking lot.

Doug stepped into the spacious building behind Frank and the four man moving crew. He noticed the huge open structure echoing their voices. The sound of the truck's engine reverberated through it. It seemed enormous. He turned and looked at the gleaming ship sitting on the bed of the heavy steel trailer, then at the tarps and rigging lying beside it on the concrete tarmac. Around the array of transport equipment were bits of grass growing through the cracks of the cement. He stared at the ship for a long moment, highlighted against the row of sixty-foot tall wind breaking trees in the distance. The heavy nylon lifting equipment attached to it made it look like it was being delivered gift-wrapped. He glanced at the floor for a moment then up at the steel girders supporting the roof of the ancient building.

"Earth Base One," Doug said out loud. The others looked around the building. "This is Earth Base One." Doug repeated. He saw agreement in Frank's eyes. The group moved to the side of the spacious building when they heard the sounds of the trailer's air brakes being released. The truck began inching backward. The driver, a long time friend of Frank Gordon, was delivering the first spacecraft to Earth Base One.

Frank climbed the ladder to the overhead crane.

Thomas Thornton, getting no response when he knocked on Allen Brewster's apartment door, entered the bar across the street, located the phone and dialed the agent's number. No answer. He was about to explode. He hadn't slept in two days. Last night he'd seen some kind of craft. A hidden flying saucer; a real one. It was awesome. Something big, really big, was going down and he discovered it. He'd take Mr. Brewster there tonight and show it to him. Thomas Thornton had his break. He'd be somebody, like Mr. Brewster, after tonight. Tom looked at his watch. One-fifteen pm. He'd get some lunch then call again.

Doug and Dave sat before the computer keyboards of Research One going over programs. Frank and Marvin had all the inspection plates off the rotor pod. Marvin was turning the rotors by hand while Frank carefully inspected each magnet and its mounting. Isaac and Al were examining each of the tanks and their respective plumbing and valves. It was well into the night when they were satisfied that all was well with Research One. Whoever had turned on the safety system had turned it off as soon as they realized the computer had begun to do its job. Nothing else was amiss.

"What a day," Frank said as he wrenched his neck then looked around the spacious building. The support equipment lay on the floor along one side, stacked in waist high piles with just walking room between them. On the opposite wall three forklifts had been parked randomly. Along with them were assorted jigs his workman used for the construction of magnetic assembly lines. Toward the opposite end of the building were the offices and associated facilities. He looked back at Research One. It was a futuristic entry into the panorama of the building.

"It's going to take a few days to get Earth Base One into shape," Frank said. A cool breeze ruffled Frank's thinning hair. He ran a hand through it.

There was a loud clap of thunder. A moment later rain started falling in windswept waves. The group looked toward the open doors and lighted parking lot and into the darkness beyond. A puff of cool air toppled a metal canister off a stack of equipment. It hit the floor and rolled several feet. They hurried to the doors and rolled them along their tracks until they met, closing out the driving rain.

"Tomorrow we'll set things in motion to get living facilities in here," Frank said. "Everything can be set up in the offices." He glanced up in response to the sound of the rain falling on the metal roof. The others followed his gaze.

"This is perfect," Dave said. "It's private, roomy; great to test the ship."

"Earth Base One," Isaac said. "I love it."

Thomas Thornton parked his car behind the adjacent building to Gordon & Gordon Magnetics as he'd done twice previously. Allen Brewster sat in the passenger seat. Torrents of rain swept across the windshield as Agent Thornton pulled on his leather gloves with finality. Brewster pulled a pair of gloves from his inside coat pocket and laid them on his knee. He looked at the windshield.

It was raining harder. He finally said, "This better be good."

Tom smiled at him. "What's in that building is the biggest thing the CIA has ever discovered. You'll see for yourself in a few minutes, Sir."

Brewster began putting on his gloves, thinking that Thornton may really have something here, something big. But he didn't know what Brewster had known for thirty years. Tom was a child when the 'really big' discovery was made. Of the eight agents present in that meeting, him and the seven assigned to him, only two were still alive. The other living member, Paul Mason, was paralyzed in an auto accident two years ago. Allen was now alone with the assignment, however, he had an open ticket to get the job done. He glanced at Tom again. The kid sure was pushing to be somebody. *"Let's see if he's found something really significant."* He thought.

"Okay," Brewster said. "Take me to your flying saucer."

Tom glanced at Brewster with a look of resentment. Brewster read the thought, slid his hand inside his coat, and touched his gun. Tom acted as if he didn't notice.

They exited the car and made their way to the fence. The young agent was over it quicker than ever, then watched and waited for his superior. Brewster was a little slower, but with extra effort, almost matched the speed. They crept to the back door. Tom had it open in seconds and they were inside the test room. They paused for a moment in the stillness, both soaked form the torrential rain. Lightning flashed in the distance. The bright flash of light through the test room window illuminated the silvery disc shape of the plywood mock-up. The shape seemed to remain for a few seconds after the light had subsided. Brewster's eyes widened.

"Oh my God!" he whispered.

"I told you, Mr. Brewster," Tom said. "It's a spaceship. A real flying saucer." Tom pulled out his flashlight and outlined the ship again.

"Let's go inside it," Brewster said.

"The entrance is around here," Tom said then led the way. Tom hurried up the ramp; Brewster moved slowly and cautiously. At the top of the ramp Tom stepped inside the mock-up and disappeared from view. There was a crashing sound. Tom fell on the bottom of the plywood construction knocking a sheet of the plywood loose from the framework. He and the sheet of plywood hit the floor below. Brewster crouched down from instinct, pulled his gun, and then hopped off the ramp onto the floor to a squatting position.

"Tom!" he said in an intense whisper. Tom moaned. "Tom," Brewster said again. "You okay?" Tom rose up from his stomach to his hands and knees. His flashlight was lying on the floor four feet away illuminating one of the legs of the mock-up saucer. It was a wooden four by four inch block. He stared at it for a long moment then looked up at the 'ship' above him. He saw the four by eight foot hole he'd fallen through, taking out one of the plywood panels, and then the interior of the wooden vessel. He looked around at Brewster crouched on the floor of the facility.

"You okay?" Brewster asked sarcastically.

Marvin, Doug, and Dave, clustered together in the cramped overhead crane, gritted their teeth to maintain silence. They watched the two men on the test room floor argue violently in whispers, then leave through the same door they'd came in moments before. One minute later, by Marvin's watch, they burst out laughing.

## Chapter 12

*"No great discovery, no great adventure, no great stride forward, is ever made as a Community effort. The Community is always far too busy tending itself. However, within every Community there's always that daring few...."*

## - FLIGHT TESTS -

## SATURDAY MORNING, EIGHT O'CLOCK A.M - INITIAL TESTS.

| | | |
|---|---|---|
| *Colonel Marvin Andrews* | -- | *Pilot* |
| *Frank Gordon* | -- | *Propulsion* |
| *Douglas Hastings* | -- | *Computer* |
| *Controls* | | |
| *Dave Henson* | -- | *Flight Safety* |
| *Isaac Henson* | -- | *Ship's* |
| *Atmosphere* | | |

The crew of Research One had each studied their respective assignments diligently. Each member knew the absence of competence would mean disaster. The astronaut member of the crew was impressed with the discipline, rivaling that of the trainees at the NASA facility. There was electricity in the air as the entire group sat around a line of tables in the popular Breakfast Fork Café. Breakfast finished, they went directly to Earth Base One.

Today was christening day, then the crew would take it out and fly it. Today it became absolutely real. The two hanger doors were rolled to the end of their tracks leaving a forty-foot opening to the concrete apron behind Earth Base One. The group stood in a semicircle in front of the massive windshield, the bow, of Research One. Karen Hastings raised her arm, gripping the neck of a bottle of champagne, then paused and glanced from face to face. Each nodded, smiling. She turned and faced the bow of the vessel.

"I dub thee Research One!" She swung the bottle against the heavy acrylic windshield. The bottle shattered a splash of champagne across the windshield. The group cheered and clapped their hands then gradually grew quiet.

The five member crew would board the ship. The others would witness the first time that Research One broke the bonds of Earth and rose into the air.

Marvin bowed and extended his left hand, palm up, toward the ramp. "Mr. Gordon."

"Thank you, Colonel," Frank said. He marched up the ramp followed by Marvin, Doug, and Dave.

Isaac stuck his right arm straight up, gripped his fist, and jerked it down. "Yes!" He bounded up the ramp like a man half his age.

The witnesses cheered as the crew seated themselves, enjoying the moment, but as the seconds ticked by, a serious note invaded the atmosphere of the spacecraft.

The seats were lined across the front in a semicircle with the contour of the ship, each so arranged to be facing ahead. Each would rotate on its base and face a twelve by twenty inch table mounted just behind it on a pedestal. Half way down the pedestal, opposite the seat, a similar sized bench would fold down for seating behind the table, also facing ahead. A bench by the air lock would accommodate two more people. Research One would seat fourteen people in leisurely flight, six people in space flight with complete belts and harnesses. In front of the seats was a cushioned console table twelve inches wide, blending into the COMM panel, loaded with gauges, digital readouts, controls, monitors, keyboards and square keypads by the controls. Just above the pilot's flight screen was a rear view monitor.

Centered in front of the pilot was a computer screen with a three coordinate display; the x axis, the y axis, and the z axis. There was a duplicate in front of the copilot's seat and another on the end in front of the navigator. The positions were manned by Marvin, Frank, and Doug respectively.

"We've studied the computer control specs that you and Dave prepared for us," Marvin said, "But go over just the basics as a refresher."

Doug nodded, and then laid his hand on the pilot's monitor.

"Research One is designed to be computer controlled although it could be flown without the use of a computer at all. Due to the design of the power plant, if it were flown without the aid of computers, forward would be always on one point of the compass. If you changed directions, you would have to fly sideways or backward, or manually rotate the cabin to be facing the direction of flight. By using computer control, forward is always the way the windshield is facing, just like a conventional aircraft. The computer trims and alters the controls so that the crew is always facing the direction of flight. This is done by using three points of reference. They are called axis's; the x axis, the y axis, and the z axis.

"The X is left and right, the Y is up and down, and the Z is forward and backward. The two handles are for manual control. The one on the right hand is forward, backward, left and right. The one on the left hand is up and down. The keypads just below the controls instruct the computer. If you want to go up three feet, you can use the manual control and raise the ship until the altimeter reads three, or you can type the number three on the keypad and the computer will do it.

"To go forward, just push the control forward; the further forward, the faster the ship will go. Backward is the same. For left and right, move the stick to the left, the computers will bank the ship according to its speed, rotate it around the rotor pod, then engage the correct controls to make the ship go that way.

"When you lift off, the computer will automatically determine the weight of the ship by how much power it takes to lift it. The computer will set itself and use that figure for one gravity of acceleration.

"If you pushed the stick all the way forward, the ship will continue to gain speed until the full power of the rotor pod is offset by the resistance of the air in front of the ship. Dave will explain how fast the ship will accelerate."

Dave cleared his throat. "Safety factors have been programmed into the computers. The computers won't allow any motion or maneuver of the ship that would injure its passengers. For example, the ship won't gain speed quicker than three *Gs*. If more than that, there's a risk of blackout. Three *Gs* is gaining speed at about the rate of a hundred feet per second. That acceleration is used by the computers only in the event of an emergency. Normal acceleration is one *G*. The ship will automatically do that unless you push the emergency button, or the ship is about to hit something and has to use that much power to miss it.

"Research One has a built in avoidance radar. If you are flying along and are about to hit something, or even come too close, the ship will automatically make a course correction around the object. If the ship is moving slow enough that it can stop in place without exceeding the allowable *G* forces, when it encounters an obstruction in its flight path, it will cancel forward motion and wait for your instructions.

"You can set altitude, say fifty feet, and the ship will maintain that altitude. If there's something in the way, the ship will go up over it and then return back to the altitude of fifty feet.

"One other thing," Dave continued, "the ship has a program for automatic return to point of origin. When you start the ship and leave, the computer knows where you are and remembers it. You raise this cover," Dave flipped the small cover on the control panel revealing two buttons marked, Ret P O -- Cancel, "push this button, and the ship will return to the point of origin automatically. Research One will take the shortest route back to its starting place. It remembers all the turns you make."

Doug caught Dave's eye, then nodded.

Dave resumed speaking in a serious tone. "Doug and I discussed it at length and decided to install another program. We call it Imminent Collision. Here's how it works. If something unexpected happens and the ship's about to collide with something at high speed, the computers will use whatever power it takes to avoid the collision. We felt we all have a better chance of surviving, say ten *Gs* for a few seconds, than we do of surviving a high speed collision."

The last instruction had a disquieting effect on the crew, but Doug noticed the perceptible nods.

"Mr. Gordon." Marvin said, "Start the Engines."
Frank responded by turning on the square

readout marked Propulsion. The display lit up, reading systems one, two, and three. He pushed the button marked one. A red light came on and then seconds later, turned green.

"Booster units running, engaging rotor pod," Frank reported. The rotor rpm digital readout began climbing, slowly at first, then, when the rotors passed critical velocity and the field coils engaged, it very quickly went to over five thousand RPM. A faint hum filled the ship. The rotor pod light turned green.

Isaac Henson's eyes sparkled.

Marvin said. "Okay, gentlemen, let's find out if everything works. Frank, this baby's your dream. Let Doug and Dave talk you through some trials."

Frank smiled. "Okay, Doug, let's find out if Magnetic Inertial Propulsion will deliver."

Doug glanced at his monitor, then at Dave. Dave looked up from his and nodded. Doug looked around at the others then out the windshield at the group standing fifty feet away on the floor of Earth Base One.

"Frank, type three on your altitude keypad." Frank nervously reached up and pushed the key marked '3.'

The ship rose 3 feet.

The strong surge of one gravity of acceleration briefly doubled their body weight. One G of acceleration plus one G compliments of Mother Earth. The discomfort was on all their faces. Doug and Dave glanced at each other.

"I'm reducing the power acceleration setting to one quarter G," Dave said.

Doug watched Dave make the entry, then turned to Frank, "Open the red cover and push the Return to Point of Origin button." Frank complied. The ship remained stationary momentarily. They heard the faint whine of electric motors. The tripod gear was lowering itself. No one had heard it come up. The ship gently settled back to the floor.

"That's much better," Isaac said.

"Frank, key in three on the keypad again," Dave said.

Frank confidently pushed the button. Research One rose gently to 3 feet. The motors whined again.

"Okay, turn the ship around," Doug instructed. "Just push the stick to the left. With no instructions to go forward, the computer will rotate the ship around the Y axis."

Frank moved the stick to the left. The ship began rotating in place. The crew watched the wall of Earth Base One pass by their field of view, then the hanger doors went by. Frank released the stick and then moved it to the right; the rotation reversed. When the hanger doors were centered in his view, he returned the control to neutral.

"I like this!" Frank said. He looked around the ship, then at the floor three feet below it. Research One was completely motionless, as if it was still sitting on the floor.

"Okay," Doug said. "We're ready to go outside and put it through its paces, Colonel."

Marvin looked out the windshield. Across the open field, a quarter mile away, was a stand of tall trees. To the right was more open field.

"Suppose we're seen?" Isaac said.

"It won't matter," Marvin said. "There are so many UFO reports now that it'll just be another one. A lot of people simply won't report it, and besides, those that see the name, Research One, on the side will think it's just a test vehicle by the government, or a promotion by some company. Michael said he was

139

surprised how easily it was to get an agreement of confidence from all of our suppliers. This is the nineties folks. All of you are from the sixties."

"And fifties," Isaac said, holding up his hand.

"Okay," Frank said, "let's go."

Doug turned to Frank. "The farther forward you push the stick, the faster the ship will go. If you let go of the stick, the ship will slow down until it stops. If you want the ship to keep going without holding the stick at, say fifty miles per hour, when you get to that speed, push the button on the top of the stick and the ship will hold that speed until you change it. If you punch fifty into the computer, it will accelerate the ship, at a quarter $G$, until we're at that velocity and then maintain it.

"Cruise Control," Isaac said. Doug looked at him, blinked, and then nodded.

Frank pushed the stick forward cautiously. The ship moved out of the hanger and into the sunlight. Frank released the stick; the ship eased to a stop and became motionless. He eased the stick to the right and rotated the ship one hundred and eighty degrees until they were looking back into Earth Base One. Michael, Al, Karen, Jean, and Sandra waved, smiling broadly. The crew all returned a thumbs-up. Frank rotated the ship back to its original heading.

"Punch in fifty on the altitude, Frank," Dave said.

Research One rose gently and hovered. The altitude read fifty. Frank eased the stick forward. The ship began smooth forward motion, the speed constantly increasing at a quarter $G$.

They were coming up on a tree line very quickly. A red light began flashing and the ship rose. Doug thought of an elevator leaving floor one. The gauge beside the red light read: AV-S Engaged. The stand of trees passed underneath them. The ship sank.

The gauge read: Return to Y50. The red light stopped flashing. Doug and Dave nodded to each other. Doug saw Isaac look up and down the COMM panel then out the windshield again. He was smiling and breathing with his mouth open.

"Take a right and head for open country." Marvin said.

Frank eased the stick to the right. The ship banked and began turning. He moved the stick back to center then pushed it forward a little. The pilot, copilot, navigator, flight safety officer, and life support officer watched the countryside passing under the ship, mesmerized by the smooth, silent ride above it.

"Punch one hundred into the altimeter," Dave said in an even tone.

Frank, taking his eyes off the windshield just long enough, pushed the buttons. The ship rose smoothly and leveled off. Frank glanced at the square digital window in the console marked Speed.

""We're going a hundred and seventy," he said.

"Ease it up to three hundred," Marvin said.

Frank pushed the stick forward and watched the digits climb. Abruptly, a pond, silo, and farmhouse passed under them. Doug pictured himself standing by the silo watching Research One fly over. He glanced at Frank.

"Pull the stick back to zero," he said, watching his monitor.

The ship decelerated gently to a dead stop, hovering, a hundred feet above the ground.

As Doug and Dave watched their monitors, Frank and Marvin took the ship through all maneuvers; forward, backward, left and right. They executed climbing turns and descending turns. The ship performed flawlessly. Then came the crucial test the programmers were seeking to verify before any high speed flight; the collision avoidance system programmed into the ship's computers.

Marvin deliberately put the ship on a collision course with a small hill, prepared to avoid flying into it if necessary. The AV-S system sensed the oncoming obstruction, canceled the manual controls and kept a hundred feet safety clearance of the obstacle, then when the flight path was clear, re-engaged them. The programmers were satisfied the systems were functional. Following the extensive tests, the ship hovered again at a hundred feet.

Dave smiled. "Okay, Mr. Frank Gordon, you're in a ship powered by Magnetic Inertial Propulsion; your invention. Have fun with it."

Frank punched fifty into the altimeter, then twenty into the Speed control. The ship responded smoothly, sinking to fifty feet above the ground and gliding along at twenty miles per hour. The eighteen foot wide windshield afforded a panoramic view of the countryside. Several birds flew along ahead of the ship for some time, then turned and flew away at an angle to the ship's line of flight. The crew watched, enjoying a feeling of accomplishment.

"I visualized this moment twenty-five years ago," Frank said. "I was in college when I first conceived the idea of creating a power supply for flight, free of a whirling propeller, jet thrust, or a fast moving airfoil or an airplane wing, to cause lift." The crew's eyes were pulled from the scenery to Frank. He glanced around at his colleagues and continued. "And here it is. Inertial force is canceling gravity and keeping us airborne."

"And," Marvin added, "that harnessed inertial force will supply gravity for us on the way to the Moon."

Research One abruptly halted in place. All eyes went to the windshield.

"It's a kite," Doug said. Frank rotated the ship to the right and their eyes followed the string in a gentle sway to the ground. At the operator end of the kite string were two boys that appeared to be ten to twelve years old. One was holding the string in one hand and shielding his eyes against the Sun with the other, staring at Research One. The other young man was shielding his eyes with both hands and staring also. Two hundred yards behind them was the back of a small farmhouse.

Frank glanced at Doug and smiled then moved Research One close to the kite, opened the outer doors, then moved closer until the kite was dancing over the ramp, dragging its tail across it. He pulled out his wallet, retrieved two ten dollar bills, and stepped out onto the ramp. He captured the kite and lodged the money behind the wooden center strut and then released it. He waved at the two kite flyers. They looked at each other and waved back. Frank moved the ship, closed the outer doors, and proceeded to fly away.

All eyes aboard Research One went to the rear view monitor. The boys were hurriedly reeling in the kite. It was doing loop-de-loops on the rapid descent. Marvin turned to Frank, his hands open in front of him.

"Is that what you spent half a lifetime and a couple million dollars to do?" he said tauntingly. Frank answered, looking straight out the windshield.

"Without the research, I'd still be flying a kite." Marvin nodded, smiling. The crew laughed approvingly.

Research One glided effortlessly across the terrain, its space-worthy outer shell shutting out the noises of civilization. It seemed a world apart, protecting its crew from the outside environment, a technological haven of refuge, a place to be safe and secure. In its heart, inside the eight-foot diameter black sphere, awesome power was poised, waiting to be summoned. When called upon, jealous of its crew, it would measure that power to guarantee their safety and, when necessary, use whatever it took to protect them.

The vessel topped a hill, then sank gently, maintaining the set altitude.

"Look!" Isaac said, pointing.

A hundred yards ahead, sitting on an asphalt road, was a large white car with its hood up. A heavy-set man, wearing faded jeans and a black T-shirt, stomach hanging over his belt, was bent over with his head under the hood.

Frank typed in twenty then zero on the COMM panel. The ship slowed to a stop fifteen feet in front of the car, twenty feet up. Frank opened the outer doors.

"Hello there, need some help?"

The man, startled, bumped his head on the hood, then straightened up and glanced over his shoulder, then around in all directions.

"Up here," Frank called down to the man.

The man looked up. His mouth dropped open, and then he staggered backward and sat down in the middle of the black top road.

"I'm sorry," Frank said. "I didn't mean to scare you. I saw you were having car trouble and wanted to see if I could help."

The man looked at his car, back at the ship, eyed the name on the side, and let out a deep breath. "Ah, yeah," he said, "it died on me. The battery's dead and it won't start. Say, what kind of airplane is that?

I never seen one before."

"This is a research craft; we're trying to get the bugs out of it. You got jumper cables?"

"Yeah, in the back." The man got up and went to the trunk, patted his trousers pocket, returned to the door, pulled the keys out of the ignition, then got the cables out of the trunk.

Frank moved the ship down to three feet and over to within five feet of the car. The man hooked the cables to the car's battery and handed Frank the other ends. Frank removed the cover of the battery compartment and clamped the cables on the terminals of the nearest battery. Research One's starboard booster unit sensed the depleted cells in the car's battery and adjusted its output to re-energize them. Frank looked down and nodded to the man.

The man blinked, went back to the driver's door, opened it, paused and looked both up and down the black top road, then up at the saucer and grinned. Frank raised an eyebrow. The motorist entered his car and engaged the starter. The car's engine burst into life. He looked up at Frank leaning up against the door seal of Research One and smiled. Frank made a waving gesture, and then tossed the cables to the ground. The man returned the gesture, then opened the car door and stepped out on one foot.

"Thanks," he said. Good luck with that thing." Frank smiled and nodded at the pot-bellied man with the big car. He closed the doors, punched in 'fifty' altitude and 'twenty' speed, and Research One rose and gilded smoothly away. In the rear view monitor, the crew saw the man on the ground drop the jumper cables into the trunk, then get behind the wheel, turn and watch the saucer for a few moments, then drive away.

After a couple of minutes of the roller coaster ride provided by the Avoidance System, Dave pointed out that it would be much smoother at five hundred feet. Frank entered the digits. The others still looked at him and smiled about the 'first' in road service they had just witnessed.

Marvin pulled a cell phone from his breast pocket and dialed a number. After a moment, he spoke into it.

"Daniel, this is Colonel Andrews, I'm on my way. I'll have some friends with me; the people I was telling you about…Good, be there in an hour."

Marvin pocketed the phone. "Daniel's expecting us." He patted the console of the ship. "I can't think of a better way to challenge the man then this. We're going to a little place called Red Oak, Texas. Frank, May I?" Frank gestured toward the controls. Marvin placed his hand on the stick.

"Texas in an hour?" Dave said. "Colonel, we're in Illinois."

"Yeah, I know." Marvin typed in five hundred, then one thousand on the COMM panel.

As the ship began its quarter *G* acceleration, Doug turned to Marvin.

"Colonel, you're about to go visit a friend and you will be arriving in a flying saucer. Does this man have a strong heart?" Doug looked around at the others and smiled. They all smiled and looked at Marvin.

"He's got a good one," Marvin said.

# Chapter 13

*"As if fate has dictated that someone must know, a pool of consciousness, protected in a crypt of stone, sleeps on...waiting..."*

## - CREW MEMBER # 6 -

Daniel Stubblefield was five feet eight inches tall, stocky, and thirty-six years old. He had curly, dusty blonde hair, glasses...Nerd, Egghead, Brain. Daniel had heard these references to himself ever since he'd fallen in love with mathematics at age nine. He didn't care; he was consumed with the order of mathematics. Working out the trajectories for the two Voyager series missions had been pure dessert for him. The intricate entries into the data banks of the systems were delicious and he loved it.

He'd fantasized about being a spaceman like his friend, Marvin Andrews, but knew it would never happen--Daniel Stubblefield was not physical, not tough, not commanding like the colonel. He'd never be considered for space flight.

When Daniel sat down at a Computer to program telemetry, he got his ego food. He was good and he knew it. He determined how the spaceships got to their destination, the 'route' they would take, and when they would arrive. But still, it wasn't like getting into a spacecraft and going yourself.

He glanced at the clock on the mantle; one thirty pm. The colonel said he would come by in the afternoon to say hello and tell him about a project he'd gotten involved with just outside Chicago. He knew Colonel Andrews had retired from the Air Force and the space program. Daniel remembered the disagreement with their reasons and Marvin's arguments for staying on. But Marvin had told him in confidence that he felt he didn't have full support from the powers that be and decided to accept retirement.

The colonel was rugged, tough, and he was Daniel's friend. Daniel liked being with him.

There was a knock on the back door. Daniel got up, set down his glass of lemon tea, then went and opened it.

"Colonel...why'd you come to the back door?"

Marvin didn't answer. He gestured for Daniel to follow him, then turned and walked off the patio, straight out and around a plush vine arbor, and up the ramp into Research One. Daniel followed. Confused, he stepped around the vine arbor, saw the ship, recoiled, read the name on the side, and then stared up into the spacecraft as the colonel held the airlock door. Marvin gestured for him to come into the ship. Daniel swallowed and slowly walked up the ramp and through the airlock door into the ship. The whine of electric motors accompanied the closing doors. Becoming immersed in the moment, Daniel scanned the line of people sitting in the row of plush, high back seats arranged in front of the windshield. His eyes, going down the line, rested on Isaac Henson.

"I.J.!" Daniel said. Isaac just waved and smiled. Marvin pointed to the empty seat between Frank and Doug. Daniel mechanically walked over and sat down in it.

Doug extended his hand, "Douglas Hastings."

Daniel, a blank look on his face, replied, "Daniel Stubblefield."

Frank Gordon did the same. Same response.

Daniel heard the clicking of computer keys. The ship started rising. He grabbed the arms of the men adjacent to him. Doug and Frank looked at his hands. Daniel removed them. The ship stopped rising and held. Daniel looked around at the community below, and then his eyes went to the array of instruments in the COMM panel. Research One rotated a quarter turn. Facing south, it began to accelerate. Daniel leaned forward, turned to Isaac and spoke softly.

"Where are we going?"

"To the Moon," Colonel Andrews answered, punching keys on the console.

"Ah, what?" Daniel said in a weak voice.

The ship descended in the middle of a pasture and settled in among a grove of trees. Daniel watched the ground come up at them and stop. Following the faint whine of the landing gear, the ship touched down. He saw a cottontail rabbit scurry away across the grass. The trees were completely still, undisturbed by the presence of the craft.

"Daniel," the colonel said, "I want to talk to you about something very important."

"Colonel," Daniel said, and then swallowed, "You have my attention."

Marvin smiled. Daniel returned the smile and glanced at the others.

"We need a good telemetry man to join the crew for a research project. I'm asking you to join us. Before you answer, let's go back to the place where this ship was built and we'll show you everything."

Daniel turned and looked at the rotor pod centered in the craft behind the seats, listening to the faint hum coming from it. He imagined a sprawling development center at Chicago, something secret that he hadn't heard about, and the colonel was one of their astronauts.

"Okay," Daniel said and settled back in his seat.

Marvin flipped the cover, pushed the Point of Origin, and then began the introductions.

Allen Brewster sat in the concealment of the underbrush of the line of wind breaking trees a quarter of a mile from the open hanger doors of Technical Research Association's Earth Base One. The saucer that Thomas Thornton had described had come out of those doors two hours earlier and glided away. He patiently waited for its return. He dropped another cigarette butt on the pile already on the ground in front of him and stepped on it. He swept the area again with the binoculars.

He'd threatened to kill Tom for dragging him to the outskirts of Chicago to see a plywood flying saucer. Tom had been adamantly persistent that this craft did exist and it had been switched. Brewster had leaned on him unmercifully about trying to claim the premise that the group had spirited away a real spacecraft and built a plywood model in its place in one day. He'd fired Tom although he believed him. Tom had obviously made a mistake somewhere. The group knew he'd been there. He made it clear that Tom was no longer involved. If he did anything else at all regarding this case, he was a dead man. He meant it and Thomas Thornton knew he meant it. However, since Tom was right, after this thing was resolved, he'd pick him up later. It'd be a lesson to the young agent. Don't make mistakes. If you do, clean them up--permanently.

Brewster saw the silvery pin dot a mile away. He put the binoculars on it. It was the ship, coming in fast a hundred feet above the ground. A chill went up his spine as he watched it decelerate and descend before the hanger doors, then enter the building and settle to the floor with such precision. A moment later, the side of it opened like a giant mouth. Two guys came out of it and closed the outside doors.

Brewster felt like he did years earlier when he was first assigned this task. New energy swept through his body. He stood, kicked some dirt over the pile of cigarette butts and tamped it, then looked back at the faded building housing the threat to the keeping of the secret. He carefully began making his way through the trees and brush to his car. He had a serious phone call to make and then a subsequent meeting to attend. This was going to be ugly, but, it had to be done. He recalled what he'd seen decades earlier and his first act to conceal it. And there were his instructions: *This must never be known.*

Doug went over the entire sequence of the discovery of the artifacts on the Moon with crew member number six. Daniel was very excited about the possible discoveries that lie ahead of them. Frank showed him the small test model, the full size prototype, and the wheel inside the wheel being utilized in the ship. Technical Research Association arranged an apartment for him near Gordon & Gordon Magnetics. Daniel Stubblefield went to work on the telemetry for the research project.

The full crew now selected for the research mission, Marvin addressed the ship's company in the conference room at Earth Base One.

"There are two things I want us to do, then come back here and evaluate. One: Let's take the ship out and operate it under emergency conditions. And two: let's suit up in the excursion gear and take the air lock down to zero atmospheres and verify the space suits and communications equipment."

The crew went to the ship for the first test; emergency acceleration. Marvin raised the ship to a thousand feet and headed for the open country of Kansas. In half an hour, they were hovering a thousand feet above a wide flat area of sprawling wheat fields: the solid sea of greenery was interrupted only occasionally every few miles by the ribbon of a Farm to Market road. There was nothing to be seen, save a farm house or two, all the way to the horizon in all directions. Marvin descended to five hundred feet.

"Okay," Marvin said to Doug. "Let me be sure I'm clear on this. The emergency button automatically engages the power at three *Gs*?"

"Provided," Doug said, "the ship has instructions to move in a direction. If none are given, like now, it won't do anything. If you go forward, then hit emergency, the acceleration will be at three *Gs*. Until you cancel, all directional controls would be obeyed at that acceleration. If you hit Point of Origin, the ship would return home accelerating at three *Gs*, automatically reversing power to stop at the point of origin."

"Okay," Marvin said, "be sure your belts are tight. Let's make a short emergency run."

The six men pulled on their belts again. Marvin checked the row of seats; the crew nodded.

"Engaging power." He pushed the stick all the way forward and the ship began accelerating at one-quarter *G*. He flipped the protective cover and pushed the red button. They were pinned back into the seats firmly as the terrain started passing under them rapidly, getting more so constantly.

Doug, Dave, and Daniel were watching the terrain below, glancing at the readouts as a terrace or small hill would pass under the ship. The numerals would spin, reflecting the true distance from Research One to the ground below.

The pressure of the seats on their backs, 3

Gs--three times their body weight, was constant. The effort to concentrate and do their jobs under that acceleration was clear evidence of the seriousness of the machine they had collectively developed at Gordon & Gordon Magnetics.

Marvin glanced at Frank. He was watching the terrain, every few seconds glancing down at the rotor pod readouts, then back at the terrain. The hum of the rotor pod was unchanged under the constantly increasing power demand; the power needed to push a wall of air in front of the ship faster and faster.

Marvin looked at the speed: six hundred, a thousand, climbing rapidly. A farmhouse passed under them. He glanced at the rear view monitor to watch it quickly disappear into the distance. His eyes went back to the speed: twenty-five hundred, three thousand. There was no buffeting, no foreign stress, just dead smooth lateral acceleration. Frank's words formed in his mind: *"the gyroscopic design gives it complete stability."* Marvin glanced at the rear view monitor again. Thirty-five hundred, then four thousand. The wake of air behind the ship reached the ground. The wheat was being bent over. It looked like the wake behind a speedboat on a lake; the sea of wheat bending toward the speeding ship after it passed over then returning to straight up. The AV-S light blinked. He glanced at it and back at the scene ahead as the ship sank a few feet. Five thousand miles per hour and climbing. He barely had time to recognize the small private plane as it passed over them. The ship rose quickly and resumed altitude. He glanced at the rear view monitor; the eyes of the crew followed. The wake of air behind Research One pushed the private plane skyward a thousand feet. It was dancing in the sky like a dragonfly and then was out of sight.

The speed of Research One had just passed six thousand when Marvin pushed cancel. The ship quickly slowed; the computer adjusted the controls to keep the speed change at a quarter *G*.

"The wake behind the ship," Marvin said. "We almost blew that small plane out of the sky."

"He'll have a story to tell when he lands, won't he," Doug said as he checked the emergency system readouts.

Marvin watched Frank read the propulsion system instruments and nod.

"We're in Colorado," Daniel said.

Marvin looked at the mountain range ahead, turned the ship around and took it up to ten thousand feet, then headed back toward home. Up ahead, he saw a twin turboprop commuter plane on a heading for the mountains.

"They're radar has probably picked us up," Marvin said. He pulled up beside the aircraft and paced it long enough for the pilots to see the name on the side of the saucer. The co-pilot of the twin-engine craft saw Research One and recoiled, then said something to the pilot; he leaned forward and eyed the saucer. The two airline pilots in the commuter plane studied the silvery disc. Marvin waved. The two men waved back. Marvin did the 'wing wave' with Research One then pushed the stick forward and sped away from the airliner. He then descended to five hundred feet and pushed the Point of Origin button.

Back in the hanger facility, the crew looked at Research One with a new respect and a little awe.

"How fast do you think it would go, wide open?" Isaac said.

"I can tell you," Daniel said, "when I get back to my computer."

"Let's get some lunch and come back and check out the excursion system," Marvin said.

Following lunch, they were all at Earth Base One again.

Isaac liked the suits. Al had put Michael in touch with one of the passed-over bidders of NASA's space suit contract. The suits were relative light and simple. They were designed for short usage, one hour with a maximum survival time of four hours. They were different from NASA's version in that there were two tanks mounted on them. One was on the back with natural compressed air, coupled with a system to maintain air temperature and pressure in the suit. The other, smaller tank was mounted on the left leg. It released oxygen inside the suit as needed. The tether on the back allowed a hundred feet excursions from the ship, unless detached purposely.

Isaac also favored the electronics installed in the excursion system. When anyone talked in the suit, it could be heard by all the other suited partners and on the intercom in the ship. Everything said in the ship could be heard in all the suits. One other thing that touched his fatherly instincts; a sensor, hooked to the intake valve of the air supply to the suit, monitored the breathing of the excursion group. Tied into the console on the ship, a green light was on while inhaling and a blue light when exhaling. His eyes fell on the one marked, 'Dave.'

Frank started the booster units, engaged the rotor pod, and closed the outer doors. He verified the readouts and nodded. Isaac closed the vents and put the ship on the internal air supply, sealing the vessel from the outside atmosphere. He turned on the excursion system and he, Frank, and Daniel began helping the three crewmembers get into the suits.

The heavy zippers were stiff to operate. They pressed soft rubber surfaces together to affect a seal. When all three were inside the suits, minus the helmets, they took a few steps wobbling like penguins.

"They're very heavy," Dave said. Doug nodded and attempted to bend forward. With extra effort and a half squat, he was able to touch the floor.

"They won't be this heavy on the Moon," Marvin said. Doug and Dave nodded, and then walked back and forth again.

Isaac went from person to person, read the small gauges on the tanks of the suits and turned on the valves that supplied the air. He set their helmets in place and flipped the sealing latch. He pushed the darkened visor up and down on each one after it was in place.

Starting with the colonel, Isaac patted the side of his helmet. "Can you hear me?"

"Yes, perfectly."

How's the compressed air?"

"Smells like downtown Chicago." Marvin said and grinned.

Isaac smiled at the colonel then motioned toward the airlock. Marvin, Doug, and Dave, wobbled into it and turned to face the transparent door. Isaac closed it and flipped the latches, sealing them in.

"Okay," he said, "I'm going to pump the air out now."

They nodded, bending from the waist. Isaac started the pump and watched them. As the gauges moved slowly toward zero, he saw them working their lower jaws and swallowing.

"Everybody okay?" Isaac asked.

"It's like driving up into the mountains," Doug said. "My ears popped."

"Mine, too," Dave said.

"I can barely hear the suit pump working," Marvin said. "It came on right after you started taking out the air."

I'm fine now," Doug said. Marvin and Dave nodded.

"You're at zero," Isaac said. "Everything looks good."

The three in the air lock put their arms and hands out, thumbs up. Daniel and Frank returned the gesture, then Daniel turned to Frank and held out his hand, palm up. Frank slapped it and extended his. Daniel accommodated. Isaac smiled and reversed the pump.

Marvin stood at the window of his apartment looking across a baseball field; grass, with a half moon wire net behind home plate and bags for bases. Center was the pitcher's mound. There was a young man on it. He was burning the ball across home plate into an older man's catcher's mitt. The Sun, almost touching the horizon, highlighted the boy's swift movements. Marvin was impressed with the speed. The kid had it. The older man would stand and throw the ball back in a high arc. The kid would catch it, pause a moment, then with smooth form, rifle another one across home plate. Marvin seemed to feel the old man's pride each time the ball impacted the catcher's mitt.

*"Someday he'll sit in the stands and watch that boy play,"* he thought. His mind went back to Marvin, Jr., just briefly. He shook his head in a silent 'no, no more pain,' and then looked beyond the playing field toward the industrial area. Far in the distance he could see the roofs of the buildings of the Gordon & Gordon Magnetics complex.

A ship was built there; his ship and he was the

Captain. A magnificent ship, capable of reaching the stars. He wondered if the others realized that. Going to the Moon was a major thing. But, on this ship, there was no fuel problem. It would never run out. All you would have to do is multiply its size by twenty times to carry enough equipment to replace worn parts and the stars were within reach.

Marvin's mind soared into the heavens. His imagination saw the Solar System behind them and Alpha Centauri dead ahead....

The ring of his cell phone brought him back to Earth. He answered it.

"Colonel, you busy?" Daniel asked. There was something in Daniel's voice that Marvin hadn't heard before. Marvin turned away from the window and switched the phone to the other ear. He could hear soft music in the background.

"No, Daniel."

"I was wondering if I could buy you a drink."

"Yes, I'd love a drink. Where are you?"

"I'm at the Holiday Inn."

"I'll be there in a few minutes," Marvin said.

Marvin walked through the lobby, down the hall and left into the club. He spotted Daniel sitting in the corner. He made his way through the maze of tables and chairs, nodding to several people, and approached Daniel's table.

"Ah, Colonel, have a seat. You like Jim Bean and Coke, don't you." Marvin nodded and smiled. Daniel raised his hand, holding his Gin and Tonic. The bartender raised his eyebrows.

"A Jim Bean and Coke for the astronaut here," Daniel said loudly, "and another Gin and Tonic." The bartender nodded. Several people glanced at Marvin and Daniel for a moment. Marvin nodded and smiled.

The patrons smiled and nodded then went back to their own affairs. Marvin picked up his drink and took a sip, then noticed a stack of coasters by Daniel's left hand.

"How many have you had?"

"Four, no, five...this," Daniel said pointing at his glass, "is number six."

"What's the occasion?"

"I'm celebrating coming back from the Moon," Daniel said defiantly.

Marvin nodded slowly, smiling.

Daniel looked straight into Marvin's eyes. "We will be coming back, won't we?" Marvin held his eyes.

"Yeah, we'll be coming back." Marvin said.

Daniel stared at Marvin's eyes for an awkward moment, then glanced at his drink, then back to Marvin. He nodded. Marvin held his glass up, Daniel tagged it with his. They took a sip together.

Daniel picked up the stack of coasters. "I want to show you something." He placed a coaster at the edge of the table to his left, then one in the center, then another half way to the edge of the table above the center one. He pointed at the one at edge of the table. "This is the Sun." Then Daniel pointed at the coaster in the center of the table and then at the one above it, "This is the Earth and the Moon."

Marvin nodded. Daniel retrieved a quarter from his pocket; put his fingertip of his left hand on it and the fingertip of his right hand on the 'Moon'. Marvin glanced at Daniel then focused on the pattern on the table.

"The Apollo astronauts," Daniel began, "circled the Earth and then fired a blunderbuss rocket and pushed themselves away from the Earth's gravity in the direction of the Moon." Daniel was moving the respective pieces as he spoke. "Then when they were close to the Moon, they turned around and fired the rocket again to slow down and let the Moon's gravity capture them. Three and a half days--floating."

Then Daniel moved the pieces back to their starting points, put the quarter on its edge against the 'Earth' with heads toward the Moon and tails toward the Earth, and then looked at Marvin.

"We, on the other hand, Colonel, have constant power. We will go straight up for just over ten minutes," he said, moving the quarter, on its edge, along the surface of the table, "then begin a parabolic curve, reaching almost to the half way point between here and the Moon. This parabolic curve will put us on a trajectory that will have us moving sideways relative to the North South axis of the orbital plane...."

"Hold up a minute," Marvin said in a jovial manner, "let me take another sip of this drink." Marvin did so dramatically. "Okay, he said, "continue." Daniel grinned.

"....sideways, relative to the North South axis of the orbital plane at the same speed that the Moon is moving sideways relative to a North South axis of the orbital plane. During all this time, we will be gaining speed constantly--getting faster and faster. Then when we reach half way, we'll cut power and rotate the ship." Daniel rotated the quarter on its edge until heads was toward the Earth and tails was toward the Moon. "Then we'll re-engage power and start slowing down. From there it's a straight shot to the Moon." Marvin eyes stayed on the display momentarily, and then went to Daniel's face.

"How long?"

"Four hours, fifty-one minutes, twenty-three seconds."

Marvin glanced back at the coaster pattern on the tabletop, then back to Daniel, in wide eyed innocence. "Could you be a little more precise?"

Daniel stared at Marvin through slightly glazed eyes momentarily, and then it registered. He burst out laughing, causing Marvin to join in. Daniel rolled his drink between his hands in an awkward silence for a few moments before looking at Marvin.

"Colonel, I'm not scared, because you're going to be on the ship."

"Daniel, my friend, I'm not scared because you're going to be on the ship. We won't get lost. We'll get to the Moon."

"Colonel, I can hit it dead center."

"I know."

"Less than five hours," Daniel said to the group.

"Research One will get there that fast?" Karen said.

"It's the capability of the constant acceleration of one gravity unit that reduces the time to the Moon so dramatically." Daniel said. "You see, the first second the ship will move thirty-two feet, the next second, it will move sixty-four feet, the third second it will move ninety-six feet, and each following second it will get thirty-two feet, per second, faster. We'll accelerate half way, then turn around and decelerate the other half. We'll be weightless for thirty seconds during the turn-around. When we stop at the Moon, we'll be hovering one hundred miles above the surface. We'll be at one-sixth gravity. The AV-S system will keep us in the clear in case something is sticking up that high."

Daniel Stubblefield, *astronaut*, was a very excited and motivated man.

Marvin, Charles, Melvin, Michael, Doug, Karen, Dave, Jean, Isaac, Al, Frank, Sandra, and Daniel sat in a group in the now familiar meeting place of Frank and Sandra Gordon's home. Daniel was bubbling over with excitement explaining the road map to the Moon and the time factors, acceleration factors, and answering questions on details of the mission.

"We need to decide when we're going to leave," he said and glanced at Marvin.

Marvin agreed. "Let's board Research One as we promised our new passengers and we can talk on the ship," he said as he got to his feet. "Also, I want to pick up one more person."

"Renee?" Doug said. Marvin nodded.

"I'd like to meet her," Karen said.

"Yes," Jean and Sandra echoed.

The group occupied three cars on the drive to Earth Base One. On board the ship, Marvin occupied the pilot's position. Sandra, Karen, and Jean sat on his right. Al and Charles sat on his left. Frank, Doug, Dave, Michael, Melvin, and Daniel sat behind the utility tables. Isaac sat on the bench by the air lock. Marvin glanced at Dave. Dave nodded. Marvin raised the ship three feet, rotated, and moved out the hanger doors. The guests aboard Research One were all smiling and enjoying the moment as the craft moved out into the sunlight. Marvin punched in one hundred, then fifty. The ship rose smoothly and began a gentle acceleration.

Michael watched the terrain roll under their feet for a few moments.

"This if fantastic!" he said, "How fast will it go?"

"Daniel figured out the drag coefficient of the design with the power of the rotor pod," Marvin said, glancing over his shoulder. "At a low altitude, as we are now, Research One would do a little over eight thousand miles per hour."

Michael whistled.

"In the stratosphere," Marvin continued in a

monotone, "it would reach twelve thousand." He paused. "In space, it'll keep accelerating constantly until you stop it. There's no drag in space."

Michael glanced at Frank. "We have something here that will go to the Moon, don't we."

Daniel answered. "Yes, Sir."

Marvin turned the ship southwest and punched in five hundred, then one thousand. The guests watched the terrain drop away and begin to speed by faster and faster. After half an hour of sightseeing, Marvin canceled forward motion. Research One glided to a stop, then hovered at five hundred feet. In the distance, the occupants saw a wood framed country home sitting a hundred yards off a Farm to Market road. To their right, eight miles away, was the Wichita, Kansas skyline.

"Colonel," Daniel said. "You have this thing of landing a flying saucer in people's backyards." The group laughed. Marvin glanced around at the ship's company, then retrieved his cell phone and dialed Renee's number.

"Go out into the backyard," Marvin said into the phone.

"What?" came from the receiver.

"It's me," Marvin said, "go out into the back yard and look up." Marvin pocketed the phone and eased the ship forward and made a gradual descent. The group watched a slender woman, hair in a pony tail, wearing jeans, a T-shirt, and sneakers, come out the back door of the house. Marvin eased the ship down in front of her. The landing gear lowered itself and Research One settled on the grass. Renee Blanchart cradled her hands on her hips and grinned at Marvin through the windshield. Isaac triggered the controls and the outer doors opened. Marvin walked down the ramp and to the front of the ship.

163

"Hi, honey," he said and kissed her, "let's go for a ride." Renee scanned the people's faces through the windshield and smiled.

"Marvin, you got style," she said and laughed. "Let me tell Uncle Jason I'll be gone for a while."

Marvin made the introductions. Daniel joined Isaac on the air lock bench; Renee sat beside Marvin; Karen sat on the bench beside Doug, behind Renee. The four women began talking as Marvin steered the ship southeast and headed for Arkansas. A half hour later he punched in fifty and zero.

"Ladies and gentlemen, the Ozarks." he said.

"Beautiful!" Charles said approvingly as the ship gently settled above the rolling mountains of the Arkansas landscape. Marvin began rotating the ship slowly on its axis, the panorama passing in front of the windshield.

"It's gorgeous," Sandra said. "It's like watching it on the big screen."

Marvin completed a full revolution of the ship above the magnificent scenery of the pristine hills of Arkansas then steered Research One into a valley nestled in by three dominate mountains. The ship hovered fifty feet above the ground. He glanced at the enhanced photograph Doug had mounted by the navigator's seat on the end. It was covered with a heavy clear plastic sheet with directional gridlines on it. Doug had attached a small chain beside it. On the end of the chain was a grease pencil inserted into its holder.

"Okay, we're ready to do it," Marvin said. "We need a definite launch date so Daniel can set up our telemetry computers and we can tend to all the details for the mission."

"How about we set the launch date for the

twenty-fifth," Michael said. "That's when Melvin and I are doing another financial review of Technical Research Association."

The crew nodded. Michael turned to Doug.

"Should I do a press release?" All eyes went to Doug.

"I don't know," Doug said glancing from face to face. "Thinking about it makes me nervous. How would you do it?"

"I know an Illinois state senator I could ask to sit in with me. I'd wait until you've launched and then contact him and explain the research project and ask him to endorse the release."

"Would he do it?" the professor said.

"He wouldn't have much of a choice. I could just call the press myself and tell them the senator refused to acknowledge the project and he would look bad, especially after the discovery becomes known. When I explain that to him, he's going to have to take some kind of a position."

"Any way you look at it, this is going to start a brush fire," Doug said.

"There's a way," Daniel said. The group focused on Daniel. He cleared his throat and continued.

"Think about it," he said. "The discovery on the Moon is Earth shaking news; proof absolute that mankind is not alone. The Apollo missions discovered it and a decision was made not to release it to the public. It's history now. Trying to find out who did it and why would be a long drawn out process. I don't think we should get involved with that. We shouldn't announce that we're going to the Moon. I think we should go, get something that NASA took there on the Apollo Missions, bring it back, and turn it over to Congress and let them deal with the problem.

We're interested in research.   Something brought back from the Moon, that could only have come from the Moon, will establish that Technical Research Association and this research mission, is not a hoax.

There was silence for a few moments.   Michael nodded, all the others agreed.

"What about radar picking us up leaving the Earth?" Isaac said.

"They'll think it's a bogus blimp on their radar screens because of the straight up ascent and the constant acceleration or they'll peg it as a weather balloon," Marvin said.   He glanced at Daniel.   "How long will it take us to leave the atmosphere?"

"Three minutes," Daniel answered.   "We'll be going almost four thousand miles per hour, straight up, and getting faster every second."

"Another thing," Marvin said, "we're going in the wrong direction to be a threat.   Anything threatening would be coming in, not going away and getting faster at the same time.   My guess is, they will think it's just a fluke and treat it as such."

"I hope you're right," Jean said.

"I am.   The radar operator himself will probably never mention it because of the readouts he gets."

Daniel," Dave asked, "have you figured the time of day we need to leave for the best trajectory?"

Daniel nodded. He pulled a note pad from his breast pocket.   "I worked out the telemetry for the next month, just in case.   On the twenty-fifth… here it is. We engage power at five twenty-one a.m., Saturday the twenty-fifth.   That will take us to the place in the sky were the Moon will be when we arrive."

"Well," Karen said, "when one takes a long trip, one should get an early start.

Marvin spoke quietly to Renee.   She got up and

motioned for Michael Sheridan to take the co-pilot's seat. Michael took the seat. Renee then occupied the bench behind Marvin. Marvin typed in five hundred on the altitude and the ship complied and hovered. Marvin looked at Michael and gestured toward the stick. Michael turned to Frank and pointed at himself. Frank nodded.

Michael placed his hand gently on the stick then looked around at Doug. "The computers won't let me mess up?"

Doug shook his head.

Samuel J. McNeal sat in his second story office at McNeal Ceramics. As he was going over his books, a shadow slowly passed over his desk. He glanced up at the picture window, then back down at his work, and then paused. He looked back at a saucer shaped craft hovering outside the building. Inside the shining silvery ship, there was a group of people waving at him. Recognizing the man sitting at the controls, a big smile formed on his lips.

DAN HOLT

# Chapter 14

*"To dare the impossible is to serve notice of change."*

## - THE POWERS THAT BE -

At one o'clock in the afternoon, Research one crossed the border into Kansas. On its way to the secluded area for one final test prior to the morning launch the next day, the ship cruised along at five thousand feet, three hundred miles per hour, as the crew discussed the one *G* launch test to be conducted shortly.

They were going to start from the ground at one g until they reached one hundred thousand feet. The cabin was to be fully pressurized. They would hold at that altitude and operate the air lock doors. Isaac had been through many trial runs but wanted it to be the real thing prior to launch. Daniel was enjoying the view afforded by the ship's design. Suddenly his head snapped to the right.

"Colonel," Daniel shouted. Marvin recoiled at the strained cry from his friend and looked in the direction he indicated.

Two F-16's were pacing the ship. The atmosphere dependent machines doodled as compared to Research One's dead smooth lateral flight. The crew of the spacecraft could hear no sound through the thick insulated outer hull.

Marvin saw the nearest pilot taking into his headset. He put his hand on the knob of Research One's radio and turned the control through its frequencies. Suddenly the pilot's voice boomed into the cabin. "...instructed to follow us. I repeat, you are instructed to follow us. Please acknowledge."

Marvin pressed the transmit button.

"Afraid not fella's. You're interfering with private research and development."

"Marvin, ole buddy," came over the radio.

"Odell?!" Marvin said.

"Yeah, it's me." was the response. "I've missed dancing the skies with you. How have you been?"

The crew of Research One looked at each other, at Marvin, then back to the two armed fighters pacing the spacecraft.

"I'm doing fine," Marvin said. "Now, why don't you fella's go home; we have work to do."

"Can't do it, Marvin. We have orders to take you to a test facility in Nevada." Marvin glanced at his crewmates. All their faces were fixed on him, their eyes wide and concerned. Marvin's face hardened.

"Sorry, can't help you."

"Now, wait a minute, Marvin," Odell said solicitously. "They're very interested in that craft, and in you. They want to talk to you about re-instatement. You'll be wearing a star, ole buddy." Marvin glanced at Daniel. His face was pale and his eyes were filled with fear. Marvin winked. Daniel blinked and took a breath. Marvin leaned toward the radio.

"Sorry," he said. Odell's voice became strained and hard.

"Marvin, I have orders to shoot you down if you don't follow us." Marvin didn't answer. He glanced at the crew, after a second's pause, they straightened in their seats and pulled their safety harnesses tight.

"Marvin," Odell raised his voice, "I hope you fly that thing as good as you used to fly one of these. Goodbye, ole buddy."

"Odell," Marvin said into the radio, "you're not going to believe what you're about to see." Marvin flipped the cover of the emergency button and pushed it. Research One accelerated ahead of the fighters. In the rear view monitor the crew saw the engines of the fighters belch smoke. The two F-16's swung on line with Research One. Odell's aircraft fired two missiles. When they closed on Research One, the spacecraft darted upward and then left a hundred feet. The missiles passed by harmlessly. The second fighter corrected his heading and fired. Research One dropped rapidly and quickly slowed. The two missiles passed over, and then the F-16's passed ahead of the ship. They banked in opposite directions.

"Pressurize!" Marvin shouted. Isaac triggered the controls. Marvin pushed the ascent button. Research One shot skyward at 3 *Gs*--space shuttle velocity--and was quickly out of sight before the F-16's could complete their turns. The crew of the spacecraft looked through the bottom of the windshield and watched the two tiny black specks pass each other in the empty air space then bank for another turn.

At a hundred thousand feet of altitude Marvin pushed Cancel on the emergency system. Research One slowed its ascent, adjusting to a quarter *G*, then came to a stop at a hundred and twenty thousand feet. Doug glanced at Marvin.

"They were going to take this ship!" He said with indignation.

"Can't take it if you can't catch it," Marvin said, grinning. He unbuckled his belts, stepped over to the rotor pod, patted it with his hand, kissed it, and then grinned at his crewmates. Frank smiled as he collected himself.

"They tried to buy me," Marvin said. "That means they are getting pressure from some of Michael's friends in Washington. By the time they cook up an alternative plan, we'll already be on the

Moon.  Let's do our tests and go back to Earth Base One and prepare for launch tomorrow morning.

# PART 3

# UNDERNEATH THE MOON

DAN HOLT

## Chapter 15

## - LAUNCH -

Isaac stood in the open air lock bay of Research One. It was less than an hour and a half until launch. He'd made arrangements with Al and June for Thelma to stay with June during his absence. Thelma was on daily medication associated with her age and health. He felt comfortable about the arrangement. And, he just had to do this.

He stood confidently in the air lock of the silvery disc, hand on his hips, checking, one more time, the three spools with tether lines hooked to the back of the space suits. The tethers were attached between the shoulders to thick reinforced material. He'd gone over the six pressure suits a dozen times; a suit and a back-up for each Marvin, Doug, and Dave. He'd checked and rechecked everything else related to the excursion equipment--monitoring gauges, safety locks, exit and entering procedures, and valve opening and closing sequences to vent the ship. He'd reviewed the changing of the scrubber filters that kept Research One's air clean. There were handholds mounted throughout the air lock and ramp area. He pulled on each of them. He checked the batteries in the marine lanterns that were attached to the airlock wall. He started whistling as he considered what it might be like to put on one of the suits and walk around on the Moon. He held one of them up to himself for size. It weighed almost half his body weight of 142 pounds. He liked its rugged feel and appearance. He put it back in its compartment.

He, Frank, and Daniel would remain with the ship at all times as the pilot, navigator, and life support in the event of the unthinkable, to get Research One home. Isaac accepted the thought, but would not consider it. None the less, he opened the two medical supplies cabinets and checked the contents; satisfied, he closed them.

Each member of the crew was busy going over his assignments, checking and rechecking to be sure nothing was missed. Doug, Dave, and Daniel ran the programs again and agreed that everything was right. Frank checked gears, lubricating systems, control valves, and air connections. The compressed air reserves were filled to capacity. Isaac inspected the bank of compressed air tanks and oxygen tanks, reading the gauges and comparing their settings to the specs on his clipboard. Doug tightened the retaining straps again after inspecting the parachute silk tarps to be used to secure the treasures to be returned to Earth. He and Dave went over the video system again. The outside lighting was check again. Dave swiveled the searchlight mounted for detailed pinpoint lighting.

Marvin and Daniel rechecked the supply of food and water.

The ship's ready," Marvin said. "Let's get some breakfast and prepare to leave."

As they walked down the ramp, a camera flashed. Michael smiled and took several pictures of them from different angles, then of the ship from a distance.

The crew of the spacecraft sat around the conference table at Earth Base One eating the breakfast prepared in the newly constructed facilities. Each had a small serving of scrambled eggs, one piece of bacon, and orange juice. Too excited and nervous to eat, they ate a few bites and drank the orange juice.

Karen, Jean, Sandra, Renee, Melvin, Michael,

Charles, and Al admired the crew, enjoying the moment.

"You're not getting the send-off that the NASA astronauts got," Al said. "But I think the day's coming when you'll have all the publicity you can handle."

"I don't know if I'm looking forward to that or not," Karen said.

"It'll be okay," Michael said. "When it comes, I'll handle it. That's what I do."

"Michael," Frank said, "Research One is about to put you on the stage. You may as well get ready."

"I'm ready," Michael said with passion. "I've been ready ever since we saw that enhanced photograph Doug showed us in my office over a year ago and the image of those twin bells in that test room popped into my mind."

"Did everybody get some sleep last night?" Charles said.

Marvin saw everyone nod. He had finally dozed off himself after a couple of hours of going over everything in his mind. He felt good about the equipment and the crew who would be occupying it, and operating it.

Allen Brewster steered his car into the hidden space at the tree line a quarter of a mile from Technical Research Association's Earth Base One. He would have to destroy the saucer himself. The effort by the Agency to simply take the spacecraft had failed; the agile craft had easily eluded the fighters. He'd waited too long to act and now he had a serious problem. He'd have to blow it up while it was on the ground. The chief had recalled Thomas Thornton, so he was alone.

Brewster cradled the two-pound block of explosive and its timer under his left arm and hurriedly made his way toward his spot in the trees.  He worked his way into position then pointed his binoculars at the hanger.  The saucer was outside.  The hanger doors were open and there were a dozen people there. He'd wait until they took it inside.  He wanted it to look like something had gone wrong and the explosion had leveled the whole place.

At 5:20 a.m., Marvin scanned the console in front of him.  He read off the checklist one by one.
"Engine."
"Ready," Frank said.
"Computer."
"Ready," Doug reported.
"Safety."
"Ready," Dave responded.
"Life Support."
"Ready," Isaac said.
"Telemetry."
"Ready," Daniel said.

The colonel eyed the ship's chronometer.  He began the count down from ten seconds.  At zero he engaged power.
The ship's strong upward movement was there instantly.  Soon their bodies caught up with it and they were rising straight up.  Doug watched Earth Base One drop away through the bottom of the Lead filled Acrylic windshield, slowly at first, then getting faster.

Brewster cupped his hands to light a cigarette. When he looked back up at the saucer, it suddenly left the ground, rising straight up.  He threw the cigarette down and grabbed the binoculars.  When he found it through the eyepiece, it was a hundred feet above the ground and climbing rapidly.  He kept the binoculars on it as it continued straight up, faster and faster, until it was out of sight.  He focused back on the building.  A group of people walked into it and disappeared into the interior.  He aimed the binoculars upward again and squinted his eyes; a silvery dot blinked on, then quickly grew tiny, then disappeared.  He moved the binoculars to the right and adjusted the focus on the full Moon.  A trapped, subdued feeling crept up his spine....

Research One burst into sunlight.  Frank saw an airliner in the distance.  It quickly dropped below the plane of view.  He glanced over his shoulder at the rotor pod.  He listened at the faint hum as it delivered the smooth power that was pushing the ship and its crew toward the sky at the constant acceleration of one gravity unit.

"I've realized my dream," Frank said softly.

"What's that, Frank," Doug said, leaning toward him.

"This is what I've always wanted.  I'm realizing a dream that I've been carrying around for years."

"Me, too," Doug said.  "And that engine is making it possible."

A red light started flashing on the console.  The ship moved backward relative to the windshield, while accelerating straight up.  A silvery object zipped past, from top to bottom, a hundred feet away.  Research One returned to the telemetry flight path.

"What was that?" Daniel said.

"A weather balloon," Marvin said.  "Check your safety harnesses.  We'd better stay buckled in our seats until we get out of the atmosphere and out of the satellite belts."

"Satellite belts?" Isaac said.

"Yes.  Mapping satellites are from two hundred

to two thousand miles above the Earth and communications satellites are twenty-two thousand miles up. Also, there's a lot of junk in orbit, left there from the space program. We could get some strong AV-S movements before we're in the clear."

The young private picked up the blip on the radar screen at 1000 feet, then 1500, then quickly 2000. He glanced over his shoulder. The room was empty; the corporal had made his usual early morning trip to the vending machines. He turned back to the screen and watched the blip quickly rising straight upward. When it reached 60,000, he leaned backward and looked down the hall. Still no sigh of the corporal. The private checked the screen again. Nothing. Gone. He stretched and rubbed the back of his neck, then looked at his watch. He'd be off duty in half an hour.

"Three minutes," Daniel Stubblefield said, "We're out of the atmosphere."
"How fast are we going?" Frank asked.
"Just over a mile a second," Daniel reported. "About 4000 miles per hour."
"Look at the Earth." Dave said. "Isn't that beautiful? It's blue and white just like the photographs."
"Awesome," Doug said.
"This is the first time I've seen it while I was comfortable," Marvin said. "This time I don't have the nagging sensation of weightlessness. Frank," he added. "I like your ship better than I do theirs."
"*Come in Research One*," a voice said through the intercom speakers.
"Research One, go ahead," Frank said.
"*Frank, this is Al, how's it going?*"

"Just fine. We just flew by a weather balloon, but the system took us around it. Everything's okay."

"Al, you ought to see the Earth from up here," Isaac said. "It's beautiful!"

*"I'll go up and take a look when you get back."*

*"Frank,"* Sandra's voice came over the speakers. *"How do you feel?"*

"Fantastic," Frank said with excitement in his voice. "It's hard to believe that I'm out of the atmosphere of the earth and I've been gone from home three minutes."

*"You took a shortcut,"* Michael said. *"Straight up."*

"Michael, no news flashes on TV or radio, huh?" Marvin said.

*"No. Business as usual on planet Earth."*

"Okay. We'll check in with you every thirty minutes."

As they talked with the ground crew about the view through the massive windshield and the magnificence of the experience there was a gentle nudge of the ship to the left. Doug, talking to Karen on the radio, abruptly stopped and checked with Daniel. Daniel held up the palm of his hand.

"Intersection number one on the road to the Moon. We just entered a telemetric parabolic curve." Then Daniel grinned at Marvin. "And, I might add, the computer hit it right on the second." Marvin smiled and nodded.

After closing the radio link, there was silence for some time as they watched the scene unfolding. Marvin scanned across the curvature of the Earth and glanced at Daniel. He had a look of awe on his face.

"We're on our way, let's review what we're going to do when we get there," Marvin said. He released his seat and rotated it around. The others did the same and were facing a narrow table in a conference room that was accelerating into the void of space. The crew focused on the astronaut.

"Daniel, where on the Moon will we arrive? I know we'll be a hundred miles above it, but at what location?"

"Dead center, give or take a degree. We'll be right above that crater that has a triangle inside it." Daniel said, pointing at the photograph mounted on the cabin wall. "The crater's eighteen miles across, so we should be able to see it very well from a hundred miles up and verify the check point."

"Which way will we be facing when we come to a stop?"

"Due north, north being straight up from the orbital plane relative to the Earth."

Marvin left his seat and stepped to the map. "We'll be facing north," he said as he studied the grid lines superimposed over the map. "Good, we can establish some check points and verify returning to the same place later. It appears that the main objectives we've discussed the last few months are north of an east-west line through that crater."

Doug rotated his seat toward the map, pulled the attached grease pencil from its holder. "I'd like to check under the Castle. It's now hanging from the rigging of the dome, thirty miles high above the surface. Since it was such a huge structure, there's sure to be a lot of support equipment underground. I think we'll find rooms underground; areas dug out to house all the equipment necessary to service such a structure. If we're lucky enough to find an open entrance into them, maybe we can retrieve some of it.

"There's also a long structure, twenty miles or so, that looks like an apartment or office complex.

You can see here on the picture that a meteor's gone through it since the dome was destroyed and made a hole wide enough that I think Research One can fly right through it."

Marvin frowned. "We'll have to move the ship very slowly. The glass is apparently very strong, and is now broken up, probably with sharp edges sticking out everywhere."

The crew continued to plan their activities as the Earth dropped further and further away from the tiny ship.

When the Sun peeped over the horizon and bathed Earth Base One with its warming rays, Karen, Jean, Sandra, and Renee sat around a table by the bank of radios, sipping a cup of coffee and talking idly among themselves. Research One had been on the way to the Moon for a little over an hour. Michael and Melvin were in the conference room on the phone. Al and Charles were at a local grocery store picking up additional supplies.

"Marvin is so alive since he started with this project," Renee said. "He'd been hurting for a long time." The other ladies nodded.

"Frank's been looking at the sky ever since I've known him," Sandra said. "I expected to see something like this with him."

"Since Doug made the discovery, he's been consumed with it," Karen added.

"Dave's the same," Jean said. "He and Doug could have been like brothers."

"Well, Renee said, "They're all up there now, in outer space."

"Boy, I hope nothing goes wrong," Sandra said. The girls looked at her. There was something creeping into their eyes, something that had been suppressed. Sandra glanced from face to face, and then took a breath. "I mean...."

"Marvin's been up there before," Renee said quickly.

`Al and Charles returned and entered the building through the hanger doors carrying three bags of supplies. Al stepped up to the table, set the bag of groceries down and looked at the women. He picked up on the atmosphere of their conversation.

"They'll be back," he said. "Research One has been thoroughly tested. The engine had been running for over a year without stopping. The ship performs the same no matter where it is. And, the crew on board is made up of all highly qualified experts. They know that ship inside and out." The women were focused on his face. He looked from face to face. "Research One will bring them home."

Al triggered the radio. "Research One, come in."

*Research One, go ahead*, Marvin said

"How's it going," Al asked.

*Good. We were just studying the map of Moon City*, Doug responded.

Al laughed. "Moon City?"

*That's what we're calling it,* Marvin said, *until we get there and check the city limit sign.* Karen, Jean, Renee, and Sandra glanced at each other and laughed.

"Okay," Al said. "Check in with us regularly."

*Will do.*


On board Research One the crew's anticipation grew concerning what might await them upon reaching the ancient city. Having exhausted the subject, they were quiet for a while. Then they began to relive the experiences of developing the research project. From its inception to the present, a closely knit crew, rushing into the void in a saucer shaped research craft, relating incidences that brought laughter, others the understanding of concern and moments of doubt. The radio checks with Earth Base One would trigger more discussion.

Into the second hour, as the telemetry program dutifully obeyed the numbers of Daniel Stubblefield, the crew gradually became quiet again.

*A million miles away, a giant ball of deep frozen ice tumbled slowly in its elongated orbit around the sun. On its snowflake-like surface, tiny dots of reflected lights danced from ice crystal to ice crystal. One of them was changing patterns slightly different than the rest. It was defying the laws of orbital science. It was gaining speed constantly, crossing the void between the Earth and the Moon.*

The immense star speckled void made the twenty-four-foot diameter Research One seem very small; its crewmembers, smaller still. From inside the tiny ship, the Moon in the upper right windshield was getting slowly larger. The Earth, dead center of the bottom windshield, was growing smaller.

"It's like watching a movie," Dave said softly. "The beauty's hard to describe."

Doug nodded. "You know, these people that built the Arcology on the Moon saw this scene many times as they transported supplies and equipment from Earth. Crews of workers, technicians, and robotics experts no doubt, were needed to build it and get it functional."

"I wonder what type of ships they had," Frank said.

"It wouldn't surprise me if they were very similar to this one," Daniel said. "You could take a much larger model of this ship and make a cargo run every day if you wanted to."

"And the trip would be comfortable," Marvin said.

"One of their ships may still be there in an underground hanger," Doug said.

"I sure hope we can be that lucky," Frank said. The crew became silent again, a silence broken when the voice mode of the telemetry program engaged.

*"Twenty minutes until zero G transfer to deceleration phase."*

The crew came alive and began checking the ship. Everything had to be secure. Each followed a prearranged routine. When they were satisfied that Research One was prepared for the absence of gravity, they returned to their seats, fastened their belts, and waited with anticipation for the mid-trajectory reverse of power.

*"Five minutes to zero G transfer to deceleration phase."*

As a former astronaut Colonel Andrews knew about weightlessness. He also knew he couldn't explain the sensation of sustained weightlessness to the crew and they be ready for it. He knew that all of them, at one time or another, had experienced the feeling. Amusement park rides offered a taste of it. Isaac said that he rode one of them with a weightless duration of a full three seconds.

Although those experiences gave some idea of what it was like, they were not the real thing. The mind knew that it would have gravity back right away and held on to that fact. When this crew went into about the fifth second and gravity wasn't back, the body was going to protest and start to make changes. The blood pressure in the legs would get lower and the midsection would begin to swell with more of the body's fluids. It would be very slight in only thirty seconds, but the inner feelings would be there; the nausea that some feel more than others.

*"One minute to zero G transfer to deceleration phase."*

"Try not to hold your breath," Marvin said to the crew. "It's a natural reaction. You'll be more comfortable if you continue to breathe normally. If you hold your breath it gives your body one more thing that's wrong."

As the voice mode of the program counted down the final seconds to zero *G*, Marvin glanced around the ship and then at the crew. Out of the corner of his eye he saw Daniel Stubblefield take a deep breath.

The telemetry program disengaged power.

Research One floated free at 187,000 miles per hour.

Marvin felt the seat cushion rise when he became weightless. His body remembered the feeling. He glanced at each crewmember. They seemed to be dealing with the dilemma of zero *G*. Isaac repeated with his lips: *"I'm doing fine, I'm doing fine."* Doug and Dave looked at each other. Marvin watched Daniel.

The telemetry program began the rotation of the ship.

Suddenly, Daniel began groping with his arms.

His body was lashing under the belts without gravity to counter the inertial mass of his arms. Marvin released his belts and watched him closely. Daniel grabbed at his harness, found the latch, and released it. Trying to jump up, his upper body being heavier, his legs came up and hit the underside of the console prying his upper body forward from the seat.

The colonel's left arm went across Daniel's chest and then around him. Using his right arm, Marvin grasped the back of Daniel's seat and pulled the both of them over it and onto the floor. Daniel was fighting to free himself as Marvin forced his body to a prone position, and then turned him on his back.

The programmed rotation stopped.

*"Five seconds until one G deceleration."*

When the colonel heard the voice mode counting down, he stuck his legs under Daniel's seat and pinned the programmer to the floor, himself on top of him.

The telemetry program engaged power.

The crew sank back into the cushions. Daniel grunted, reacting to the weight of his friend. His breathing was rapid. He blinked his eyes and took a breath.

"What happened?" he said.

Marvin got to his feet. "You like gravity more that you like computers."

Daniel wiped his mouth and swallowed. "I've never been without it before."

"I believe you," Marvin said, extending his hand. Daniel reached up and grasped Marvin's hand and was lifted to his feet. Marvin patted his shoulder and released his hand. Daniel adjusted his clothing and wiped his mouth again.

"Frank, how'd you do?" Marvin said.

"I was fine. I just looked straight ahead,

breathed slowly, and counted seconds. By the way, you stepped in my lap."

"Sorry."

"It's okay."

Smiles played on the lips of the crew as they checked the console readings.

"How fast are we going now, Daniel?" Marvin asked.

Daniel ran the fingers of both hands through his hair and cleared his throat. "A hundred and eighty-seven thousand two hundred sixty-one miles per hour..." Daniel paused and looked at the faces of his crewmates; they were staring. Marvin grinned. Daniel's face cracked a smile. "But we're slowing down now," he added. "We'll be stopped at the Moon in about two hours and twenty minutes."

"We're now the world's fastest humans aren't we." Isaac said.

Marvin nodded. "We sure are. Apollo never got near this fast. Escape velocity from Earth is twenty-five thousand miles per hour. They coasted to the Moon. I took them three days to get there."

Daniel checked his console read-outs. The group was now standing behind the seats talking about the experience.

"Colonel," Daniel said, "thanks."

"Don't' mention it my friend. You'll be ready for it next time."

"*Research One, this is Earth Base One, come in.*"

Daniel touched the button on the console.

"Research One, go ahead."

"*Research One, this is Michael, how was the mid-point turnaround?*"

"Well," Daniel said into the radio, "I just wrestled the astronaut and he won." The crew laughed and

189

gathered around the radio.

"*What was that?*" Michael said.

"It's nothing," Daniel said. "Zero *G* caught me by surprise. I had an overwhelming urge to run so I unbuckled my belt and tried to get up. The colonel put me flat of my back on the floor."

A silent endorsement of Colonel Andrews swept throughout the crew and reached over the radio to the ground.

"*You tell him I said pick on somebody his own size,*" Al said.

Marvin heard laughter near the radio down on the Earth. He glanced around at the crew and smiled.

The deceleration phase of the mission sparked more conversation among the crew. The Earth was now up and the Moon was down. They soon reached the point where the Earth and the Moon appeared to be the same size.

"It's no wonder that some have referred to the Earth and Moon as a dual planet system," Daniel said. "The Moon is enormous to be a satellite of Earth."

"Makes you wonder if it formed naturally," Doug said, "or if it was arranged by someone--someone awesome. Did you know that the Moon is an exact fit over the Sun during an eclipse? What are the chances of that happening randomly?"

"That's beyond me," Isaac said. "I have to take this thing one step at a time." Marvin nodded.

"I'm trained to deal with and react to unknowns," he said, "but that's a little staggering for me to think about."

The mid morning Sun warmed the interior of Earth Base One. Al crossed the floor to the electrical panel on the far wall and turned on the four exhaust fans mounted in the ceiling. They felt the gentle breeze began to enter the open hanger doors, bringing in cooler air. Al returned to the table and took another sip of his Coke, then another bite of the half sandwich, their mid-morning snack. He glanced out the hanger doors when the Sun flashed off a car window. A cab pulled up onto the concrete apron. Two women got out.

"June! Thelma!" Al said then jumped to his feet and hurried toward the car. The rest of the group followed. "Is everything okay?" Al said. June nodded.

"We're okay." she said hurriedly, "Thelma kept insisting that we come here. I had to bring her."

"That's fine." Al responded. He hugged June then Thelma. "Are you okay?" Thelma nodded, and then lifted her purse in front of her. "I brought my medicine." Al smiled warmly and introduced everyone. Thelma smiled and nodded to each member of Earth Base One then looked at Al again.

"Come on in, we'll radio the ship and you can talk to I.J.," Al said.

"How long have they been gone?"

"They're almost there," Al said. The group seated themselves around the radios. Al contacted the ship, explained to Isaac about June and Thelma arriving at Earth Base One, and all were okay.

Isaac was very pleased that Thelma was there now, especially now. They talked at length, Isaac giving her a brief summary of the mission so far. Then Isaac got personal. "Thelma, forty-two years ago I promised you the Moon if you'd marry me. Well...guess what..." Thelma laughed.

"Isaac Jacob Henson, you're hopeless."

"I'm going to bring you something."

DAN HOLT

Chapter 16

-THE CASTLE -

Research One hovered motionless a hundred miles above the central most crater of the Moon.

"Telemetry program is disengaged," Daniel said.

"Let's run a complete check on the ship," Marvin said, scanning the console.

"Rotor pod and booster units functioning normally," Frank responded, looking up from his read-outs.

"Oxygen at ninety-six point six percent," Isaac reported.

"Computers on line and ready," Doug said. "I'm turning on the video monitoring system." He flipped two switches and watched the lights come on. The video equipment, compliments of Chicago Imaging systems, began recording everything on all six points of reference to Research One.

"Okay," Marvin said, "let's check in with Earth Base One and then go see what's underneath the Moon. Remember," Marvin paused and looked around at the crewmembers, "you're too strong for the gravity here. When you move, move very slowly and carefully."

Research One notified Earth Base One of its arrival. Doug described the Moon to the ground crew as seen from a hundred miles up. Then they prepared to descend.

"Look at those stars," Daniel said. "They're so bright and odd shaped. That one," he pointed, "it's fat on one end and small on the other." Doug looked in the direction, then across the upper windshield.

"Those are pieces of glass hanging on the

latticework of the dome."

"But they're above us!"

We're inside the dome," Doug said, leaning over the console and looking around at the scene below. "It's just almost all been eaten away by the solar wind. Sunlight, without an atmosphere and an ozone layer to filter it, is very abrasive on a microscopic scale. Let's go down in the central crater."

Marvin took the controls and started easing the ship straight down. As Research One began sinking toward the crater, the radar screen was littered with odd shaped images. Doug glanced at the crew. Six sets of uncensored human eyes, counting his, scanned the full width of the huge windshield, charged with excitement, trying to see, for real, the city they knew was here. A magnificent city, that the latest computer enhancing technology had revealed to him. As the twenty-four foot silvery craft continued its descent, the ruins of the crystalline city began to take identifiable context below them.

"It looks like it was melted form the top!" Daniel exclaimed.

"It was," Doug said. "One tiny microscopic piece at a time. The slowest melting process that ever took place."

Marvin glanced at Doug, then back to the scene unfolding below. "it looks like a city that was bombed continuously around the clock for weeks."

"I'll bet that's what the Apollo astronauts thought," Isaac said. "I'll bet that's what they told Houston."

Doug kept looking at the ruins.

"There are the roads," Dave pointed out. "They're a long way apart, but go exactly the same way, same curves and all. Looks like they go from the crater to that mountain range, and on the other side, they go from the crater to the hanging castle-like structure.

Doug looked to the left. "Those are not mountains. It's the complex. It's been melted down by the Sun's radiation making it round, like mountain tops."

Doug pointed at one end of the twenty-mile long structure. "See that giant hole in the end of it. A meteor opened the door for us. We're going in after we look at the crater and investigate the Castle." They looked at him as if he was a tour guide explaining the next exciting part of a ticketed tour.

The crater grew larger as they descended.

The AV-S system light began flashing. Research One stopped and hovered.

"What is it?" Daniel said.

"The ship stopped automatically," Marvin said. "There must be something in the way."

The colonel glanced at the rear view monitor, and then moved the ship backward slowly. A hundred feet below them, an enormous black tube came into view. Doug searched the object for detail. It was thirty feet in diameter, larger than the ship. The surface of the tube was pock marked in places. He followed it with his eyes, leaning to his right. It went down toward the surface of the Moon, disappearing from view. Leaning the other way, he saw the end of it two hundred feet away. It was jagged where it stopped, the edges rounded.

"The latticework of the dome," he said. Isaac examined the black material arcing across their field of view.

"What kept the Apollo astronauts from hitting it?" he said. They didn't have a craft like this." Daniel glanced at Isaac, then back at the scene outside.

"The Apollo spacecraft entered orbit upon

195

arriving." he said. "They would pass by the side of the dome to do that. Then when they circled the Moon, they would come across the face of it at about seventy miles altitude."

"There are just so many holes in the latticework of the dome," Doug joined in, "that they didn't hit anything. They were lucky."

Marvin backed the ship farther away, and then eased downward. The edge of the tube came into view. There was a groove recessed into it twenty feet wide from top to bottom.

"The panes of glass of the dome fit in that groove," Doug said.

"The panes were twenty feet thick?" Daniel said.

"Yeah," Doug said, "that rigging held up thousands of them. We've got to find a piece of that black stuff to take home."

"It must be really strong," Dave said.

"The metallurgist will lick their chops over that," Daniel said.

"It's going to the people who helped us build Research One," Frank said, with appreciation in his voice.

Marvin resumed the downward descent. Doug searched the area below for detail. A huge triangle dominated the bottom of the crater. He could see bright spots in the center of each of its sides. The walls of the crater came up beside them. Next to the rim, equal distances from each other, he could see huge pilings of the same black material. Mounted on top of the pilings were enormous transparent tubes running across the edge of the crater to another piling, and then to a third. They looked like giant fluorescent light bulbs constructed in a triangle inside the crater. In the middle of each one, there was an object that resembled a satellite dish. It was of enormous scale.

There was one on each transparent tube. All three were pointing at the middle of the crater.

As Research One continued its descent, he could see a huge square below. There were walls on all four sides twenty feet high. The surface inside the walls was concave.

"It's where they made the panes of glass for the dome!" Dave said breathlessly.

"The big dishes mounted on the transparent tubes are pointing at the square," Isaac said supportively.

"Lasers," Doug almost screamed. "they melted the sand into glass with lasers beamed from Earth!"

Doug and Dave looked at the Earth centered in the upper windshield, and then back at each other.

"Stonehenge!" they both said at the same time.

"Stonehenge was a laser station," Doug said loudly.

Daniel looked at the giant square below. "Doug, that square's a couple of miles across. How would they get them up to the dome and fasten them in?"

Doug examined the badly degraded remains of the dish to his left, and then the huge mold. "Maybe we can find some clues somewhere. I wish we'd gotten here before it was all eaten away like this." Doug glanced at Marvin. "Colonel, set the ship down in the center of the mold and let's look at our map."

Marvin eased the ship down toward the concave surface below them. As they got close to touchdown Doug could see hundreds of potholes where meteorites had left their marks on the smooth surface. Marvin picked an unblemished area. The gear motors whined and Research One came to rest. Frank checked all the read-outs for the rotor pod.

Doug radioed Earth Base One and excitedly

explained the significance of the triangle inside the crater; the awesome system of manufacturing the airtight dome over the city eons ago.

The crew ate while discussing procedure for examining the ruins.

"First, let's go up to the castle, examine it, and see what's holding it up," Doug said.

Marvin nodded then looked around at the crew. "I don't think we should go inside it with it hanging like that; the slightest disturbance could cause it to come down.

"We could get a good look at it, and then check for artifacts on the ground at its base," Doug said. The crew secured everything then positioned themselves for liftoff.

Research One rose out of the crater. Doug watched the huge glass tubes pass by the ship, and then the walls of the crater drop below them. He scanned across the lunar landscape as Marvin rotated the ship toward the northeast. As the craft moved away from the crater, it appeared that hundreds of flashlights were being flashed at them from the sprawling ruins on the surface. There were spires sticking up everywhere, many of them with beveled edges. They had the appearance of enormous transparent pipes from a pipe organ that had been stuck into the surface randomly around the ruins. The scene was mass devastation.

"What happened here?" Doug muttered. The question went unanswered. The ships company was scanning the scene below in awe.

"The flashing AV-S light caught Doug's eye. The ship stopped and held. He scanned the width of the windshield.

"Why did it stop?" Daniel said, "There's nothing

out there."

Dave pulled up a diagnostic screen on his monitor. He scanned it and another, and then another. "All programs are running. There's something blocking our path."

Doug leaned back and looked up. The others followed his gaze. High above the ship, he could see the edge of the giant pane of glass. It looked like a faint line of black crayon drawn across the Earth.

"It's a pane of glass from the dome," Doug said. "It must've landed edgewise when it fell to the surface."

"But you can't see it," Isaac said. "It's completely clear."

"NASA did a study several years ago," Daniel said. "It established that glass made in a vacuum would have no impurities." Doug nodded.

"And have the structural strength of steel," Doug added, searching the giant pane of glass standing vertical ahead of the ship for a visible blemish; a verification that it was actually there.

Marvin initiated an ascent toward the top of the pane of glass. As the ship rose, Doug saw pockmarks here and there. Then the top edge of the pane came into view. As the ship rose above it, he saw the hanging building in the distance. It looked like a odd shaped point of light. Marvin eased the stick forward. As the crew watched the structure slowly take shape, Dave scanned the lunar surface to the left.

"Look at that," he said, pointing and moving his arm side to side.

To the left were the remains of sprawling surface buildings. There were streets between them and blocks in a perfect geometric pattern. Down through the middle of it there was a wide road. In the center of the road, there were mile high columns spaced evenly apart like streetlights. Many were leaning on their foundations, others stood exactly straight. There were tanks, in clusters of three, scattered throughout the neighborhood. Doug looked at the three tank clusters, then at the enhanced print inside the ship. "The spots on the photograph," he said.

Dave glanced at the map and nodded. Doug then focused on the hanging structure ahead. It was much closer now. It looked like it was made of candle wax, partially melted and hanging by its wick. Out of the corner of his eye, Doug saw Marvin checking the video lights. He saw that they were getting everything. Marvin raised the ship to parallel with the structure, then eased closer and closer.

"It's enormous!" Doug said. "Up at the top, there's a black rod that goes through it and on up to the rigging. That rod's about three feet in diameter. That's what's holding it up."

Doug's eyes followed the rod downward below the structure. It continued toward the surface of the Moon, disappearing from view.

"That black stuff doesn't reflect light." Dave said. "It's hard to see."

"A thirty mile high building," Daniel said. "Wonder why the top of it is still here and the bottom is gone."

"Probably," Doug said, "a meteor hit the bottom and weakened it. Take us in closer, Colonel."

Marvin looked up and down the structure, raised the ship a hundred feet, and eased forward. As they got closer, Doug could see the lines where the joints and sections of the structure were put together. Through the transparent walls, he could see jumbled up square pieces of glass where they had fallen on each other. The view was blurry from the melting effect on the outside wall of glass. Marvin moved

Research One along the side of the structure, keeping a distance of fifty feet from the glass walls. As they progressed, they came to a long flat side. He adjusted the ship's direction, maintaining the distance between the ship and the magnificent structure.

The passing wall suddenly changed. Doug caught his breath. "Look!" he said, "there's an opening!"

Marvin moved the ship to the center of the place where a whole wall section had fallen out of the structure. The hole was a hundred feet square. Doug could see objects inside. He looked at Marvin excitedly.

"We can't go in there, Doug," Marvin said firmly.

Doug paused, breathing with his mouth open, and then turned back to the open chamber. "Okay...take us up real close."

Marvin nodded and glanced at the rear view monitor. "Everybody, buckle your belts." he said. "If anything happens, we're going straight backwards."

Marvin glanced to his left and right, checking the safety harnesses. With his right hand on the stick, he flipped the cover and placed his left hand over the emergency button, and then inched the ship forward. At ten feet from the edge of the exposed floor of the structure, Research One hovered.

Doug and the crew leaned against the belts and strained to see the contents of the room. On the left wall there was a box-shaped object sitting on one cylinder-shaped leg. The leg appeared to go right into the floor. On the face of the ten-foot square box were buttons or dials. A black pipe or cable came out of the top of the box, went over to the wall and up through the ceiling. On the right hand wall was an enormous flat board, also suspended by the one leg, which also disappeared into the floor. Above the board, there was a rectangle, fifty feet long and ten feet high, raised from the otherwise flat wall of the room. Doug could also see a black hose or cable coming out of the end of the huge flat board and going up into one end of the raised monitor.

On the opposite wall there was an outline of a door, from the floor to just over half way up the wall. Doug could see a line down the center of it.

"They look like elevator doors," Dave said.

"They must be fifty or sixty feet tall and thirty or forty feet wide," Doug said.

"Maybe it's a freight elevator," Daniel said.

Isaac agreed. "It's big enough."

"Is that an emblem on the doors?" Doug asked.

Dave squinted his eyes and studied it. "It looks like it. I can barely see it; it looks like a triangle with circles on the points of it, and there's something in the center. I can't see what it is."

"The video's getting it. We can work with it when we get home," Doug said.

"I'd sure like to read those dials on that big box," Daniel said.

"It appears to be some type of machine," Marvin said. "It's huge."

"If there was some way we could get closer," Doug said.

"We'd have to have a remote controlled robot ship to get close up pictures or maybe even retrieve it," Marvin said. "Maybe there'll be another one on the ground somewhere."

Doug looked down toward the lunar surface far below.

Chapter 17

- THE FOUNDATION -

"Okay," Doug said, "let's go down to the base where the building sat on the surface and look there."

The Colonel backed the ship away from the structure a hundred feet, closed the cover over the emergency button, and began a descent toward the lunar surface.  As the bottom of the structure past above the ship, Doug looked up into the mostly hollow, conical, parts of the once immense building.  He could see several cables hanging free.  There was a box with a square opening on one side, attached to the end of one of them.  He estimated it to be fifty foot square. It was cocked at an angle and hanging completely motionless.

"That's the elevator," Dave said.

Daniel turned to Doug.  "Maybe that's for cars," he said.

Doug was looking closely at the suspended elevator.

"Think about it," Daniel said.  "When they drive into the parking lot down on the surface, they'd still be thirty miles from the office.  Maybe they drove right into the elevator and it took them up there to indoor parking."

Doug nodded as his eyes went downward again.  As the miles to the surface diminished, the outline of the base of the structure began to take shape.  They were a hundred feet away from the edge of the suspended remains of the building, but well within the boundaries of the base on which it had stood.  The structure had been larger, much larger, at the base.  The entire base outline looked like a grid drawn on the lunar sand.  The perimeter was a continuous mound of blue-gray dust that circled the entire foundation outline. Inside, smaller mounds of the same color dust formed hundreds of squares, all identical in size. Craters left by tiny meteor impacts interrupted the continuous pattern in several places.

"Colonel, land the ship just outside the outline of the base," Doug said. "Let's suit up and go out there. I think some of that black stuff will be under that dust. We can collect some of it."

Marvin moved several hundred feet farther back until the outline passed from under Research One. He descended until he saw the light indicator signaling and heard the whine of the landing gear. Then he eased the ship onto the lunar surface. Doug looked up at the tiny spot of light thirty miles above. He was awed again at just how enormous the building once was.

Doug and Marvin went into the air lock and began suiting up for the excursion. Doug noticed how much lighter the suit felt than it did when they were testing them back home. He watched Isaac check the tanks again, and then start helping the colonel get his helmet on. Doug was next. Fully in the suit, he lowered the darkened visor and raised it again to check it. His pulse was rapid as he considered what he might find.

"Are you ready?" he heard Isaac's electronic voice say through the system. Doug nodded and glanced at the colonel. He nodded.

"Close the air lock and depressurize," Marvin said.

Isaac closed the air lock door, secured it, and turned on the pumps. The crew watched the two men as the gauge dropped toward zero atmospheres.

"Are you Okay?" Isaac asked.

Doug's nod was more of a bow. "Yes, I'm fine."

"You're at zero on the gauges," Isaac said.

"We're okay for exit," Marvin said. "Open the outer doors." Doug watched the outer doors open and the ramp settle on the lunar sand.

Doug looked across the lunar landscape in its stark clarity. There was something eerie about its absolute stillness. It looked like a desert sprinkled with gray geometric patterns. It was beautiful in a gripping way. The degraded remains of the ancient structures made it look like an abstract painting. Doug stood transfixed, staring out of the open doors of Research One, holding his breath as if at any moment a bird would fly by chirping loudly.

"Doug," Marvin said. "You okay?"

Doug turned toward Marvin. Yeah."

Marvin walked down the ramp and onto the sand, bounced a couple of times maintaining his balance, then turned and waited for Doug. Doug walked slowly, adjusting to the cumbersome suit and the low gravity, bounced on his toes several times, until he began to get the feel of being so light on his feet.

The two men made their way around to the front of the ship, turned and looked at Research One with its tripod landing gear, then up at their crewmates lined across the windshield. Doug stuck his arm out, thumb up. The four, in the ship, matched the gesture.

"How do you feel?" Dave said from the ship.

"Like an astronaut!" Doug said. He then jumped effortlessly and went up four feet, then fell back to the surface in slow motion and bounded once. He then turned and looked across the three quarter mile wide remains of the foundation.

Just twenty feet away was a terrace of blue-gray dust; the remains of a wall that someone built long ago; so long ago that the unfiltered sunlight had reduced it to nothing but dust. He followed it with his eyes to his left. It went hundreds of feet, straight as an arrow, into the distance. In his field of view, were his and Marvin's tethers lying half buried in the fine lunar dust. He leaned on the tether to feel it on his back and watch it slide in the sand. It gave him a sense of security. He turned to his right and followed the terrace with his eyes.

Thirty feet away an impact had occurred. There was a crater about ten feet wide. The projectile had struck the center of the mound of dust and splashed it in a circular pattern. He leaned back as far as he could and looked for the suspended top portion of the building thirty miles above. He could barely see the point of light in the top of his faceplate.

Doug scanned the foundation again, and then bounced over to the terrace of dark blue dust. It was almost waist high. He reached out to touch it. His fingers went right into it. It was a fine powder. The colonel started pushing the dust to the side, digging for whatever may be underneath. Doug joined him. They had dug two feet into it when they hit something solid. They cleaned out around it. It was more of the black material. Doug pulled on it; it didn't move. He picked himself up in the low gravity trying to twist it free.

"What is it?" Frank asked from the ship.

"It appears to be the same black material," Doug said. "It's a square bar. I can't get it to come loose."

"It must be secured in the bedrock below," Marvin said. "Let's go down to that break in the terrace. Maybe the meteor broke some of it loose."

Doug looked to his right, went around at the ship, and then slowly made his way to the small crater. Marvin followed.

"I see a piece of it sticking up!" Doug said. "I'm going to get it."

"Be careful," Dave said into the system.

Doug crouched down and made his way down the slope of the impact crater the few feet toward the bottom. He reached down and grasped the piece of material with both hands and pulled. When it came free, he staggered a couple of steps and sat down on the slope of the crater.

"Doug!" Dave said.

"I'm okay. I got it."

Doug rolled over, got to his feet and climbed out of the crater. He then examined the artifact, turning it over and over in his hands. It was two feet long, eight inches square, and jagged on each end.

"It seems light for its size," Doug said, "even in this gravity." He handed it to Marvin. Marvin held it up for the crew in the ship to see then examined it himself.

"It looks kind of like charcoal, only it's a very dull black, no light reflection at all," Doug added. Marvin made his way around to the ramp of the ship and put the artifact in the airlock, then rejoined Doug. Doug was eyeing the smaller squares of dust across the outside perimeter of the foundation.

"Let's cross over the terrace to the inside and see if there's more we can get." Marvin nodded.

"You've been out twenty minutes." Isaac reported.

"Okay," Marvin said. Doug and Marvin worked their way over the mound and moved on to the first smaller terrace of dust. They brushed aside the dust and found the same beam in a scaled down version. It would not come free. Doug straightened up and looked for another impact site. The next terrace had a broken place in it. He and Marvin stepped over the beam and started for the break.

Frank watched his two colleagues moving in slow motion in the thick space suits, their tethers snaking through the lunar sand as they made progress. They bounced forward, leaning against the tethers as they lengthened and got heavier. He heard Isaac's voice.

"Doug, Colonel, you have twenty feet of tether left. You've been out thirty-six minutes."

Doug and Marvin stopped and turned. Marvin responded.

"Okay, we're less than ten feet from..."

Frank saw the surface collapse under Doug and Marvin. They dropped out of sight. The two tethers snaked through the sand until the slack was gone and then became taut.

The ten-foot diameter hole they had fallen into was filled with a blinding bright light!

Frank was stunned, staring at the scene. The change in the respiratory lights on the console pulled his eyes down. The colonel's had increased slightly; Doug's were flashing rapidly. Frank's eyes snapped back to the circle of bright light.

"Doug, Doug!" Dave said.

"Colonel!" Daniel shouted.

Then Frank heard the Colonel's voice:

"Close your visor, close your visor!, Doug, close your visor."

"Okay!...I still can't see!" Doug said.

"Your eyes have been flashed; your vision will come back in a few minutes," Marvin said.

"Are you hurt!" Isaac shouted.

"Doug!" Dave said, "are you okay?"

"Yes," Doug said. "The bright light blinded me; I can't see a thing."

"Frank," Marvin said, "We're hanging in a brilliantly lighted chamber."

Frank looked at the system lights on the console; the blinking lights by Doug's name begin to slow down. He looked back at the brightly illuminated hole in the lunar surface.

"Colonel, we can see the light from here," Frank said. "The hole you fell through is about ten feet wide. Do you want me to send out Dave to help you?" Frank glanced around; Dave was on his feet.

"No. We can climb up the tethers easy enough in this low gravity," Marvin said. "There's a floor about twenty-five or thirty feet below us. It looks like a grid of some kind."

"A grid?" Dave said.

"Yeah. It's a brownish color. It has black lines in it."

"What do you think it is?"

"I don't know," Marvin said. "We need to be closer to see it clearly."

"How can there be light in that room," Daniel said. "Everything here has been dead for ages."

"I don't know," Marvin said, "but it's very bright. Something is supplying the power."

"I'm getting my vision back," Doug said. "My eyes are starting to clear up. I want to find out where that light is coming from."

"You've been out forty minutes," Isaac said.

"Frank, we're about thirty feet above the grid," Marvin said. "Move Research One toward the hole and ease us down to it."

Frank looked at the other crew members and then back at the hole.

"I don't know about that, Colonel. The tethers might snap."

"Oh, no, Frank," Marvin said. "They're very strong. We weigh thirty-five pounds apiece in this gravity. They'll be fine."

209

Frank checked the respiratory lights again, then out the windshield at the two taut parallel tethers running from the open bay of the ship through two of the terraces of dust, cutting into them, then down into a hole in the lunar surface. He turned to Isaac.

"What do you think?"

Isaac nodded. "The tethers are two thousand pound test."

Frank nodded. "Colonel," Frank said. "Do you think that grid will support your weight?"

"Probably in this low gravity. If it doesn't, the tethers will catch us."

"Okay," he said. "I'll have to raise the ship a few feet. It will pull you up a little. Keep talking to me so I will know you're in the clear."

"Okay," Marvin said. "All clear here, go ahead."

Doug was hanging three feet from the colonel when his vision began clearing up. When the surface gave way, the fall was in slow motion and didn't shock him near as much as the sudden overwhelmingly bright light. He instinctively closed his eyes, but the light was so strong it seemed to overpower his eyelids. Surprised, he'd forgotten about the visor until the colonel reminded him. As his vision cleared, he could see the floor.

"Okay, Colonel, I'm raising the ship," Frank said.

"Okay, we're ready," Marvin said. "I'll relay distance as you lower us down."

Doug felt himself and the colonel being hoisted upward a couple of feet, then they stopped, swinging gently for a moment, then he and the colonel started going downward as Marvin kept relaying distance to Frank. He watched the floor come up and meet their feet. The tethers went slack.

"We're on the floor," Marvin reported. "Bring

the ship close to the hole and give us slack to move around."

The tethers threaded down in through the hole and piled up behind them.

"How's that?" Frank asked.

"That's good, hold right there. The floor seems solid."

"What's down there, Doug?" Dave said.

Doug, his vision back now, studied the chamber and reported. "The room's about fifty feet on each side and about that tall. It looks like a perfect cube. There are tall, narrow, oval shaped mirrors in each corner of the room with a series of small mirrors spaced up and down each side of them. The smaller mirrors are pointing at different angles. There's a pyramid shaped, transparent object, with mirrors inside it, suspended on rods just above the floor on the room. It's in the center. I get the impression it's exactly dead center." Doug paused and turned from side to side, studying the walls.

"The floor and three of the walls are a brown grid-like material. The other wall is different. It's covered, floor to ceiling and end to end, with what looks like black metal squares, each on about twelve inches square. In the middle of each of the squares, there's a hose coming out of it. The hoses are secured in groups of threes and go up through the edge of the ceiling.

"In the middle of the metal wall, there's a hole that goes into it. It's brilliantly lighted and about two foot in diameter. There's a black circle around it. Inside the large tube, there are oval shaped mirrors, placed like fish scales, overlapping each other. The hole is directing the light at the bottom of the transparent pyramid."

Doug and Marvin studied the giant cubicle for a

few moments.

"What do you make of it?" Marvin asked.

Doug tapped the floor with his foot and looked at it from side to side.

"This looks like a giant solar cell," he said. Marvin examined the floor, the three walls with the same pattern, different from the odd wall.

"That wall," Doug said, "I think, is a huge battery. The wires going up through the ceiling must carry the power to the building." Marvin walked over to the brightly lighted hole coming into the room through the metal wall. He held up his hand against the light.

"That tube in the wall goes toward the center of the base of the building," Doug continued. "I think we are looking at the bottom of that rod that went through the Castle. I think it gathered sunlight above the dome and sent it here to these solar cells."

"Fiber optics?" Marvin asked.

"Yes. Amplified by the multiple mirrors on its way here."

"Brilliant!" Daniel said over the radio.

"Yeah," Doug said, "it is. The Moon has two weeks of day and two weeks of night. Maybe this equipment stored power for the two weeks of darkness."

Marvin eased over to the odd wall and reached up and touched several of the terminals. One of the hoses popped loose when his gloved hand came in contact with it. Doug pulled one of them loose and used his other hand to grasp it. He then broke off a piece several inches long. A handful of crystalline dust, sparkling in the bright light of the room, slowly settled to the floor. He turned and held up the piece of hose for Marvin to see, and then he looked inside it. It also had tiny mirrors inside, like scales.

Doug held the open end toward Marvin. "This

is not an electrical wire." he said. "It's a mirrored tube like the big one."

Marvin studied the end of the hose. "I don't think that battery stored electricity," Doug said. "It must've stored light in some form that could be recovered, as light, later."

"How do you store light?" Daniel asked from the ship.

Doug said, "We'll have to come back and excavate and dismantle that battery to find out." He put the piece of hose in the right leg pouch of his pressure suit. "Let's see if we can get one of those mirrors." He said, pointing at the corner of the room.

They moved over to the forty-foot mirror. Doug reached out and touched it with his gloved hand, then leaned back and looked up at its size. It was flawlessly smooth. The small mirrors were mounted on pencil sized rods attached to the center of the backs of them. Doug pulled on one. It didn't budge. Marvin positioned himself and bumped it with the heel of his hand. It snapped loose and slowly went over and hit the wall. It then bounced back to the floor at his feet. Marvin braced himself on the center mirror and carefully bent down, picked up the six-inch long, three-inch wide oval mirror, and handed it to Doug. Doug turned it over and over in his hands as he examined it. He then held it in front of his face. His image was upside down and tiny. Beside his image, he saw a dark circle. He leaned on the huge mirror and looked up at the hole in the surface they'd fallen through. Marvin followed his gesture.

"Isaac," Marvin said, "how long we been in the suits?"

"Fifty-eight minutes, Colonel. You'd better come back in and let me check them and refill the supply tanks."

213

"Let's get back to the ship," Marvin said.

They climbed up their tethers and returned to the ship. The crew spent a few minutes examining the finds, marveling at the intricate interior of the piece of recovered hose from the underground chamber. Frank held the end of it over the green light on the video system switch. It put an amplified green circle on the ceiling of Research One. They secured the artifacts in the rigging organized on board the ship. Isaac refilled the tanks on the excursion suits as Doug raised Earth Base One on the radio for a full report.

Michael received the news of the discoveries enthusiastically and requested frequent reports. He said he would begin making contacts with the concerned parties. Frank reported Research One's performance. After half an hour in communications with Earth Base One, Doug outlined the next objective: the surface structures and enormous columns.

Research One lifted off the lunar surface.

## Chapter 18

## - THE CITY -

In the distance, Doug saw the huge transparent pane of glass they flew over on their way to the Castle. The pane had fallen edgewise and cut into the lunar surface like a giant knife, long ago. It was now an enormous transparent billboard. Doug wondered again how this culture managed to get it two hundred miles above the surface and mount it in the rigging. There were thousands of them.

Doug experienced some anxious moments at the base of the Castle, but the find was fantastic. This culture devised a way to use the energy of the Sun to power this huge crystalline city and store light for the long lunar nights. They must find something with writing on it. He had to know more about this ancient, advanced culture.

The colonel turned the ship north toward the sprawling ruins with the tall columns in the middle of the road.

"Take us along the wide road." Doug said. "Let's get a close look at those columns."

"We've seen lots of roads and streets." Daniel said. "Have you noticed that there are no cars? Why haven't we seen any cars?"

"Maybe they didn't stand the enormous amount of time they've been exposed to the Sun's radiation," Doug said. "Maybe they were made of such light material because of the low gravity that they completely degraded."

"Or," Dave offered, "they were built of such light material that they would collapse down to something that could be hand carried with you. Have you noticed that there are also no parking lots either?"

Marvin initiated a descent. Spires were everywhere, sticking up several feet above the melted down structures. Flickering lights played different patterns across the devastation below.

"How could they see?" Daniel asked. "With this city completely intact, the light reflection would be blinding."

"Don't forget," Doug said, "they had a dome over them and an atmosphere inside it to diffuse the Sun's rays. In fact, standing on the surface, you probably couldn't see the dome. It probably looked like the sky on Earth, clouds and all. They had forests. It was a huge greenhouse."

The AV-S blinked; the computer canceled forward motion. The colonel squinted and scanned ahead.

"I see it," Dave said. "It's one of the rods."

Doug leaned forward. "There's one of the columns right below us. Let's go down and get a close look."

Marvin made a descent down the rod, moving backwards as they got close to the column. Doug watched the column come into view. It was sparkling from the inside, the light blurred and diffused by the melted exterior. There were hundreds of rooms, many of them, with the geometry still correct. It appeared to be an office building that would accommodate hundreds of personnel. He could see objects in the rooms, blurred through the melted exterior, but varying from room to room. He wished he could walk through the rooms and look around.

The colonel spiraled around the column slowly as they strained to see the objects inside until the ship was fifty feet above the surface. He moved the ship down the wide, clear area of the road. Their eyes searched the ruins for any opportunity. They examined column after column, trying to see more detail. Then Isaac sat straight up in his seat.

"Look at that!" he exclaimed. Doug stood and leaned toward the windshield as Research One got closer. One of the huge panes of glass had fallen from the dome. It landed at an angle and the corner of it dug out a deep trench in the lunar surface. Once stopped, it fell over on top of a flat-topped building. It now rested on top of the ancient structure like a giant hat. The top of the glass pane was badly melted. The building under it appeared amazingly well preserved. The area was littered with broken glass shattered by the impact of the enormous pane. Much of it was shielded from the sun's radiation. The broken pieces of glass sparkled brightly as Research One moved closer.

"They look like diamonds!" Doug said. "That big pane of glass from the dome protected the broken glass. This is what we've been looking for. We can collect a lot of lunar glass right here."

The edge of the pane was over a hundred feet above the street. The colonel eased the ship up under the edge of it and touched down twenty feet from the well preserved wall of the building.

Dave joined the excursion party this time. The three donned the suits, moved into the air lock, and anxiously waited to be processed outside the ship. Isaac removed the atmosphere and opened the outer doors. All three walked out of the ship and into the bright sunlight.

"Don't forget to move slowly," Marvin reminded Dave. Dave nodded then bounced a few times to get the 'feel'.

Doug rotated his body from side to side and scanned the area. There were unblemished pieces of lunar glass scattered about. As he watched them glisten and sparkle in the sunlight, he thought about how much more valuable they were than real diamonds. There were pieces the size of his fist up to pieces two and three feet long. The suited members of the crew struggled at first but soon learned to help each other pick up the scattered pieces and take them into the air lock. Within a few minutes they had a pile waist high in the side of the entrance ramp. Doug turned to the ancient building.

"Let's see if we can get inside."

Marvin bounced around the corner of the building. Doug and Dave followed. The ditch, dug out by the falling pane, caused the debris to fall away from the side of the building. It exposed a vent. The screen-like vent cover was six foot square, made up of quarter-sized circles connected together with the familiar black rods. Marvin bounced over to the vent and pushed on it. It fell slowly into the building. They stared inside. The interior of the structure was well lighted.

"The lighting must be coming from one of the columns; it's still intact and working," Doug said. He then climbed over the four-foot wall. Marvin and Dave followed. The three men surveyed the gymnasium-sized room.

"What do you see?" Isaac said into the system.

"This room's about fifty feet high," Doug said. "It's much bigger than the other underground chamber. It's about a hundred feet square." Doug walked out into the room thirty feet and caught his breath.

Books!" he shouted. "There are hundreds of books!" Marvin and Dave hurried to where Doug was standing.

"My God! Look at that!" Dave exclaimed. Doug turned around. The wall behind him was an enormous map of the Solar System a hundred feet wide and fifty feet high.

"What is it?" Daniel said excitedly.

"It's a huge map," Doug said. "A map of the Solar System. It covers the whole wall."

"A map and books." Isaac said. "Is it a library?" Doug scanned the room, turning around in a complete circle and studying the interior.

"Yeah," he said as he walked a few feet toward the opposite wall from the map. "Three of the walls are covered with books. On each of the three walls there are three huge books, about six of seven feet square, mounted up high, evenly spaced apart. Then under them are hundreds of regular sized books. Each of the big books is in a separate section with hundreds of the regular books. All three walls are the same, floor to ceiling. I count nine of the big books. It's a very unusual layout."

"Maybe the big books are the master record and the regular books are the details," Dave offered.

Doug nodded then turned to study the map again. "Wait a minute," He said. He motioned to Marvin and pointed at the map. "There are only eight planets. Surely these people knew about Pluto."

"I've been studying the map," Marvin said. "Look at it closely. There's a planet between Mars and Jupiter. It's bigger than Earth but a lot smaller than Jupiter. It has two moons." Doug moved a few steps toward the map, examining it. He glanced at Marvin, then back to the huge panorama of the Solar System.

"That's where the asteroid belt is supposed to be," Doug said.

Marvin nodded, and then pointed. "Now, notice that, on their map, Mercury and Pluto are missing, and the asteroid belt is a planet with two moons."

"My God," Dave said. "It exploded!"

"That's a theory that's been circulating for a long time," Daniel said from the ship. "I wonder if they did it."

"God, what a horrible mistake," Dave said. "If that's what happened."

"We need to find out," Doug said.

They all stared at the map for a few minutes. Then Doug moved over to the shelf of books to the left of the vent where they'd entered the underground room. He tried to get one of the books out of its shelf but he was unable to get his thick-gloved hand between them. He struggled with it momentarily, and then saw Marvin looking around the room. The colonel went over to the grate he'd pushed in and came back with a piece of connecting rod. He pushed it in between two of the books and forced one out a couple of inches. Doug eagerly grasped it and pulled it out. He struggled awkwardly until he got it open. Marvin and Dave stood on each side of him.

It opened in the middle. The two pages were covered with circles and triangles interlaced with each other in hundreds of different patterns. Dave helped him hold it while he thumbed through the pages. They were all the same, thousands of different patterns of circle and triangles.

"It appears that their language is all circles and triangles and their arrangement has meaning," Doug said. "I can't wait to get this home to Karen!"

"Let's check another one," Dave said. Marvin already had it in his hand; he opened it. It was the same.

Doug glanced up at the huge book, then around at the other walls. "I wonder what's in the big ones."

"Doug," Marvin said. "There are nine big books and nine bodies on that map. I'll bet this room is a record of the Solar System."

Doug nodded. "Let's get some samples from all the sections."

They began retrieving books and stacking them outside the vent hole at the end of the building. Dave put a hand full of books outside the vent and started back for more. He glanced to his left.

"Hey," he said, 'look at that." He pointed at a six-foot square object at the bottom left corner of the map. Its color blended in perfectly with the map background. The three men made their way over to it.

"It's some type of a machine," Doug said. "There's a hose connected to the side and the other end is connected to the map. Here's a slot; it looks like a chute in a mailbox." Doug had several of the books in his left arm. He picked up one of them and tried it in the slot. It fit exactly.

"Look at this," Marvin said, "it looks like a place to plug something into the machine just below the chute."

"A machine that reads books?" Doug asked. "It's connected to the map, or screen. Maybe it reads books and puts the story on the big screen. Can we get this machine in the ship?" Doug and Marvin tried to lift it. It didn't move. They shoved on it. It remained solidly in place.

"It must be made into the wall," Marvin said. "We'll have to come back with the right equipment to work with it."

The three men resumed moving the books outside. While working down the wall, they came to the end of the tethers. They had the books on the far wall yet to retrieve. Doug turned his back to Marvin. "Unhook me, I'll get them." Dave also turned his back to Marvin.

"Frank," Marvin said into the communications

equipment, "I'm unhooking the tethers from Doug's and Dave's suits so they can get the books that are out of our reach. They'll be out of communications for a few minutes."

"Colonel, will you be able to see them all the time," Isaac said.

"Yes," Marvin said. "They will be in my view all the time."

"Okay," Frank said. "Keep us informed."

Marvin released the heavy latches on each side of the plugs at the end of the tethers and pulled. The plugs popped out and the two tethers snaked around in the vacuum and low gravity, and then slowly arced downward. A cover snapped closed over the ports in the back of their suits.

Doug walked a few feet away from Marvin, and then bounced a few steps, adjusting to the different balance of the suit without the weight of the tether. He turned and looked back at Marvin. He was standing there watching them, holding the two tethers that ran across a dust covered floor and out a window. There were dozens of tether trails in the dust.

Each of the bottom shelves on the adjacent walls were missing a few books. It was evident that they'd been here, in this library, study room, or whatever it was to the culture that built it.

Dave tapped Doug on the shoulder. He turned and saw his lips moving. He was pointing up toward the big book at the top of the wall. Doug, remembering a briefing session back on Earth, reached up and grasped Dave's helmet and pulled him over until their helmets were touching on the faceplates. He then spoke: "What?" He saw Dave's reaction and then heard the tinny sound of his voice vibrating through his helmet and to his ears.

"I forgot about being unplugged," Dave said. He then pointed awkwardly. "There's a box at the bottom of that book up there."

Doug released his helmet, leaned back, and looked up at the big book again. Scanning across the bottom of the seven foot book, he saw it. It was a black box six inches square. It was sitting in a shelf just above the top shelf of the regular sized books. His eyes scanned the other big books around the room. They all had the same type of box sitting near them. He placed his helmet against Dave's again.

"I'll lift you up there so you can get it. Place your hands on the bookshelves to keep your balance."

"Okay," Dave said. He faced the bookshelves and readied himself. Doug motioned to Marvin what he was about to do. Marvin nodded. Doug saw his lips moving, keeping the crew in the ship informed. Doug turned back toward Dave, leaned forward and grasped his lower legs, but then stopped. He rose back up and tapped Dave on the shoulder again. When Dave turned to face him Doug tagged his helmet.

"I won't be able to see what you're doing," he said. "When you have the box in your hand, move your right foot and I'll lower you to the floor."

Dave faced the shelving again and put both hands on it. Doug grasped his legs and easily lifted him upward. Dave walked up the rack; hand over hand, until the box was in front of him. He reached to get it. Unable to open his hand far enough to grasp it, he reached up with both hands and picked it up. His body slowly went forward toward the bookshelves. He placed the box against his suit and held it with one hand while he pushed himself back up straight with the other. Then he moved his right foot. Doug lowered him to the floor.

Dave turned the box over and over in his hands looking for a latch. Finding none, he handed it to Doug. Doug inspected it and handed it back to Dave. Doug looked at Marvin; he was still talking into the headset, giving a move by move report to the ship's company still on board. Doug retrieved several books from the shelves. Dave placed the box on top of them and Doug took them to the vent and laid them outside. Doug and Dave returned to the far wall and got the other two boxes and corresponding books. They returned with the recovered bounty in hand and plugged back into the ends of the tethers.

With Doug and Dave's communications restored, the three men recovered the other six boxes from their positions high on the walls.

"You've been in the suits a little over an hour," Isaac said from the ship. "You have to return to the ship and let me refill the tanks."

"Okay," Marvin said. "We're on our way. We'll come back out to get everything we've gathered here."

"I'm going to take one of each to the ship for them to see," Doug said.

Chapter 19

- THE MACHINE -

Back inside Research One, the three crewmembers got out of their suits. Doug handed the six-inch square box to Frank. Daniel and Isaac focused on the alien container in anticipation. Frank turned it over and over in his hands. It was perfectly smooth with no sign of a crack or indication of a lid. He clasped a hand on each side and pulled. Nothing happened. He turned it the other way and pulled again. A crack formed around the center and the two halves slid smoothly apart.

Daniel and Isaac bumped their heads trying to look inside. There was a black piece of cloth covering something. Frank reached down into the box with two fingers, grasped the object and pulled the piece of material out of the box. Frank unwrapped the ancient artifact and held it up.

"A bracelet!" Daniel said.

It was a bracelet sized transparent ring with continuous overlapped circles and triangles carved into it all around. On top was a cluster of crystalline circles and triangles in a tight configuration. The setting was mounted on top of a square shaped pedestal.

"A bracelet?" Daniel repeated. They passed it around and examined it.

"Why would a bracelet be at the bottom of those big books?" Doug said.

"It doesn't make any sense," Dave said. He turned toward the building. "That appears to be a place where one could study the Solar System."

Daniel stared at the book in Doug's hand. Doug handed it to him. Daniel eagerly opened it and

225

looked from page to page at the grouping of the symbols.

"It appears that all of their writing is just the two symbols." Doug nodded.

"It'll take a computer to decipher it." Daniel handed it to Frank. Frank leafed through the pages then handed it back to Doug. Marvin was examining the bracelet closely.

"Wait a minute," Marvin said holding up the bracelet. "This looks like it would fit into the square hole in that machine we saw in there. When we go back in, let's try it."

"Hey," Daniel said, "look at this." He was examining the small piece of cloth that had wrapped the bracelet. "This is the finest weave of cloth I've ever seen. It feels like cloth but seems solid like paper or foil. The weave is so fine you can't see it." The others passed the piece around and examined it closely.

Isaac began refilling the oxygen and compressed air tanks from the master cylinders. Frank looked at the explorers.

"You fella's look tired," he said. Marvin stretched and rotated his shoulders and neck. "What time is it?" Frank glanced at the ship's chronometer.

"On Earth it's nine-twenty in the evening."

The crew looked up at the Earth, then out across the brilliantly lighted ruins.

"How's everything with the ship?" Marvin asked.

"Everything's fine," Frank said. "While you were inside, Daniel and I tested the back-up booster units and Isaac vented the ship and changed the scrubber filters.

"Say, why don't we eat," Frank continued, "then everybody rest for a while; maybe lie down and get some sleep. After we eat we can check in with Michael and bring them up to date."

"Okay, "Marvin said. "I'm hungry and I imagine that everyone is."

The crew of Research One had a meal while discussing the day's events among themselves. As they relaxed, Frank noticed it was becoming evident that they were exhausted. Their adrenaline had been pumping at its peak throughout the day. Frank felt tired himself, but his day had been filled with a lot less physical activity than the three who had been outside. The suits were rugged and stiff; a safety edge of toughness, and it took manpower, calories, to function in them.

They contacted Michael and filled him in on the finds. The crew answered the many questions that were asked. The ladies back home insisted on a detailed description of the bracelets and placed stake on six of the nine. Doug explained how and where they were discovered and described them in detail. Michael asked Frank for a weight estimate of the lunar glass. Frank filled him in.

"Everybody, get some sleep," Frank said. "Daniel and I will keep watch on the ship."

They spread out some of the restraining tarps and then the rest of the crew laid down and relaxed. Minutes later they were sleeping soundly. Once in a while one would turn over, using more than the muscle power necessary and bounce themselves a little, then settle back to sleep.

Frank and Daniel sat and looked at the ruins glistening in the sunlight. The ship was very quiet. The ever present hum of the rotor pod, that their ears had tuned out hours earlier, came back to keep them company.  The minutes turned into an hour, then two.

In the distance, a piece of glass that had been waiting for thousands of years for the hard particle to sever its last restriction, fell fifty yards to the surface, flickering a final signal to Research One.  Frank glanced at Daniel; he'd been watching it, too.  Daniel nodded.

Almost through the third hour, Marvin and Doug tapped them on the shoulders.

"You and Daniel lie down for a while," Marvin said.  "Doug and I will watch the ship."

Doug sat in Frank's seat as they looked at the black sky and the lunar surface.  They were quiet, alone with their thoughts for some time.

Doug imagined the city still intact with huge sparkling buildings and people everywhere walking back and forth leisurely in the low gravity.  He imagined them greeting each other as they passed, going about their daily business.  He envisioned some of them noticing Research One, walking up to the windshield, cupping their hands around their eyes and peering through the glass curiously, then turning and smiling at each other, then going on with their daily routine.  Doug, into the vision, smiled.  Marvin noticed.

"This was really something before it was torn up," Doug said.

Marvin nodded.  "Just imagine the work to put all this together."

"Yeah," Doug said.  "First they had to put up the dome, then pump it full of air, then come in and fertilize and plant it.  Then bring in workmen to build all this. The project must have spanned decades."

"I wonder what they did here," Marvin joined. "Is it just a place to live, like maybe when you retire.

The gravity here would be favorable for when a persons' older."

"Yeah, it would."

"On the other hand," Marvin continued. "There are a lot of structures here that look, sort of, academic. I get the feeling of advanced research or something like that."

"There's so much we don't know," Doug said.

"We're going to learn a lot when we decipher their language that's for sure," Marvin said.

Doug and Marvin were quiet for a while, looking at the details of the scene spread out before them. Doug broke the silence.

"Colonel, did you know that when this was all intact and the air was still in the dome; if you had a pair of wings, having the strength you have from Earth's gravity, here, you could fly like a bird."

"Oh, yeah?"

Doug nodded.

Marvin shifted in his seat then took a breath. "When I was a kid, I built me a pair of wings and tried to fly."

Doug turned to him and smiled. "Well, Colonel, when you got grown, you did fly."

"Yeah, I did, didn't I."

"All the way to the Moon," Doug added.

The crew stirred behind him. He looked around and they were all sitting up and stretching. Doug glanced at the chronometer. Three fifteen am.

They folded the silk tarps and returned them to their harness. They ate breakfast, contacted Earth Base One with their itinerary, and went about readying the ship for the day's activities. They secured all the lunar glass samples in the harness and arranged a place for the books to be brought on board.

Marvin touched his shoulder to Dave's. "Would you mind if Daniel borrowed your suit?"

Dave glanced at Daniel. "No," he said and then smiled at Daniel.

Daniel's eyes widened. "Do you think I could do it!" he said. "I mean…will it fit?"

"We're about the same size," Dave said.

"Suit up my friend," Marvin said. Isaac and Dave helped him into the thick protective pressure suit. Daniel was breathing deep. He looked at the COMM lights marked 'Dave', took a deep breath, and then deliberately slowed his breathing. Isaac patted the side of his helmet.

"You okay?" he said.

"Yeah," Daniel said. "I feel like a goldfish looking through the side of his bowl."

"You look like an astronaut," Dave said and grinned. "Bring the suit back when you're done."

"Oh, he'll be coming back," Isaac said then patted one of the oxygen tanks. Daniel glanced at Dave and Isaac then turned to the colonel.

"Let's go," Marvin said, and Isaac processed them to zero atmospheres and opened the outer doors. Daniel started down the ramp, staggered, lost his balance, and reached for Marvin. Marvin and Doug up righted him.

"Take your time," Marvin said. Get used to the weight and stiffness of the suit."

Daniel took a step at a time, cautiously, until he walked unaided onto the lunar sand. He moved away from the ship twenty feet, turned and looked at Research One. He then jumped cautiously, bouncing several times.

"This is great!" he exclaimed. "I'm walking on the Moon."

"Yeah," Marvin said. "Let's go back into the

building and try these bracelets in that machine."

Marvin led the way; Daniel followed next and then Doug. At the vent hole, Marvin positioned his hands as a step for Daniel. Daniel made his way over the wall and into the room. Doug and Marvin followed. Daniel bounced out into the library and looked around.

"Holy Jesus," he said. "This is fantastic." He turned until he was looking at the wall-sized map. Doug and Marvin moved to his side. They waited while the expert in orbital science studied the map for a few moments.

"So that's how Mercury got that close to the Sun without being absorbed by the Sun's powerful gravity well," Daniel said. "It was ejected into orbit already formed. And Pluto; that's why it's so far off the orbital plane of the Solar System. Telemetry to Pluto is very complicated because of it."

Marvin turned to Doug. "I told you he was smart."

"Okay, he's smart," Doug said.

Daniel looked from Marvin to Doug. They were grinning. Daniel smiled.

They headed for the machine in the corner, carrying the nine bracelets. Doug watched Marvin insert one of the bracelets into the slot just below the chute. The map changed to a huge image of Jupiter.

Daniel took a breath. "It can't still be working!" Doug said excitedly. He hurried over and got one of the books, returned and pushed it into the slot. The machine remained inert. The image of Jupiter did not change.

"The machine's not working." Doug said. "That image is put there by fiber optic light through the setting on the bracelet."

Marvin pulled the bracelet out of the plug and shoved in another. The image of a blue and white

231

world spread across the map. Doug frowned and pointed at the image. "Look at that, the continents are different."

"That's not Earth," Daniel said.

Marvin removed the bracelet and inserted a third. Another blue and white world appeared on the screen.

"Now that's Earth." Daniel said.

Marvin removed the bracelet and inserted the previous one.

"Venus!" Daniel said. "Venus wasn't always a hot house. I wonder if these people occupied that planet too."

Marvin removed the bracelet and inserted another. The image of the new planet filled the screen. It was twice the size of Earth. It was blue and white. The three men stared at it for a few moments. Marvin removed the bracelet and inserted one more. Another blue and white world filled the enormous screen, smaller that Earth.

Doug and Daniel glanced at each other. Marvin turned to face them. "Mars?"

Daniel nodded. Doug's eyes went from Marvin's face to the image, at the ring of the bracelet sticking out of the side of the machine, then around at the room and the hundreds of books.

"Let's get everything into the ship. We'll be coming back here with more equipment," Doug said.

"Doug, Colonel," Daniel said. "I just noticed something. There's no door. How did they get into this room? We came in through a window. It appears to be the only way in."

The three looked around the room, then at their tethers running out the vent hole.

"Maybe one of the bookshelves opens," Marvin said.

Doug leaned backward and checked the ceiling, the others followed his gesture.

"There," Doug said. There was a rectangle on the ceiling, from the middle of the room to within ten feet of the wall with the map on it. "An elevator or maybe some stairs that fold down to enter from the ceiling. We're in a basement."

They laboriously moved all the books and boxes, containing the bracelets, into the ship. Isaac processed them into the ship's atmosphere. Frank and Isaac watched Daniel get out of the suit.

"How was it?" Isaac said.

"Fantastic," Daniel said. "I've dreamed about it for years. I knew it would never happen. But, it did. Thanks, Dave, Colonel." Daniel described the interior of the alien library to Frank and Isaac with new enthusiasm.

The crew meticulously stored and secured the artifacts. Marvin produced several broken parts of the grating from the leg pouch of his suit. Dave secured them, and then they settled in their respective seats for lift-off. Marvin surveyed the ship prior to getting underway. He glanced at Doug. He was holding up four fingers.

"Four," Doug said. "Four livable planets, blue and white, in the Solar System. *Four.* One of them blew up and destroyed two more and this outpost on the Moon. Only Earth survived. God, what a disaster. We need to know what happened."

Doug raised Earth Base One on the radio and began the report. When they were finished, Marvin positioned himself to pilot the ship.

Doug watched as Marvin raised the ship from the surface, noticing the faint whine of the landing gear moving into the up position. He pictured three piles of lunar dust clinging to the tiles, now a smooth part of the bottom of the ship. Research One moved out from under the pane of lunar glass that had preserved the research library through the millenniums. He wondered if any of the first astronauts had seen the library, or even the giant hat on the building housing the records. Probably not, he thought. Thirty years ago, their ability to move around on the lunar surface was too limited…come to think of it, they hadn't seen any tracks of the lunar rover vehicle.

The colonel had begun increasing their altitude and retracing their route when Doug's eyes fell on one of the three-tank clusters they'd seen scattered around the surface neighborhood from twenty miles up.

"Colonel," he said, "let's get a close look at those tanks." Marvin steered the ship toward them, still moving very slowly, carefully watching for the black rods that ran vertically from the bits of structures below to the rigging overhead.

As Research One got closer, Doug could see that a meteor had torn part of the rounded wall off one of the tanks. Marvin eased the ship around to that side of the cluster. When the hole came into view, the inside of the damaged tank was on fire, the flame rippling as they watched. Doug's eyes widened. He got to his feet and leaned forward for a moment, then glanced at Marvin.

"My God!" Doug said, "it looks like an oil fire." Marvin, staring at the scene, stopped the ship. The rippling flame became a constant glare. Doug recoiled.

"Colonel, move the ship a little bit." Marvin moved Research One a couple of feet. The fire rippled again but then returned to a constant glare. Marvin moved the ship into position near the opening in the ruptured tank and set it down. Doug, Marvin, and Dave hurried into the suits and entered the air lock.

When the outer doors were opened, Doug went down the ramp and out of the ship thirty feet from the tanks. Marvin and Dave joined him and they made their way carefully toward the open hole, stopping after a few feet to lower the darkened visors. The landscape took on a greenish hue and detail came into focus. There was a square enclosure mounted on the side of the tank. It was six feet high, four feet wide, and two feet deep. There was a door on the oblong box. In the middle of the door was a handle three feet long.

Doug grasped the handle and pulled. The door came off in his hand, exposing the interior. There were three sections: bottom, middle, and top. Inside each section there were transparent glass donuts, a small one in the center and then larger, all the way to the full four feet of width. They looked like clear soda straws in continuous circles. Doug studied them closely. Each donut was a separate tube.

"Gauges?" Doug said. "Do you think they're gauges?"

"If they are, what were they measuring?" Dave said.

They moved on toward the hole in the side of the twenty-foot high and thirty foot diameter tank. Scattered about were parts of the tank's interior, knocked loose by the impact. Doug picked up a piece of it and held it up.

"It looks like an eight-sided shaped tea pitcher," he said.

The three looked at it and then toward the hole, then made their way to see the inside of the ruptured tank. The complete inside of it was filled with the octagon shaped cells, all glistening brightly. It looked like a giant honeycomb. In the center of the bottom was the round brilliantly lighted hole with the scale-like mirrors, but near the center top was a ten-foot diameter black ball. It had the black rods coming out of it spaced evenly all around it. The hoses went to the top of the tank, then over and down the sides between the honeycomb and the wall of the tank, into the lunar surface. It looked like a giant black spider inside the tank.

"A water heater?" Doug said. He looked around at the surrounding ruins. Magnificent; all the conveniences of Mother Earth."

"When the dome was broken open, the water would all escape into space," Daniel said from the ship.

The three men gathered several of the tea pitcher sized cells of the honeycombed shaped interior of the tank and a small piece of the material used for the tank itself and returned to the ship.

Chapter 20

## - THE BLACK BOX -

As Research One lifted off the surface, Doug addressed the ship's company.

"We need to find one of their machines that we can get into the ship. Let's go over to the other side of the central crater and down in the open hole of the complex. Maybe we'll find something there."

Marvin raised the ship to five miles altitude and flew south until they reached the line of sight between the Castle and the crater. He turned southwest toward the central crater. After passing over the vertical pane of glass, the giant transparent billboard marker, Marvin descended to fifty feet above the surface.

Doug watched the terrain passing under the ship. The scene below him had become a place he knew. It was now a place he'd been. He rubbed his armpits. He could tell that he had been in the space suit three times. The heavy suit restricted movement and strength was needed to function in it. In spite of the discomfort, he was eager to put it on again.

As the ship passed over the rim of the crater, Doug's eyes went to the huge piling on the right with the two giant glass tubes resting on top of it. Something caught his eye; he leaned forward trying to see better detail. "Stop, stop, Colonel, back up." Marvin canceled forward movement.

"What is it?"

"I saw an opening on the side of that piling. It could be a doorway; it's on the side between the piling and the crater rim."

Marvin eased the ship backward until they were in position to see between the huge black piling and the ascending wall of the crater's rim.

"I see it," Marvin said. "It is a doorway."

"There's probably machinery in there," Dave said.

The others leaned forward to study the scene. Marvin moved the ship over the rim and down beside the piling. The crater rim rose up behind them as he eased the ship down to the surface. Marvin examined the area for a smooth flat spot. It was pocked marked badly with small impact craters and scattered with debris. "I can't land close enough to the piling," he said.

Doug, searching the area also, nodded. "Let's let Frank keep Research One hovering just above the surface and you and I go out and take a quick look." Marvin glanced at Frank and Isaac. They both nodded.

"Okay," Marvin said.

Doug and Marvin got into their suits, exited the ship and carefully made their way around to the opening in the hundred-foot diameter piling. There was no door on it but the opening was ten foot wide and forty feet tall. The inside of the piling had no lighting at all. The interior was pitch black.

"Can you see anything?" Dave said.

Doug placed his hand on the edge of the door opening and stepped inside the round black structure. Marvin followed.

"It's too dark," Marvin said. "I can't see anything. Wait a minute, Doug, I'll get one of the lanterns from the air lock." Marvin made his way to the ship and returned to the piling with a marine lantern. He turned it on and entered the darkened room, then swept the interior with the beam.

"Hey!" Doug said. There are lots of crates in here. They're stacked all around the walls."

"What do they look like," Daniel said.

"Black," Marvin said, "and about two feet square. There are hundreds of them." He moved the beam of light around the structure, illuminating the neatly stacked black crates, then stopped and focused it across the piling.

"There's a square opening in the back of the piling," Doug said, "but it's full of debris."

Marvin swung the light around the structure again, then upward. There were several huge black rods that came into the piling to their left and curved sharply and went out to their right. They made their way over to the stack of crates.

"Is there anything else in there?" Dave said.

"No," Doug said, "just hundreds of black crates. We'll see if we can lift one and bring it back to the ship."

As Marvin held the light, Doug studied the stack of crates. On the edge, they were stacked three high, then stair stepped up to over fifty feet above them. Doug reached up and lifted on the top crate. He easily picked it up. It weighed almost nothing.

"Let's take one apiece, they're very light." Doug handed the crate to Marvin and got another.

Back inside Research One, the two crates sat on the floor. The crew had swiveled their seats and were examining them.

"I don't see a lid," Doug said. "How do you open it?" Marvin picked up the crate again and turned it over and over in his hands. Doug was doing the same with the other.

"Look at that one side." Dave said. He pointed at the seam around an odd side of the crate.

They studied the crate closely. It was a two-foot cube. Of the six sides, all were the same except for one. On that one side, the seam was inside the other walls, as if the side was put in last and was inside the four walls of the other sides. The crack was completely closed. There was no space to insert anything. Marvin shook the crate. It seemed solid; nothing rattled. Unable to get it open, Marvin put the crate on the metal floor and pushed down on the odd side firmly. A loud click came from inside the black box.

Research One surged upward several feet! The crew and the other crate were pitched from the floor. The crewmembers were disoriented momentarily as the ship sank back to its set hovering altitude. Marvin crouched and grasped the seats, then scanned the COMM panel. Doug and Dave's eyes went to the computer screens. Frank scanned the rotor pod readings back and forth, and then his eyes locked on the power percentage readout.

"Marvin!" he said loudly.

"What," Marvin shouted.

"We're at zero power!" Frank said. His eyes went to the lunar surface outside, then back to the readout.

Marvin glanced outside, then to Frank, then to the readout. "What do you mean, zero power?"

"We're at zero; the rotor pod's not holding the ship up. We should fall to the surface."

Doug's fingers flew over the keyboard of the control systems computer. "Nothing's wrong," he reported.

"Marvin turned to the two crates. The one he'd pushed on was still on the floor where they'd put it. The other was at the wall of the ship, leaning up at an angle.

"The crate!" Marvin said. He reached down to pick it up. He couldn't move it. It was locked securely to the floor. He motioned to Doug. They tried to lift it together. The black box remained firmly in place. Marvin paused a moment in thought.

"Everybody brace yourselves," he said. They grasped the backs of the seats. Marvin pushed firmly on the panel of the crate again. It clicked.

Research One sank a few inches and then resumed hovering altitude. The crate slid sideways a little on the metal floor under Marvin's hands.

"Power readout is normal," Frank said.

"Everybody okay?" Marvin said. They all nodded, collecting themselves.

Doug stared at the crate. He reached down cautiously and picked it up, then turned it over and over in his hands.

"Antigravity!" he said, examining the crate again. "The ship surged because it took the computer a couple of seconds to adjust for the loss of weight."

"The crew focused on the crate, beginning to comprehend its significance.

"They discovered antigravity," Doug continued. "That's how they handled all these huge pieces of glass and the enormous pieces of rigging. They knew how to take away the weight until they got them in place." Doug handed the crate to Isaac. "Wrap these securely so they can't touch the ship."

Isaac and Dave secured the crates in the parachute silk and strapped them securely to the rigging.

Doug looked again at the black piling. "We'll come back and get all of those."

DAN HOLT

Chapter 21

- THE GLASS CRATES -

Marvin moved the ship up out of the closed space between the crater rim and the piling and set it down on the bed of the huge mold. Each member of the crew checked their respective responsibilities and was satisfied. Doug and Dave straightened the books that were jostled by the surge of Research One and secured them.

All in order, the crew collected themselves and checked in with Earth Base One. After updating the members of the research effort at home, they proceeded toward the next objective: the huge complex to the northwest. When they passed over the opposite crater rim, they could see it ahead.

Marvin adjusted the altitude to fifty feet above the lunar surface as the spacecraft glided across the open terrain. They saw hundreds of melted away spires of glass, geometric patterns of piles of dust, from light gray to dark gray, then back to light gray. Perhaps plants of some type and their associated holders or planters, both, over eons of time, reduced to their simplest form--dust.

The wall of glass grew in size as they approached. Marvin moved the throttle back to zero and allowed Research One to come to a stop. Looming above them was a mountain of glass, the pattern of the puzzle pieces all jumbled up. One had fallen on another, and then the two had fallen on others. A horrible condition of architecture that was obviously magnificent when in its glory. They looked up toward the top of the huge complex, then from side to side, to see it reaching toward the horizon.

"Take us up top," Doug said, looking upward

through the curve of the windshield.   Marvin eased the ship upward.   Doug watched the bright flickering as the Sun hit the panels in front of them at different angles.

"It's like a multicolored laser show," Daniel said.

Doug glanced at the crew.   They were mesmerized by the intricate light patterns that were coming through the windshield.   He looked back at the kaleidoscope of sparkling colors.   Research One rose above the immense mountain of broken and distorted glass.   In the distance, the ruins of the surface neighborhood come into view.

Doug pointed toward the distant ruins.   "Look at the layout from this vantage point.   It's on a smaller scale than the one on the other side of the crater.   We lay out suburban neighborhoods like that on Earth." His eyes followed a single road back to the crystalline mountain below them.   It appeared to go into the complex at the center of its twenty-mile length.   Then he looked toward the end of the glass mountain.

"Colonel, there on the end; see that big hole?" Marvin leaned forward and surveyed the rupture, then turned the ship and slowly moved it over the open hole. It looked more like a giant well or cistern than an impact crater; relatively narrow for its depth.   The bottom of it was covered with gray dust and scattered with boulders.

Easing the ship down into the hole in the mountain, Marvin stopped the descent at a thousand feet and did a slow 360 degree rotation.   The complex contained much of the debris of the meteor impact. The glass cubicles surrounding the hole were filled with sand and rocks.   There were the ends of the glass walls sticking out in some spots.   The sliced apart rooms, hallways, multiple floors, and broken walls, went up a thousand feet and down as far as the eye could see.

The tiny inhabitants of Research One stared in awe.

The rotation completed, Marvin resumed the descent into the opening. The crew watched the dust filled rooms of all sizes, passing by the ship as it smoothly lowered the adventurers deeper into the chasm. Awed by the scale of the alien dwellings, Doug looked up. Above them now was an enormous jagged opening; in the middle of it, a quarter million miles away, was a blue and white sphere--Earth.

The impact shaft began to narrow. It was still over a quarter mile wide when they saw the glass stop and rock begin. Marvin stopped the descent and hovered.

"This is the surface of the Moon," Doug said, "it's solid rock."

Looking down, Marvin said: "This hole goes down about another two thousand feet, Doug."

"Take us on down a ways," Doug said. Marvin resumed the descent. Moments later a rectangular opening carved into the wall of rock came into view.

"Just what we thought!" Doug exclaimed. "Underground rooms!"

As the ship came down even with the hole in the wall, Doug studied the parameter of the huge opening. It was three hundred feet wide and seventy feet high; a perfect rectangle. Marvin stopped the descent and moved the ship toward the opening, still five hundred feet away. As they came closer, objects began to take clear shape.

"Boxes!" Daniel said excitedly. "Rows of boxes."

"Storage of supplies!" Doug shouted. "Dave, we were right."

"I wonder what's in them," Dave said.

"Whatever it is," Doug said, "it should be in good shape. This is deep underground."

Frank said with deliberate ease: "Michael's going to be glad to hear this. He made a lot of promises to a lot of people."

Marvin stopped Research One at the entrance and examined the ceiling and walls of the structure, then eased into the room, inching forward carefully.

"Look at those crates!" Dave said. "They're huge."

"Well," Doug said, "when you bring supplies so far to get it here, you bring it in large quantities."

"They stored plenty," Marvin said. "There's crates lined up as far as I can see. This must be some kind of a hallway, or tunnel." Marvin turned on the ship lights then adjusted the searchlight down the hallway. The crates continued down the hallway until they appeared solid, like a carpet. "It goes out of sight," Marvin added.

Doug studied the placement of the containers. They were arranged on each side of the center aisle. The aisle was a hundred feet wide and went down the center of the enormous hallway. On each side of the aisle, the containers were placed lengthwise with the hallway and spaced ten feet apart. He counted four crates on each side of the center aisle, then twenty feet farther into the hallway, there were four more on each side and so on, as far as he could see. There was a narrow aisle between the wall and the crates on each side of the stone tunnel.

"This hallway probably runs the full length of the complex on the surface," Doug said. Marvin stopped the forward motion of the ship. He glanced again at the ceiling and walls and floor of the chamber.

"The floor, ceiling, and walls of the tunnel seem to be all solid rock and very smooth."

"How big would you say those crates are, Colonel?" Doug asked.

Marvin rotated the ship to the right, facing one of the crates at the middle of its length, then moved in close to it. "I'd say about fifty feet long, maybe six feet wide, and about four feet high."

"Let's go out and see if we can open one," Doug said, nodding at Isaac.

Doug, Dave, and Marvin got into the space suits.

As Doug watched Isaac going through the procedures of taking the air out of the compartment, he envisioned a stock of everyday items: office supplies, small machines, lots of gadgets, protected from decay far below the lunar surface. Maybe, gadgets that they could figure out and learn from. Computers maybe; really advanced computers. He took a deep breath as he saw Isaac nod through the glass, then realized that he'd been doing that every time.

"You're at zero atmospheres," Isaac said. "I'm ready to open the outer doors."

"We're ready for exit," Marvin said.

Doug watched the top door go up, then the ramp lower and bump solidly on the smooth stone floor. He felt a faint register of a vibration, and then heard an electronic thump through the intercom system. They walked down the ramp and around the ship to the front. Doug stopped and turned from side to side, looking at the neatly arranged, evenly spaced crates on each side of the aisle. Marvin and Dave stopped behind him.

"They were careful to line them up and space them, weren't they," Dave said.

"It was probably so they could get to any crate for supplies," Doug said. He walked over to the crate next to the ship. The colonel followed behind him. He reached out and touched the crate.

"Dust," he said.

"What's that?" Daniel said from the ship.

"Dust," Doug repeated, 'they're covered with dust."

"It must have bellowed in here when the meteor hit," Marvin said. Doug wiped some of the dust from the crate with his thick gloved hand and then paused. He blinked in surprise.

"It's glass! They're made of glass. I can see through it." Dave started making his way to the crate. Doug wiped away a circle two feet wide then leaned close and studied the interior.

What Doug expected to see inside the crate and the actual image registering on the retinas of his eyes had to be reconciled inside his brain.

Seconds went by. "Aaaaah!" Doug shouted and jumped backward, leaving the stone floor in the low gravity. Dave froze in his tracks. In the ship, Frank, Daniel, and Isaac jumped to their feet. Marvin grabbed Doug around the waist and staggered backward several feet before regaining his balance. He spun Doug around.

"What!" What is it?!"

"A body! A *human body*!" Doug said, gasping for breath.

Dave backed up a couple of steps, staring at the crate.

Marvin made his way over to the glass container, wiped more of the dust away, and looked inside.

"You're right, Doug," Marvin said. "It is a human; a giant!"

"A giant human!" Daniel said from the ship. "My God!"

Marvin moved along the crate wiping away more dust and examining the body. Doug and Dave approached it and began to examine the giant figure inside. It was perfectly formed as human in appearance. The body was dressed in a dark colored robe. The material seemed to be the same as the small piece that wrapped the bracelet. The robe came to a perfect V just below the neck of the body. The face was smooth and hairless. The hair on the enormous head was short and neat. The nose was dominate, but in proper proportion to the face.

"Look," Dave said, pointing at the chest of the giant. Doug's eyes followed. There was a round transparent object with an emblem on it. It had a tight cluster of circles and triangles mounted on a square pedestal.

"Maybe it designates which planet he's from of where his family is," Dave offered.

The eyes were closed; the arms lay at his sides. Doug glanced at Frank, Daniel, and Isaac through the windshield, then back to the transparent crate.

"It's a man and he looks smart, proud, and dignified."

"He had reason to," Daniel said over the radio.

Doug nodded. "He's young."

"Young?" Frank said. Doug paused a moment, then nodded again.

Marvin spoke from the other end of the crate. "This guy's over forty feet tall. Standing up he'd look very skinny."

"That's why all those rooms were so big," Isaac said. "*They* were big."

"Doug, come look at this," Dave said. Doug turned. Dave was standing at the middle of the glass crate. Doug bounced to where he was, sliding his hand along on the top of the crate. Dave pointed at the giant's hand. There was a duplicate of the bracelets on his middle finger. Doug put his other hand on top of the crate and stared at it.

"They're not bracelets! They're rings!"

"This one's a woman," Marvin said from the next crate. Doug and Dave made their way to it.

"Her hair is the same as his," Doug said. "Very short."

The body was dressed in the identical robe and had the round pendent on the chest. Doug checked the hands, the ring was there.

"It seems that where they're from is important," Doug said.

"Do you think that maybe this whole domed city was a university and that's a student ring" Dave said.

Doug studied the ring through the glass again. "If it is, there's a wealth of knowledge here for us." Doug studied the woman's face again through the glass.

"She's young, too."

"This one's another man," Marvin said. The colonel was at the end of his tether. Doug and Dave moved to the third crate and looked at the figure inside.

"This one's young," Doug said. "I want to check some more of the containers." Doug turned his back to Marvin. "Unhook me."

"Wait, Doug," Frank said. "Let me move Research One down the hall and stay in communications so we can hear you."

The three suited crewmembers positioned themselves in the aisle and watched Frank raise the ship a few inches and advance down the hallway, giving them access to six more of the crates.

Doug went to the first crate in the second row and wiped it off.

"Another woman, young."

"A man," Marvin said from the next one. "Young, too."

They cleared the glass on all six crates. Doug went from container to container, and then turned to Marvin. "They're all young. There are no old people. Why?"

"I don't know," Marvin responded.

"If this was their burial place, there would be all ages here," Doug said. "These are all young people." He glanced around again, then back to Marvin. "Why did they die? They weren't killed when this city was destroyed; they've been prepared for burial. Why are they dead?"

The research team, both inside Research One, and those outside tethered to it, were silent for a few moments. As Doug surveyed the scene, Dave and the colonel's movements seemed animated as they moved about in the absolute stillness around them. Doug saw the colonel stop and turn to face him.

"Maybe they're not."

Doug recoiled. "What?!"

"Maybe they're not dead; maybe they're in suspended animation--asleep. Their bodies are perfectly preserved."

"Asleep for thousands of years?!" Doug said. He turned to study the face of the woman in the crate next to him.

"We don't know how much technology they had," Marvin said. Doug studied the figure in the sealed glass container again very closely then moved to the next crate and studied another.

"We have to consider the possibility," Marvin said. The colonel was looking into the glass crate next to him. Marvin, still studying the figure through the glass, said quietly: "I wonder what he would think of us?"

The crew was quiet for a few moments.

"Doug," Daniel said from the ship. Doug stopped and turned toward the windshield. "Maybe," Daniel continued, "the city fathers here knew that doom was coming. Maybe they decided to do the only thing they could do. Take the young people and put them to sleep, hoping that someday someone would find them."

"Jesus," Doug said quietly. Marvin and Dave glanced at Daniel through the windshield, then around again at the sea of glass containers.

"Frank," Doug said, looking at the windshield again, "we've got to come back with a bigger ship and take them back to Earth." He saw Frank nod, then looked back and the huge young face through the glass. Marvin moved back to the aisle, turned and looked back at Doug and Dave. Dave followed him. Marvin and Dave made their way back to the ramp of the ship, turned, and waited.

Doug stood among the crates, almost at the end of his tether. He leaned over again and looked at the figure inside the crate, laid his hand on top of it, straightened up and turned from side to side, looking at the sea of containers neatly arranged in the stone hallway. He stared down the depth of the tunnel, then turned, wiped some dust from the top of the crate and looked down on the face of the giant inside. He studied the face for a long moment.

"Who are you?" he said quietly. After a few moments, he walked toward the ramp, stopped and looked again, then walked up between Marvin and Dave standing at the base of the ramp. They turned, facing the ramp with him, and the three walked up into the ship.

Chapter 22

- THE LAB -

Research One hovered motionless, just outside the
tunnel opening, in radio communications with Earth
Base One.   Michael Sheridan had been making
phone calls as soon as the news of the discoveries was
transmitted home.   The population of Technical
Research Association's Earth Base One was growing
as those contacted made their way there.   This latest
transmission has sent to Professor Charles Liggins'
phone so he could begin waking up fellow members of
the renowned Anthropological Society.   The news of a
race of giants living on the Moon thousands of years
ago would bring them in groves, especially, since there
was a possibility that some of them were still alive.
The crew of Research One informed Earth Base One
that they would attempt to traverse the depths of the
tunnel and determine if there was equipment to
support the suspended animation theory.

Research One re-entered the tunnel.
"Okay," Marvin said, "let's do it."  He turned on
the outside lights again and tested the function of the
searchlight.  All was ready.  He began moving the
ship deeper and deeper into the tunnel.  The crew
watched the glass containers pass beneath the
spacecraft.  When they flew beyond the reach of the
long settled dust, the crates were completely
transparent.  They saw glimpses of the faces as the
ship passed above them.  They appeared to be all
young adults, and equal numbers of male and female.
The aligned crates seemed to go on forever.  Then,
abruptly, two miles in, they stopped.  Marvin held the
ship momentarily.

"There must be over a thousand of them," Doug said.

"Gives me the creeps," Daniel said. Marvin resumed forward motion. For a quarter mile the tunnel was completely bare. Then Marvin saw something ahead flickering in the lights of the ship. He slowed to a stop. He adjusted the search light on the object. It appeared to be a beam of light reflecting back to the ship. Marvin turned off the ship's exterior lights. The tunnel was plunged into total darkness. The spot of light was gone. He turned the lights back on and eased the ship forward. As the distance was reduced, Doug recognized the object. The ship's lights seemed to circle its shape in an eerie oscillation.

"It's one of the bracelets--ah--rings," he said. It was lying on top of a lean forty-foot body. The body was withered to skin and bone and then appeared to have mummified.

"This one must have been walking along the tunnel when the dome was ruptured," Dave said.

"Or he was back at the glass crates and got this far before the hard vacuum overwhelmed him," Marvin said.

"Wonder where he was running to," Daniel said.

"Let's move on," Marvin said and resumed forward movement. Farther on there were more bodies, all seemed to have been running toward something ahead. Five miles into the tunnel, the ceiling suddenly angled upward at a forty-five degree angle. The wall angled outward at the same angle. The tunnel was now a thousand feet wide and five hundred feet high.

"Jesus," Daniel said.

"They did things on a grand scale, didn't they," Isaac said. Marvin combed the walls and ceiling with the searchlight. All was smooth rock and looked solid.

He continued on, raising the ship another fifty feet. The crew moved Research One deeper and deeper into the ancient stone tunnel, occasionally seeing withered remains of the giants, some in contorted shapes.

"They were caught by surprise," Dave said. Marvin cleared his throat.

"That means that the tenders of the crates weren't told," he said.

"Or," Daniel said, "they just accepted it, then when it happened, survival instincts took over." The crew was silent for some time as the dimly lighted walls passed by the ship.

Without warning, the floor, ceiling, and walls disappeared. Marvin canceled forward flight. Research One hovered in an immense volume of blackness. The ship pieced beams of light through it until they ran out of candlepower, reaching nothing. Marvin turned off the exterior lights and searched the blackness, looking for anything at all to determine the size of the chamber. He became aware of a faint glow above. He and the crew looked upward through the lead filled acrylic. Far above, there was a ghostly, milky glow of faint light, and, barely discernible, was the distorted image of Earth.

"A transparent ceiling," Doug said, "and it's still intact." Marvin turned the lights back on and eased the ship forward again. Moments later, he stopped and began a 360 degree rotation. All eyes in the ship strained to see anything in the blackness. Then they all saw it at the same time. A circle of light on a brown grid-like object.

"That looks like the material we saw under the Castle!" Doug said excitedly.

"Yeah, it does," Marvin agreed. He eased the

ship toward it. When Research One was within sixty feet, the circle of light disappeared off the grid and brilliantly lighted a spot on the upper windshield. Suddenly, the entire five mile by five mile by one mile high chamber was brilliantly lighted.

"Ahhhhh," Daniel shouted. The crew recoiled from the light and the sound of Daniel's startled voice.

"We just turned on the lights," Doug panted. When Marvin's adrenaline began to settle down, he rotated the ship to have a look at the gigantic room they'd flown into. The crew stared in awe at the vast layout before them. To the far side of the huge cubicle were five distinct areas, left to right, cordoned off by thousand foot high walls.

A wall twice as high ran through the center of the chamber perpendicular to their line of sight. On this side of the high wall and to their left were dozens of glass cylinders or capsules from fifty feet long and ten feet in diameter down to ten feet long and three feet in diameter. They had several pipes or wires coming out of them and going up to a fifty by fifty foot square box near the ceiling of the enormous open chamber. The box had the familiar black rod, much larger, coming out of the top of it and going up to the ceiling of the underground structure.

"This is a giant laboratory!" Doug said.

"My God,' Dave said. "It's cryogenics or something like it. The giants *are* asleep."

"Just think of what it would mean if we could figure out how to wake them up," Doug said.

"I don't know if we should," Daniel said.

"Of course we should," Doug said staring at the cylinders below. "They have been waiting for thousands of years for somebody to find them."

## Chapter 23

## - EARTH'S SECRET -

Doug leaned forward and searched the width of the windshield. His eyes found something else to their right.

"What are those?" he said. Marvin rotated Research One for a better look, then descended and approached the new shapes. They were transparent cylinders, standing vertical, about the size of a home water heater. The lights reflected off them oddly. As the distance was reduced, the cylinders seemed to have something inside. Everything was dead still.

"Either they have been painted half way up or there's an amber liquid inside them," Marvin said.

"This looks like a giant Frankenstein lab," Daniel said. Marvin looked upward. The ceiling of the awesome facility was matted with plumbing, tying box shaped, cylinder shaped, and round objects together. He rotated the ship as they stared at the array of equipment. All eyes focused on the center of the ceiling. There was a pyramid shaped transparent object suspended by cables. Light was projected in all directions from it.

"These people were masters of light technology," Doug commented. Marvin rotated Research One back to the right. Below there were rows of cages several stories high. Each was a cubicle enclosed with transparent glass bars. The bars sparkled with reflected light. Marvin eased toward them. He descended in front of the hundred-cage long, twenty-cage high bank of enclosures. As he moved the ship along in front of them, Daniel suddenly took a breath.

"Colonel, stop. There's something in that one,

lying on the floor." Marvin reversed the ship and moved it in front of the cage, rotated toward it, then moved closer.

"It's a body!" Dave exclaimed, "about five feet long." The light inside the cage was dimmer than the volume of the lab. Marvin adjusted the search light on the remains.

"Oh my God, it's an ape!" Doug said. He glanced toward the vertical cylinders then back to the row of cages. "They were doing genetic research here, too."

After a moment, Marvin moved the ship slowly along the bank of enclosures. There was dozens of cages containing remains, all apes.

"What do you do genetically with apes?" Daniel said.

"Let's look around some more," Doug said. Marvin ascended until in the clear then rotated the ship toward the cordoned off areas on the far side of the lab complex, then eased the stick forward. Research One moved across the vastness of the advanced lab. The five areas were arranged left to fight, each a mile square. As they got closer the contents of each began to show detail. The one dead ahead, third from the left, had dense jungle and underbrush. There was a riverbed traversing it. It looked like a giant painting.

"That can't be real," Dave said. "It's been in the dark and in a vacuum for centuries."

"You're right," Doug said. "There's no water in the river. It has to be fake."

"But, why?" Daniel asked. "Why would they do this?"

Marvin began a descent for a closer look.

"More dead apes," Dave said. There were bodies lying randomly around the immediate area inside the enclosure. All were skin and bone.

"Let's land and check it out," Marvin said. He moved to a clear spot near the riverbed and landed Research One. They examined the surroundings through the ship's windshield. Fifty feet away were two of the bodies, in each other's arms, withered to almost nothing. Doug felt a note of sadness for the animals. They had no idea what was happening to them.

"It's like landing in the jungles of Africa," Isaac said. Everything was absolutely still, animated in appearance.

Marvin, Doug, and Dave suited up and were processed outside. They went around to the front of the ship. Doug raked the toe of his boot across the 'grass.' It stood back up as if undisturbed. He walked over to a bush and grasped its leaves between his fingers.

"It looks like the cloth we saw," he said. "Only it's green." Marvin walked to the edge of the riverbed and looked up and down it.

"It took a while to put this together," he said. "It's like a display at a zoo. What was its purpose?" The three made their way to the two bodies in embrace for a closer look. Marvin and Doug pulled the carcasses apart and studied their faces. Doug glanced up at the other two and then back to the remains.

"These are not apes; they're more human-like. Look at the faces." Doug and Dave stared at each other for a long moment, then back at the bodies on the ground. Marvin studied the faces of the Cave men's remains.

"They're black," Marvin said. "They're black cave men."

"No, no, no...now wait a minute," Daniel said from the ship, "you don't think...."

259

"Let's check the other four areas," Doug said. They re-entered the ship, ascended to clear the dividing wall and made their way down into the next enclosure. It was a wooded prop, not as dense as the jungle, but similarly constructed. It was also strewn with bodies. Marvin eased the ship down close to one of them.

"These are white," he said, then moved the ship up and into the next.

"Yellow." The next two enclosure contained brown and red skinned early man.

Marvin raised the ship to two thousand feet and hovered. The crew was quiet for a few moments. Doug broke the silence.

"The giants genetically engineered early man; Cave Men, from apes, in black, white, yellow, brown, and red skin tones."

"The five basic colors of the people on Earth," Dave added.

"This is where we came from?" Daniel said in a strained voice. "Have we found…God?"

"No, my friend," Marvin said. "They couldn't create life. All they could do is manipulate it, just as we are learning to do back on Earth. They were just much further advanced than we are at the present time. But, we're getting there."

"I don't know if I like the idea that we were manufactured in a lab," Daniel said.

"That's why the decision was made to cover it up," Doug said. "This would be an awesome bombshell to drop on the human race."
Chapter 24

- LT. COL. ROGER STAHLS -

"Mankind has a right to know who they are and where

they came from no matter what the truth is," Isaac said seriously.

"The Apollo astronauts would have to have seen this lab to know about it," Dave said.

"Colonel," Doug said. "Let's take a look around the lab floor and see if there's any evidence that they were here." Marvin began descending toward the floor. The two thousand foot high wall dividing the lab complex come up beside the ship. As they descended lower, smaller structures began to appear. Even lower, they saw walkways; hallways leading to different parts of the lab, with glassed in cubicles scattered along them.

"Look," Doug said. "Bodies. More of the giants."

"The ones that were already put in suspended animation were lucky," Isaac said. They saw several victims of the onslaught of the unforgiving hard vacuum as they made their way down the wide hallways of the lab.

"There!" Dave said, pointing, "Parked by that cubicle."

"It's the Moon Buggy!" Daniel exclaimed. "They did see all of this."

"What's it doing here?" Doug said. "Why didn't they drive it back to the landing site to leave for Earth?"

Marvin piloted Research One along the spacious hallway toward the Apollo vehicle. The Moon Buggy was parked at an angle at the edge of the hallway. The cubicle was built onto the high wall. It was fifty by fifty feet and fifty feet high; a transparent cube; small office sized to the giants. There was a door on it eight feet wide and forty feet high. The door stood open. Through the crystal clear walls of the enclosure they could see pieces of furniture, giant versions of a desk and a chair. On one end of the desk was a seven-foot square book. It was open. The cover leaned up against the back wall of the office. On the eighteen by thirty foot desktop, the book looked properly proportioned in size. On the other end of the giant desktop was a stack of papers. Beside the stack was a pencil three feet long. It had the familiar crystalline cluster where the eraser would have been. The stack of papers had jagged edges; the stack so uneven that it appeared more of a pile of near square sheets.

Marvin set the ship down next to the lunar rover vehicle. He, Doug, and Dave hurried into the suits.

"How do we get up there?" Dave said as the three men stood around the giant chair.

"The same way he must have," Marvin said. "We jump." Marvin pulled several feet of slack in his tether then squatted and jumped. He went up so that half his body was above the nine foot high chair seat, and then fell back to the floor and bounced.

"Okay," he said. "I can do it." He positioned himself close to the chair back and jumped again the same way; grasped the upright on the chair back, and wrestled himself upon the chair seat. He positioned himself at the edge of the chair, grasped his tether with both hands, and braced for the weight of his fellow climbers.

"Okay, climb up my tether." Doug clasped it and traversed the distance to the chair seat. Marvin hoisted him over the edge. Dave followed. Then Marvin reached up and grasped the edge of the desktop. Doug and Dave lifted him up. When all three were on top, they gathered around the stack of papers.

"Is it writing?" Isaac said from the ship.

"Yes," Doug said. "It's hand written. He tore

pages from the big book and ripped them up and used them to write on. The letters are printed and are two and three inches high. It's crude. We'll bring the whole stack back to the ship."

The crew of Research One sat in their seats facing the conference table. They examined the stack of hand written pages. Doug began to read aloud:

*Dear Julie,*
*I'm sorry I can't come home like I promised. I really was going to be there for your sixteenth birthday. I messed up, baby, I really messed up. I got in an argument with my commander about this place. I was going to tell when we got home. He tried to reason with me, but you know how hard headed I am sometimes. He slipped away and drove back to the landing site, then blasted off without me.*

Doug stopped reading and swallowed.
"My God," Daniel said weakly.
"But all the astronauts got back to Earth okay," Isaac said. Doug cleared his throat and resumed reading.

*When I discovered the rover was gone I ran all the way back to the landing site...over a mile. When I got there I saw that he had blasted off for Earth. He left both tanks of emergency oxygen for me but that gives me only eight hours of air. I drove the rover back here to this place. I cried for an hour. Then I decided to write you a letter in case somebody on another mission finds it and can take it to you. You have to keep it a secret baby, you can't tell anybody. I love you so much.*

*You're all I have since your mother died....*

"It's his daughter," Doug said. "Julie's his daughter." Doug looked back to the paper.

*I have to tell you about this place. I'm in a giant laboratory underground on the Moon. It's where we were made. I mean it, baby. There're chambers here where people can be made. The people that made us are giants. They're forty feet tall. I saw cave men in huge pens with trees and everything. They made theme here and took them to Earth. The missing link is here, right here in this place. I am so hungry; don't matter though. I just started on my first tank of emergency oxygen. I'm going to look around again. Maybe the giants had some oxygen stored somewhere. I'll be back...*

"His crew left him here, why? No one knew back home because it was a secret mission," Marvin said. "They were launched in secret from the Nevada Test Range. I heard talk about it. To account for the noise, they told the press that they were testing ICBM's with targets out at sea."

"I remember that on the news," Frank said.

"Wonder where he is...I mean where he died?" Dave said.

"Let's read the rest of this and we'll look for him," Doug said. He picked up the next jagged page and continued:

*I'm back, Sweetheart. I didn't find anything. I'm going to rest for a few minutes then look some more. I feel so alone. Now I know how you felt when you tried to tell me you felt alone, living with my older brother. I thank him for taking care of you, but I shouldn't have volunteered for this. I should have been there for you. They made me feel so damned important, and all the time, you were what was really important. God, I'm so sorry, baby. I'm going to look around some more....*

Doug broke off to compose himself. The crew was silent. Marvin stared at the rotor pod. His face was steel hard, his eyes unmoving. Doug cleared his throat again, and then resumed:

*I'm going to look around again. I'll be back....*

Doug turned the page over on top of the others, then picked up the next.

*I'm back, Julie. I found something. It's one of their cylinders that put people to sleep. It's a small one--only ten feet long. It's behind the big ones that we found when we first got here. It still works. I tried it. There's a brown pad in it with a beam of light shining on it. When you pass your hand through the light, the whole cylinder is filled with an eerie greenish light. I saw Cave men in several of them and they look okay--like they're asleep. It's my only chance. It might not work, but, I've got nothing to lose. My first tank of emergency oxygen is almost empty, so I have to go. I'm going to use the last one to pressurize the cylinder after I close it, so I can take my suit off. Then I'll turn it on. Maybe there'll be enough oxygen in there for me to breathe until it puts me to sleep. If this doesn't work, baby, remember, Daddy loves you.*

Doug turned the last page up at a forty-five degree angle then read the last sentence.

*If it does work, I'll tell you myself.*
        *Love,    Dad*

When Doug turned the last page over onto the stack, he saw that the back of it also contained the scribbled writing.  He picked it up again and read:

*Deliver to:*
*Julie Renee Stahls*
*c/o Jason Stahls*
*3604 Windmill Rd,*
*Wichita, Kansas*

*Lt. Col. Roger Stahls*

Marvin bolted upright in his seat.  "He's Renee's father!" he screamed.  "They told her he died in a plane crash."  Marvin jumped to his feet, picked up the stack of papers, and began scanning them.

"Doug, where did he say he found the cylinder?"  Doug shuffled through the papers, then picked up one and scanned down it.

"Here it is," he said.  "Behind the big ones that he and the Commander found when they first came in."  Marvin returned to the pilot's position. The others hurriedly swiveled their seats.  Marvin raised the ship up a hundred feet and began moving toward the wall of the lab.

"The cylinder he's in will be close to wherever they came in." Marvin said.  "They couldn't have gotten in here the way we did.  Not with Apollo equipment. There has to be another way into the lab." The crew began searching the area ahead as the ship closed on the gigantic wall. Marvin flew close to it, and then turned left and preceded slowly, searching the base of the wall. A quarter mile farther in he saw a recessed area at floor level. He descended toward it.

"That looks like an entrance," Doug said. Marvin approached it.

A moment later, Dave pointed. "The tracks of the rover! See them?"

"This is where they came in," Doug said. "That must be a descending tunnel from the surface." Marvin followed the rover's tracks. They went down a hallway straight out from the tunnel opening, then turned right and went through an opening in a hundred foot high wall. Marvin raised the ship and went over the wall, then down on the other side.

"There they are!" Isaac said excitedly. Marvin piloted Research One directly over the enormous cylinders and eased downward. Below and to their right a row of ten-foot cylinders came into view. They counted eight of them, each with a black rod coming out the top and clustering at an enormous black box suspended above.

He's in one of those," Marvin said. He lowered the ship to ten feet above and ten feet to the side of the canisters to avoid the black rods. He flew sideways while they searched the interiors. Not the first one, not the second, not the third. Then their eyes fell on a deflated spacesuit with the block shaped life support equipment on the back of it. Next to it was an oxygen bottle. On the other end of the transparent cylinder was the perfectly preserved body of Roger Stahls. The blonde haired astronaut lay on his side, legs drawn up to his chest, knees circled with his arms, and his forehead on his knees. Marvin blinked moist eyes.

"You think he's alive?" Daniel said in a broken voice.

"Maybe," Marvin said and cleared his throat. "If he is, we've got to figure out how to get him out of there and in here without killing him." Marvin studied the latches on the cylinder. There were four. They appeared to be simple over-center clamps. You lifted the arm up and the seal would be broken. He could see mirror images of the sealing arms inside the cylinder.

"The guy's got guts," Isaac said.

"He was desperate," Dave said. "Like he said in his letter; nothing to lose."

"That's one hell of a man inside there," Doug said. "If he can be saved, we've got to save him."

"Let's think," Marvin said. "How do we do it? If we suit up and open it, the vacuum will kill him in seconds. We have to have that cylinder in here before we open it." All the crewmembers looked at Marvin.

"It'll fit through the door," Isaac said, "but it's too long for the air lock."

"We'd have to have both doors open at the same time to bring it in," Dave said.

"We have the three back-up suits," Frank said. "Let's all suit up and depressurize Research One, bring the cylinder in, then pressurize the ship again."

"That'll work!" Marvin said.

"Colonel," Doug said, studying the cylinder through the windshield, "it's attached to that black rod. We'll have to take it loose from the cylinder. There's no joint or valve."

"We'll have to break it," Marvin said.

"That will leave a hole," Dave said. "The cylinder will lose its pressure."

"Plug it," Daniel said. "Take one of the squeeze bottles of water, push it through the hole, then squeeze it out until it seals it from the inside, and then tie it off."

"Brilliant," Marvin said. He landed Research One with the ramp toward the cylinder. The six crewmembers began suiting up.

"Isaac," Marvin said, "you're going to be cumbersome in the back-up suit because of you size."

"I'll manage," Isaac said. Marvin nodded and looked at the others. "Only three of us will have communications. Frank, Daniel, and Isaac will be suited up and in a vacuum. They will not be able to hear us. The three of us will have to get the cylinder in here. First, Doug, I'll lift you and Dave up top to break the rod and seal the hole. Then we'll carry Roger into the ship and put his cylinder by the porthole just past the air lock.

"Okay," Doug said then went to the artifact storage and dug out the two-foot piece of beam they recovered at the foundation of the Castle. Dave put three squeeze bottles of water, the piece of black cloth, and a six inch piece of the tiny black rod Marvin collected from the library into his leg pouch.

The crew put on their helmets. Isaac went directly to the second step for venting the ship and released the atmosphere of Research One into the lunar lab.

Doug put his hands on the side of the cylinder and waited. Marvin hoisted him upward until he climbed to the crown of the device. Doug stood up, then grasped the rod and pulled gently on it. It didn't move.

"It's rigid," he said.

"Good," Marvin said. "One hard blow next to the cylinder should break it." Marvin lifted Dave to the top of the cylinder. Dave retrieved one of the squeeze bottles from his leg pouch and readied himself.

Doug swung the black beam at the base of the rod. It impacted and bounced back. He stepped back, raised the beam higher and swung with all his strength. The rod snapped clean at the cylinder and swung out thirty feet, and then snapped fifty feet up. It fell to the floor and broke into dozens of pieces. A crystalline, sparkling flow spewed from the cylinder like a tiny fountain. Dave shoved the spongy water bottle into the hole, and then squeezed it. The base of the bottle expanded and the crystalline flow stopped.

"Okay," Dave said, "it's sealed." Dave wadded up the cloth and stuffed it into the hole above the squeeze bottle. He then tamped it with the tiny version of the black rod. Satisfied, he and Doug returned to the floor.

Marvin positioned himself at one end of the cylinder and Doug took the other. Together they tried to lift the device. It didn't move. Marvin crouched and tried with all his strength. Still no movement. Dave joined Marvin and they tried together. It remained firmly in its cradle.

"Oh my God, we can't lift it!" Marvin said breathing heavily. Doug hurried to Marvin's and Dave's position and the three tried the lift the end of it. No success. The three stopped and gasped for breath.

"We've cut off his life support," Doug said.

"We've got to do something."

"We'll have to take a chance and open it," Dave said. "He could be dying in there."

"He wouldn't last but a few seconds," Marvin said. Marvin felt a tap on his shoulder. He turned. Daniel was standing behind him with one of the black crates from the piling at the crater. Marvin looked from the box to Daniel's eyes. Daniel winked. Marvin smiled, grasped the black crate, placed the bottom of it against the transparent cylinder, and then leaned on the odd side. The crate locked itself to the side of the cylinder. Marvin and Dave took control of one end, Doug and Daniel the other. The four men easily guided the weightless cylinder into Research One. They closed the airlock door and Isaac triggered the system to pressurize the ship. Minutes later they were out of their suits.

Marvin, Doug, Dave, and Isaac tripped the locking arms of the sealing latches simultaneously. There was a faint popping sound and the top half of the transparent cylinder rose to a vertical position and stopped. A volume of cool air bathed their faces and then went away. Marvin placed his hand on the side of Roger's neck.

"He's cold," he said, then paused. "There's no pulse." Marvin quickly put his ear next to Roger's mouth. "He's not breathing! Let's get him on his back." Roger's limbs were stiff. They gently forced them to extend and rolled him on his back, then centered him on the black cloth covering on the bed in the cylinder. Marvin unzipped Roger's body suit down to the waist and pulled it open, then forced his mouth open. He put his mouth over Roger's and blew air into his lungs. He saw his chest rise. He pressed Roger's stomach, forcing him to exhale, and then repeated the procedure. Doug and Dave began rubbing the astronaut's arms and chest. After five breaths, Marvin felt the neck again. Still no pulse.

"Give him heart massage!" Marvin said, breathing heavily. He then blew another breath into Roger's lungs. Doug positioned himself and began pushing on the breastbone and counting aloud. One, two, three, four, five. Marvin repeated the breath. Doug continued. Another breath. Frank, Daniel, and Isaac stood transfixed, staring at Roger. Doug and Marvin continued. Dave was holding Roger's hand, massaging and patting the back of it.

Suddenly, Roger's hand quivered, fully opened, and then closed around Dave's.

"He's alive!" Dave shouted. "He gripped my hand!" Marvin's eyes snapped to Roger's hand closed around Dave's. Marvin rubbed the side of Roger's head.

"Roger. Roger. Can you hear me?! Roger." Marvin gently turned Roger's face toward his. "Roger, wake up. Roger!"

Roger Stahls opened his eyes, blinked slowly several times, and then looked at Marvin. Marvin smiled. "Can you hear me?" Marvin rubbed his face again. "Roger, can you hear me." Roger's lips quivered and a faint sound came from his throat. Then his eyes widened, rolled upward, then his limbs began jerking violently. Marvin slid his hands under him and pulled him into his arms, then hugged him securely.

"Hold on, Roger. Hold on. You can do it. Stay with us. Hold on." Roger jerked with seizures for a full minute before his body went completely limp. Marvin shook him. "Roger! Roger!" No response. Marvin laid him back down on the black cloth surface.

"Heart massage!" he shouted. Doug jumped into position and began the procedure. Marvin resumed the breathing assistance. They worked with him for several minutes, stopping to check pulse every thirty seconds. No response.

"Roger!" Marvin shouted. "You can't die! Not now! You beat the odds! You survived! You can't die! Stay with us. You can't die." Marvin began crying. "You can't die!" he shouted, then pushed Doug out of the way and hit Roger's breastbone with the side of his fist three times, then blew in one final breath. Nothing.

Marvin sat back, breathing heavily. He hung his head and sobbed, tears running down his face. The rest of the crew looked at Marvin, chocking back the sounds of grief....

A faint cough came from Roger Stahls, and then he took a breath and coughed several times. The crew jumped to their feet and gathered around him. Roger took another breath and moaned, then coughed again and opened his eyes. He looked up at the semicircle of faces above him, and then blinked and smiled.

"Boy, am I glad to see you guys."

Marvin laughed and blinked moist eyes. Roger looked at him.

"How do you feel?" Marvin said. Roger tried to set up, then lay back down and moaned. Marvin and Doug helped him to a sitting position. Roger put his hand on his chest.

"I feel like somebody's been beating on me," he said. The crew laughed and all knelt down,

273

looking at Roger. Roger scanned all their faces again.

"Colonel Marvin Andrews," Marvin said and extended his hand.

"Lieutenant Colonel Roger Shahls, Sir." Roger said and shook Marvin's hand.

"Yeah, we know," Marvin said. "We found your letter." Roger blinked, then smiled and looked at the rest of the crew. Marvin made the introductions.

"Colonel," Roger said, "do you think we'll get back to Earth by the twenty-second. It's Julie's sixteenth birthday. I promised her I'd be there. I've missed the last two. It's important, Sir."

Marvin blinked and hesitated. The crew all looked at Marvin, then glanced at Roger. Roger looked around at the men's faces, then back to Marvin.

"Sir," Roger pleaded, "I won't tell anybody about this place; not a word. Julie's all I got. I'm all she's got. Her mother's dead." Marvin blinked, cleared his throat, and then put his hands on Roger's shoulders.

"Roger, today is July 26$^{th}$, 1998. You've been here twenty-six years." Roger stared at Marvin for a long moment, then blinked and looked down at the cylinder, then at his hands and paused, then rubbed his face. He looked back at Marvin. Marvin continued:

"I'm not with the Air Force. I'm retired. We're here for private research. This ship belongs to Technical Research Association. It's called Research One."

Roger blinked, then looked around at the ship, then through the transparent air lock door, through the open outer doors, and saw the reflection of Research One off the huge glass cylinder outside. His eyes widened. "This is a flying saucer!"

Marvin smiled and nodded.

Roger was confused. "Has everybody got flying saucers now?"

"No." Marvin said. "This is the first."

"What kind of engine?"

Marvin pointed at the rotor pod, then gestured toward Frank. "Magnetic Inertial Propulsion," he said. "Frank invented it."

Roger looked at Frank, at the rotor pod, then back to Frank. "I hear it humming," he said.

Frank nodded and smiled.

"We'll tell you all about it," Marvin said. "Are you hungry?"

Roger touched his stomach. "I haven't had a bite in twenty-six years," he said, grinning.

The crew laughed at their new crewmate. Isaac retrieved an energy bar and squeeze bottle of water and handed it to Roger.

"Let's join him," Doug said. The ship's company, including its newest member, ate and then showed Roger around the ship. Frank briefly explained the principal of the engine powering it. Then discussions began on Doug's discovery and the history on how Technical Research Association came to be. Roger asked many questions and the explorers gradually filled in the twenty-six year gap in his experience; a twenty-six year period in which the young courageous astronaut had bet his life on an alien appliance; *and won.*

"Let's go home," Marvin said. 'And, Roger, we'll be there in less than five hours. Roger raised his eyebrows and blinked.

"We'll have artificial gravity all the way," Marvin added. Roger looked at Frank and smiled.

275

Research One rose out of the chasm and Marvin set a heading for the central crater, the launch point for a return to Earth.

"As soon as we get there I want to find Julie." Roger said. "She was fifteen when I left; she'd be...forty-two now." Roger looked around at the crew. "She was a tom-boy. She always wore her hair in a pony tail."

"She still does," Marvin said and pushed the transmit button on the radio. Roger stared at Marvin.

"Earth Base One this is Research One, come in," Marvin said.

"*This is Earth Base One, go ahead*," Michael said.

"Michael, put Renee on the radio." There was a short pause.

"*Research One, this is Renee.*"

Marvin looked at Roger and gestured toward the radio, smiling. The rest of the crew smiled as Roger scanned their faces.

"*Research One, this is Renee*," came from the radio again. Roger stared at it.

"Julie, is that you?" he said. There was a long pause.

"*Daddy*?!" Renee shrieked.

"Yeah, baby, it's me. I'm sorry I missed your sixteenth birthday."

## Chapter 25

## - EARTH BASE ONE -

As Research One descended the last hundred feet to touch down at Earth Base One, the crew was overwhelmed with the huge circle of automobiles, news vans, and network camera crews rushing about.

When Lt. Col. Roger Stahls walked down the ramp, a forty-two year old woman, ponytail bouncing from shoulder to shoulder, came running across the tarmac with the stride and zest of a sixteen year old.

DAN HOLT

## Epilogue

"Colonel," Doug said, "Military Industrial Complex?"

"It's the faction that launched the covert mission and Stahls in the first place. It was created during World War 2 when secrecy was such an important factor in winning the war. It was strengthened by the subsequent cold war and the development of the special spy planes and other equipment. Then, over time, It gradually assumed more and more authority, above it's intended function.

So that's why Congress is all over them now."

"Yeah," Marvin responded, "They need a bad guy since our discovery is all over the news. Michael's friends in D.C. told him in confidence that they are going to fund an armada of ships to return to the Moon and recover the technology there and, of course, deal with the 'giant' problem. Michael told me to be ready to command that mission. I want Research One's crew on my bridge when this happens. Trust is big with me."

"Does that include Roger?"

"Of course, he has more experience on the Moon than everyone that's been there, combined."

And the adventure
Continues.....

DAN HOLT

## ABOUT THE AUTHOR

Dan Holt is a U.S. Army veteran, having served three years as a Communications Specialist in Germany. He spent the remainder of his civilian career as a self-taught engineer, designing and testing large scale production equipment for the file folder industry.  The efficiency and durability of his designs even garnered interest from some foreign manufacturers.   In retirement, Dan has used his writing skills to express his continuing fascination with machinery and science fiction.   His zest for adventure and intrigue are evident in this work, his second novel, *SLEEP MODE* and several other novels, including UNDERNEATH THE MOON – 2, soon to be published.  In his spare time his engineering skill enabled him to build from scratch an all-electric car with seating for four.   The street-worthy "Mary Lou" can be seen all over his home town and in most holiday parades in the local area. Dan is now retired and lives in North Texas with his wife Mary.

Made in the USA
Lexington, KY
20 December 2015